THIEF

TARRYN FISHER

ONE PLACE. MANY STORIES

HQ
An imprint of HarperCollins*Publishers* Ltd
1 London Bridge Street
London SE1 9GF

www.harpercollins.co.uk

HarperCollins*Publishers*
Macken House, 39/40 Mayor Street Upper
Dublin 1, D01 C9W8, Ireland

This edition 2026

2
First published in Great Britain by HQ,
an imprint of HarperCollins*Publishers* Ltd 2013

Copyright © Tarryn Fisher 2013
Copyright © 2026 by Tarryn Fisher, revised text edition

Tarryn Fisher asserts the moral right to be identified as the author of this work.
A catalogue record for this book is available from the British Library.

ISBN: 9780008730413

This novel is entirely a work of fiction. The names, characters and incidents
portrayed in it are the work of the author's imagination. Any resemblance to
actual persons, living or dead, events or localities is entirely coincidental.

All rights reserved. No part of this publication may be reproduced, stored
in a retrieval system, or transmitted, in any form or by any means,
electronic, mechanical, photocopying, recording or otherwise,
without the prior written permission of the publishers.

Without limiting the exclusive rights of any author, contributor or the publisher of
this publication, any unauthorised use of this publication to train generative artificial
intelligence (AI) technologies is expressly prohibited. HarperCollins also exercise their
rights under Article 4(3) of the Digital Single Market Directive 2019/790 and expressly
reserve this publication from the text and data mining exception.

Printed and bound in the UK using 100%
Renewable Electricity at CPI Group (UK) Ltd

For the Passionate Little Nutcases —
This one is for you.

Similarities to actual persons, living or dead,
events, or locales are entirely coincidental.

THIEF

1

The Present

Olivia. I've lost her three times. The first was to youth . . . impatience. The second was to a lie so dense we couldn't work our way through it, and the third time—this time—I've lost her to Noah.

I stare at the face I thought I'd be waking up to for the rest of my life. Instead she's on my TV, seventy-two inches of Olivia: black hair, accusing eyes, heart-shaped lips. She sits calmly next to her client, every so often leaning over to say something in his ear as they wait for the jury to enter the room with their verdict. Seeing her this way feels like a punch to the gut, an observer of her life, not a participant. But I can't look away. She's right there, in the flesh, representing ten years of my life; every good and bad decision I've made is intertwined with that woman. It hurts so hard I have to look away. Channel 6 News is covering the story, but I wouldn't have been able to avoid it even if I wanted to, the case was all over the internet; it was trending on X. Yesterday while on my nightly walk to the liquor store two women stood at the light at an intersection discussing the case.

"He just looks evil, gives me the creeps."

"Lock him up and throw away the key," the shorter of the two agreed.

Dobson Scott Orchard is charged with the kidnapping and murder of Samantha Reid, Cashmere Bennet, and Soledad Nava, three woman who went missing from the same area of Miami and were murdered in similar ways. Watching Olivia in court fills me with a mix of pride and unease. She's brilliant, but the high-profile nature of the case terrifies me. Defending an alleged rapist and murderer has drawn an intense spotlight, and while it's a huge opportunity for her career, it also means scrutiny, criticism, and danger. Haters can be relentless, and in cases like this they're often more than just words.

The prosecution's case isn't airtight: and Olivia knew exactly where to find the cracks. There are no eyewitnesses to any of the murders, and the evidence is thin—circumstantial at best. The single fingerprint found on the sleeve of Cashmere Bennet's shirt is their strongest piece of evidence. But Olivia dismantled that on the stand with calm, calculated precision that left no room for doubt.

When Olivia questioned the forensic expert, her voice was steady. He admitted the fingerprint could have come from an innocent exchange at the dry cleaner the day before the murder. Dobson was employed at Sunshine Dry Cleaners at the time, a fact the prosecution leaned on heavily. Her line of questioning turned what seemed like a smoking gun into reasonable doubt.

No one cared if they were wrong or right about anything—it was more about having an opinion, throwing it out there, and basking in the sound of their own voice.

I'm on my second scotch, my eyes glued to the screen. I tell myself not to focus on her face—it's too much, too revealing. Instead I watch her hands, resting casually on the table in front of her. At least that's what she wants everyone to believe. But I know her better than anyone. *She's freaking out.*

Her wedding band catches the light, a faint glint that pulls my attention like a magnet. I pour myself another scotch and shoot it back in one smooth motion. The burn is sharp and familiar, but when I set the glass down, the bottle is empty. Empty bottle, empty man. The scotch is a temporary salve, but I've convinced myself it's the only one that works. There are better for me salves, of course—therapy, hiking, traveling. But none are as accessible as the bottle. There's a liquor store just a block away, close enough to walk the distance with my eyes closed—which I've done more times than I care to admit.

The screen flickers, cutting away from the courtroom to a shot of the media room. Reporters shuffle around, setting up cameras, testing microphones. My heart pounds as I lean forward, elbows on my knees, the empty glass cradled in my hands. This is it—whatever happens next will change everything.

The jury has entered the courtroom, where in a few minutes the judge will read the verdict. The newscaster's voice fills the room with feigned gravitas. *Let's go there now, Travis . . .*

I mute the TV. The sound is too much, the commentary too eager. The space behind my eyes aches, a dull throb from exhaustion, tension, and too many drinks. All I want is my bed and eight solid hours of sleep, but sleep is impossible until this is over.

Reaching for my phone I see a slew of missed calls and texts from the office. I skim the notifications briefly but don't open them. Instead I set the phone face down on the table beside me.

The courtroom onscreen comes alive with movement. The camera pans to the judge's bench, then to the attorneys. Everyone is on their feet. The newscaster, voice still muted, looks excited as he gestures toward the camera.

Dobson looms over Olivia at the defense table, his hulking frame making her appear smaller than she is. She stands perfectly still, her hair pulled back into a tight knot at the nape of her neck. Practical, professional, no-nonsense. But my mind betrays me, pulling me into another time, another place, when that same hair spilled loose over her shoulders, and my hands tangled in the soft waves. I can almost hear the deep, throaty sigh she'd make as she relaxed against me.

I drop my head as the memory cuts through me like a sharp inhale, leaving me raw and unsettled. I blink staring back at the screen. This isn't the time for nostalgia. This isn't about us.

I see her hair on my pillow, I see it in my hands, I see it in the pool where we kissed for the first time, spreading around our bodies like ink. After we broke up, I saw pictures of her on a mutual friend's Instagram. Her hair was chopped to her chin, sharp and deliberate, a complete departure from the long waves I knew so well. She wore a pink gloss on her lips. The caption read: *Dinner with this beauty!*

I took a screenshot so I could zoom in on Olivia.

When we were together, I imagined I'd care if she cut her hair. That it would bother me. But I was wrong. Seeing her in that photo, with her new hair, made me feel like a fool.

I thought I was over her, but I was wrong. She has the kind of love that can stain your soul, make you beg not to have one just to escape the spell she's put you under. I spent months slogging through the motions, pretending to move on to make everyone around me happy. Friends would comment on how well I was handling the breakup. The truth was people wanted you to be okay so they could focus on their own shit, so that's what I became: okay.

I've got more of her in my veins than blood.

Olivia loves you with her lies. She lies about how she's feeling, how she's hurting, how she wants you when she tells you she doesn't. She lies to protect you and herself. You have to know how to interpret her or you'd miss the beauty under the harsh lines of her personality. I was unprepared to realize that I was not the only man in the world who knew that about her. What a fool I'd been.

We've been running in opposite directions for the last ten years, and we collide at every turn. Sometimes, it's because we're looking for each other, other times it's fate.

Olivia doesn't flinch as the judge enters the room. The verdict: *Not guilty*. By God—she did it. I run all ten fingers through my hair suddenly feeling wide awake. I don't know whether I want to shake her or congratulate her. Olivia is wearing her shock in her eyebrows; she's not smiling, but she looks pleased. More of her hair bounces loose as she sustains the congratulations. The camera pivots to the prosecutor's face: a guy two decades older than Olivia and with a lot less hair. He looks angry . . . no, enraged. Everyone looks enraged. This is a professional win for her, but personally it would take a toll on her friendships, mental health, and safety. I want to protect her, but she's not mine. I hope Noah's up for the task.

Noah's a nice enough guy; he's what I'd call decent, the type of man you hope your daughter marries, not your ex-girlfriend—at least not when you want her back. It's hard to hate him for his character, but being a nice guy doesn't mean being the right guy. As far as I am concerned, I am the only man for this particular woman. I helped build the bomb that is Olivia Kaspen,

I GRAB MY keys and go for a run. An ambitious undertaking. The air is thick—it feels like it's pulsing. I turn left out of my building and head for the beach, dodging puddles at every intersection. It's peak hour for traffic; I cut through car bumpers to cross a street: Mercedes, BMWs, Audis—the people in my neighborhood are neither short on cash nor personality. Reggaeton blasts through someone's open window. It feels good to run. My condo is a mile from the beach. I cross the main waterway and slow down to a jog so I can enjoy the view of the ocean. When I reach the water, I make a sharp left and run along the shore. This is where I deal with my anger.

I run until I can't. Then I sit in the sand, breathing hard. I have to pull myself together. If I wade in this sewer of emotion for much longer, I might never come out. Pulling my cell from my pocket, I scroll through the numbers until I find *Mom*. My mother answers, breathless, like she's been working out. We pass through the niceties. No matter what the situation, no matter how desperate my voice could be, my mother will politely inquire how I am, expect me to say "fine, thank you" and then give me a brief update on her roses. I wait until she's finished and take a breath. "I'm going to take the job in London."

There is a moment of shocked silence before she responds. "Caleb, it's the right thing. Thank God it came around again. You turned it down the last time for that girl; what a mistake that wa—"

I cut her off, tell her I'll call tomorrow after I've spoken to the London office. I take a long look at the ocean before I head home. Tomorrow I'm going to London.

But I don't.

I WAKE UP to pounding. There is a remodel going on in unit 760. I crush my head beneath my pillow. It does nothing to mute the sound. Swearing, I toss it aside. The pounding sounds closer to home. I roll onto my back and listen. The pounding is coming from my front door. I swing my legs over the side of the bed and pull on a pair of gray pajama pants I find lying on the floor. Crossing my living room, I kick aside the piles of clothes that have been collecting on the floor for weeks. When I fling open the door the world tilts and I have to lean on the door frame.

Neither of us says a word as we size each other up. Then she's suddenly pushing past me, crossing the threshold into my living room. I try to make sense of this. Was I still dreaming? The tiles beneath my feet are cold; could you feel cold in dream? Her perfume lingers on the air; I inhale the smell, Chanel Gardenia. *You're dreaming.* I step inside and close the door. If this was a dream I was going to enjoy it. I follow her into my living room. She stops pacing and crosses her arms across her chest, turning the full battery of her eyes on me. The sound of a drill from 760 brings me back to my body. I walk to the kitchen and start the coffee, then I open the fridge and grab two bottles of water. When I return to the living room she's standing exactly where she was, looking significantly less furious.

"What are you doing here, Duchess?" I hand her the bottle. She takes it and sighs like she's disappointed. "Coffee's on," I say. "Do you need something harder?"

She shakes her head.

I take her in, absorb her. She looks wild; her hair is braided down her back, but there are pieces of it that have come loose all around her face. She's wearing black leggings and a black shirt. Her eyeliner is smudged like she's been either sleeping or crying. She throws her arms wide: it's an angry gesture. I brace myself for the string of expletives that usually come with her anger, but she surprises me.

"You don't clean anymore?"

My house looks like a college dorm. Not my best look.

I edge my way to the sofa as if this isn't my living room and I sit down, uncomfortable. She goes to the window and looks out. I wait for her to speak.

"I let him loose. I put him back on the street. He's a rapist." She slaps a fist into her open palm on the last word. Her foot touches an empty bottle of scotch, and it rolls across the hardwood. We both follow it with our eyes until it disappears under the table. "What the fuck is wrong with you?" she asks, looking around.

I lean back and link my hands behind my neck. I trace her gaze to the disaster that is my condo.

"You should have thought of that before you took the case."

She looks ready to punch me. Her eyes start at my hair, work down to my beard, linger on my chest, and scoop back up to my face. All of a sudden, she's sober. I see it fill her eyes, the realization that she came here and she shouldn't have. We both make our move at the same time. She bolts for the door; I jump up and go after her.

"Olivia . . . ?"

She stops before she reaches the front door, her head dropping to her chest.

She keeps her distance, tucking her bottom lip under her teeth, kohl eyes looking less sure.

"Your move," I say.

I see her throat spasm as she swallows her thoughts, swallows ten years of us.

"All right . . . all right!" she says finally. She walks back around the sectional and sits down on the recliner. We've begun our usual game of cat and mouse; an uncomfortable comfortable.

I sit as far away from her as I can, and stare at her expectantly. If I let her talk without interrupting her, she'll start talking. She uses her thumb to spin her wedding band. When she sees me watching, she stops. I almost laugh when she pulls up the foot of the recliner and slouches backward like she belongs here.

"Do you have a Coke?"

I did. I don't drink Coke, but I always have it in my fridge. Maybe it's for her, I don't know. To myself I refer to it as the tribute Coke.

"Yesss."

She looks gleeful when I come back with it in hand. She pops the cap, pressing the bottle against her lips and chugging. She loves the burn.

When she's done, she tries to put her empty bottle in the cupholder and finds half of a stale ham sandwich.

Judgement feels harsher early in the morning, I decide. "I need coffee . . ." I pluck the old ham and cheese from her fingers, ignoring the look she gives me.

I take my time in the kitchen, fishing two dirty mugs from the counter. I wash them with the last of the dish soap, scalding my hands under the hot water. I pour two mugs of coffee, adding sugar to hers.

"Should we try being friends?" she sighs.

I laugh.

We can't stay away, so what's the alternative? She hiccups from the Coke.

"You know, I've never met anyone that can say as much as you without a single word coming out of his mouth," she snaps.

I grin. After a long silence I ask the burning question: "Where's your husband?"

She clears her throat. "Germany."

I raise my eyebrows. "He was out of the country for the verdict?"

"We didn't know how long they'd take to deliberate. Stop looking at me like that."

"You're in my apartment and I'm not allowed to look at you?"

She frowns. "Can we not talk about our personal lives?"

"Fine, let's talk about work. Well done, you should be

celebrating. You were brilliant up there, truly." I lean back and sling both arms across the back of the couch.

She starts to cry, stoic-faced, tears pouring like an open tap. It's jarring.

I freeze. I want to comfort her, but touching her is a bad idea overall; it's hard to stop, and she's not mine to touch. "Do you remember that time you accidentally ran over a squirrel and became so hysterically upset you then ran over a mailbox . . . ?"

She snort laughs. "And then *you* cried because I was driving your car."

We both laugh. She dabs her eyes with her sleeve.

"You did your job, Duchess," I say softly. "You did it well."

She nods and stands up.

Our time is over.

"Caleb . . . I—"

I shake my head. I don't want her to say she's sorry for coming or that it won't happen again.

I walk her to the door.

"Am I supposed to say I'm sorry for what happened with Leah?" She looks at me through her lashes. Her tears have clumped her mascara together. On another woman it would look sloppy; on Olivia it looks like sex.

"I wouldn't believe you if you did."

She smiles; it starts in her eyes and spreads slowly to her lips. An easy smile is a win.

"Come over for dinner. Noah's always wanted to meet you . . ." She laughs at the skepticism on my face. "You hate that you like him, don't you?"

I glare at her.

"Bring a date."

I run my hand over my face and shake my head. "Dinner with your husband is the last fucking thing I ever want do."

"Do you think I enjoyed defending your ex-wife in a pharmaceutical lawsuit?"

I flinch. "Touché."

"See you next Tuesday at seven?" She winks before she walks out.

She knows I'll be there.

Damn.

2

The Present

park in the garage of Olivia's building and shoot a text to my date, who is running late. She's stuck in traffic so she responds right away.

Tell them I'm sorry, I'll be there as soon as the road opens. Looks like a bad accident ☹

Okay, drive safe and see you soon.
I remembered the wine!

Good job ☺

After Olivia showed up at my apartment it took me a few weeks to clean up my act. Let's be honest—there's nothing quite as motivating as your ex seeing you at your absolute worst. The day after she left, I stopped drinking and started a cleanse. I trimmed my beard, cleaned my apartment, and eased my way back into the gym. Enter Evan, my friend-slash-reluctant trainer. He's a postal worker by day and a recently divorced guy with too much free time. His new hobby? Torturing me with dumbbells and unsolicited life advice. Our gym sessions mostly consist of me wheezing on the treadmill while Evan yells things like, "This is where the growth happens!" Which is a bold statement for someone who probably spent his morning crying into his protein shake. Evan had the same over-the-top enthusiasm for supplements that my other divorced friend, Tom, had for church. If you take this and do this your life will be changed.

I'm ten minutes late. I hate being late. It makes me feel like I'm letting everyone down before I even walk through the door. I jab at the elevator button watching the numbers above the door crawl down at an infuriating pace. As I wait, I reach for my wedding band with my thumb, a habit I haven't shaken, and find it missing.

Forever became five years; until death do us part dissolved into irreconcilable differences. I don't know if I miss it—the marriage—or just the idea of it. My mother always said I was born to be married.

The elevator dings and I step inside, pressing the button for the twenty-third floor. I came here once during Leah's trial. It's about three times the size of my place, with floor-to-ceiling windows that stretch the length of the unit, offering a perfect view of the ocean. Olivia doesn't go in the ocean; she just likes to look at it. I clutch the bottle of wine as the elevator pings and the door slides open. I make my way to the door. It's already propped open like they're waiting for me.

"Hello . . ." I call, slipping off my shoes. The floor is pristine, marble tiles lead to the living room and kitchen.

I take inventory of the hallway: a pair of men's tennis

shoes remind me that her husband will very much be here tonight, that means no flirting, no undressing her with my eyes.

Before I can let my imagination run any further, a man steps into view filling the space at the end of the hallway. He's taller than I expected, with broad shoulders and the casual confidence of someone who belongs here. We stare at each other for a good five seconds, the silence stretching awkwardly. Did she forget to tell him that I was coming? Then he runs a hand through dark wavy hair, and his face shifting into an easy smile.

"Caleb," he says, like we're old friends.

Haon.

"Hey, Noah." I say, grabbing the hand he extends. His grip is firm, the kid of handshake that sees a lot of board-rooms.

His smile is pleasant, disarming even. He's wearing a short-sleeve collared shirt, a gold Star of David around his neck.

"She sent me out here to get these," he says, scooping up the tennis shoes. "Before you got here. Don't tell her you saw them."

"Ha!"

I follow him inside. It's different from the last time I was here. Gone are the cold whites and blacks, the sterile perfection. She's replaced it all with warm tones and soft rugs. It's a home. Jealousy twists in my chest, sharp and unwelcome.

She comes out of the kitchen, pulling off an apron. She tosses it aside and comes straight for me.

She hugs me. I have to taper my smile, which always

spreads hard and fast when she's near. Noah is watching us, standing just a few feet away.

"Hello, Du—Olivia. I wasn't sure what was for dinner, so I brought red."

"Malbec," she says, grinning at Noah. "Your favorite." I see genuine affection in her eyes when she looks at him. Had I ever looked at Leah like that? I don't think so.

"We're having lamb," she says. "So it's just perfect."

The living room is expansive; there's a large sectional the color of oatmeal. The room blends into the dining area. A sliding glass door opens onto a private terrace.

"I'm going to open this bottle," Noah says, lifting the Malbec and heading to the kitchen.

I wander over to a wall where framed black-and-white prints are hung in a meticulous grid, each one evenly spaced, perfectly aligned.

"Noah took those," Olivia says. She comes to stand next to me and we admire them together. "They're from all of the places he goes for work."

A fisherman hauling in his catch along a foggy coast, a street in Paris, a market in Marrakesh.

"They're great, really good."

She grins.

"Do you ever go with him to these places?"

She looks back at the photographs and sighs softly, her expression somewhere between wistful and resigned. "Once or twice," she says. "I can't really leave because of work."

Noah walks over then, with two glasses of wine and hands one to each of us. I notice the way his fingers brush hers so casually.

"These are impressive," I tell him.

"Thanks—it's just a hobby I picked up to keep me busy. It gets lonely being on the road."

The doorbell rings.

"Your date?" she asks.

"Yep." Olivia's gaze shoots toward me sharp and searching. I can feel her trying to piece together what I'm up to. I allow a slow smile to spread across my face. Noah retreats a few steps to open the door, and we stay with our eyes locked.

Her body is frozen, every muscle tense as if bracing for impact. I hear my date's voice behind me. Olivia's eyes flick past me toward Noah, who is temporarily blocking her view from the woman behind him. Noah steps aside, and the moment I've been waiting for arrives.

I see it all at once: Olivia shocked, Olivia disarmed, Olivia angry. The color drains from her face, and her hand shoots up to her collarbone to grab at her necklace—a simple diamond on a chain. She's rattled. Noah steps up beside me, his curiosity palatable. And there's Jessica, my date, beaming and radiant.

"Jess, you remember Olivia," I say. She nods and genuinely beams at Olivia who now looks like she's been hit by a truck. "Hello, stranger," Jessica says, wrapping her arms around Olivia in a surprise hug. Olivia's arms hang stiffly at her sides.

"It's been a while." Jessica releases Olivia and steps back. "It's been a while."

"Oh, it has," Olivia manages. She's clutching her necklace so hard I half expect it to snap. I take a sip of my wine, suppressing my grin.

Jessica Alexander found me on Facebook. It was out of the blue, a name I hadn't thought about in years. She messaged me to say she was living in the Miami area again and wanted to get together for drinks. I was drunk when I read the message and responded with my number before thinking it through.

We met up the next day at Bar Louie, a casual low-pressure spot. She looked the same: long hair, long legs, short skirt. The kind of woman who could walk into any room and turn heads without trying.

She was sweeter than I remembered, funny.

I needed a nice, long dose of sweet.

I watch Olivia's face over Jess's shoulder. She has always had a knack for self-control. And then she does the damnedest thing. She laughs and hugs Jess back, like they're old friends. I'm in such a state of shock I almost take a step back. Noah is watching everything unfold with mild curiosity. We are all just characters to him, no doubt.

"Come in, come in." She ushers us into the living room and makes us sit. Noah gets Jess a glass of wine.

Touché. There is still fun to be had.

Jess runs off to help Olivia in the kitchen, which leaves Noah and me with a plate of Brie and crackers. We do the small talk thing for about ten minutes. The go-to topics for men—Marlins, Heat, Dolphins . . . quarterbacks, starters, pitchers—things I couldn't care less about anymore. At one point he leaves to get us both another drink.

When there's a lull in the conversation, he asks, "Are you uncomfortable at all, being here and doing this?"

I look at him in surprise.

"Yeah, I guess it's a little weird. Would you be?" I accept the whiskey he hands me. Single malt, black label—decent.

He sits down across from me and grins. "Sure."

I don't bother him, so how much could he really know? Unless . . . unless he's so secure in their relationship he feels like there is nothing to worry about. I sit back and eye the situation with a new perspective. He's not the jealous type, obviously.

"If you don't have a problem with me being here, I don't either," I say.

He throws his ankle across his knee and settles back in his chair. "Did you have me checked out when we got married?"

"Background check in three different countries." I take a sip and curl my tongue around the flavor.

Noah nods like he expected this. "Find anything you didn't like?"

I shrug. "You married my first love. I already didn't like you."

He tucks in one corner of his mouth in a knowing smile and nods slowly. "You care about her, Caleb. That's fine with me."

The girls come in. We stand. Olivia can sense there has been an exchange. Her ever-cold eyes travel between the two of us.

Choose me.

Her gaze lands on Noah. Their intimacy makes me jealous. Rageful. I grind my teeth until Olivia notices. I stop as soon as her eyes trace my jaw, but it's too late. She's seen what I'm feeling.

A perfect eyebrow arches up.
God. I hate it when she does that.

THE LAMB IS overcooked and the asparagus is mushy. I am so impressed that her spiteful little hands are now cooking; I clean my plate and have seconds. She drinks three glasses of wine so casually I wonder if it has become a habit or if this dinner is making her nervous. We talk about her clients, and she has everyone laughing. Noah is clearly infatuated with her. He watches everything she does with a slight smile on his lips. It reminds me of myself. She asks Jessica questions about what she has been doing with her life. It makes me uncomfortable. I am careful not to speak only to her, not to look at her too much, not to look away when she interacts with Noah, because it bothers me. It's hard not to study their dynamic. She is genuinely fond of him. I notice that her personality is softer when he's around. She has not cussed once since I stepped through their door—which is the longest her mouth has ever been clean in the history of Olivia.

Her mouth.

Noah is one of those rare personalities that has a calming effect on a potentially tense situation. I can't help but like the guy even though he has my girl. He has the balls to threaten me too.

As we say our goodbyes in their foyer, Olivia refuses to meet my eyes. She looks exhausted, like the night has taken its toll on her emotionally. She stands close to Noah, and I see her reach for his hand. I want to know what she's feeling. I want to be the one to comfort her.

Jess comes home with me and spends the night. My mother has left four messages asking about my move to London.

I WAKE UP to the smell of bacon. I can hear the clang of pots and water running in the sink. I walk naked to the kitchen. Jess is making breakfast. I lean over the counter and watch her. I was married to a woman for five years and rarely did I see her crack an egg. She's wearing one of my T-shirts. Her hair is pulled up in a messy knot. It's very sexy. I eye her legs; they go on forever. I'm a leg guy. The scene in *Pretty Woman* where Vivian is telling Edward the exact measurement of her legs is one of the best scenes in the movie. A lot can be forgiven if a woman has a great set of legs.

Jessica's are unparalleled.

I sit as she hands me a mug of coffee and smiles shyly like we've never done this before. I really like her. I loved her once; it would be easy to fall into this woman again. She's beautiful—more beautiful than Leah, more beautiful than Olivia. *Can anyone be more beautiful than Olivia?*

"I didn't want to wake you," she says. "So I kept myself busy with feeding you."

"Feeding me," I repeat. I like that.

"I like doing things for you." She smiles coyly. "I've missed you, Caleb."

I blink at her. What would have happened if she had told me she was pregnant, instead of going to get an abortion? We'd have a ten-year-old.

I pull her to me and kiss her. She never fights, never acts

like she doesn't want me. I take her to the couch and we let the toast burn.

Later, I'm sitting at the café down the street, drinking espresso. Jess had to go to work. My phone pings, signaling a text message.

O: Well?

I smile to myself and finish my espresso before answering.

Well, what?

There is a long pause. She's thinking about how to suck the information out of me without sounding like she cares.

O: Don't play games!

I remember the last time you asked me not to do that. I think we were in an orange grove.

O: What did you think of Noah?

Nice

What did you think of Jess?

O: Meh

I crack up. The other patrons of the café turn to see what I'm laughing at.

I gather up my things to leave. She always did get right

to the point. I am almost to my car when my phone pings again.

O: Don't fall in love with her.

I stare at that message for a long time. One minute—three. It pisses me off . . . and makes me happy at the same time. I hate myself for the latter. For the rest of the day I ask myself the same question: What does she want from me? Was she asking me to stay single and wait for her? She'd looked pretty comfortable with Noah that night; there'd been no sign of trouble between them. *Olivia loves you with her lies.* She could be feeling any number of things and none of us would have a clue . . . if she didn't want us to. I don't respond. I feel like she's punched me.

And that's it. I don't hear from her for another year.

3

___

The Past

The first time I saw her—my God—it was like I'd never seen another woman in all my life. It was the way she walked that caught my eye. She moved like water: fluid, determined. Everything else blended together in a blur and all I saw was her. The only solid in all that color. I smiled when she stopped under this grotesque, twisted-looking tree and gave it the single dirtiest look I had ever seen. I'd never even noticed the tree before, though it was one of those things that when you see it, you wonder how you'd ever missed it. One of my friends punched me on the arm to get my attention. We'd been talking about a game we had coming up. The coach put half the team on suspension for smoking pot, and now we had to get through the last few games with our best players benched for the rest of the season. But the conversation had ended for me the minute I saw her. My friends followed my eyes, gave each other knowing looks. I had a reputation in regard to women. They were still calling out remarks when I stepped under the tree. Her back was to me. She had the type of hair you wanted to wrap your hands in—dark and wild, all the way to her tiny waist. My first words to her should have been: *Will you marry me?* Instead, I went with: "Why are you angry with the tree?"

She spun on me so fast I drew back. She set me off my axis, wobbling and unsure. A feeling I was not well acquainted with. The rest of our exchange pockmarked my ego.

"Just a question, Sunshine, don't attack." Holy shit, she was hostile.

"Can I help you with something?" she snapped.

"I was interested in finding out why this tree made you frown." It was lame, but what the hell else was I supposed to say? She'd either had a really bad day, or she was always like this, and either way I was compelled to stand in the shade and talk to her.

Suddenly, she looked tired. "Are you trying to flirt with me?"

Damn. This was turning into one of the strangest female encounters I'd ever had.

When I told her my name it was to buy a few seconds to think. I wanted to say something strong enough to keep her there.

"I'm sorry, what?"

"My name . . ." I offered her my hand. Her skin was ice-cold. When she pulled her hand away I was disappointed. "I was trying to flirt with you. Bad idea?"

Her brow lifted in amusement. I could tell she was considering it. I was hyperaware of the space between us,

"Bad idea," she confirmed.

"Sorry," I said. "It's just that I love bad ideas, I'm full of them."

Her mouth twitched and then . . . she frowned. I could be love-drunk, but it looked to me like her eyes were smiling.

She sighed; it was deep and tired and sad if I were to be honest.

I slapped at a mosquito that landed on my arm. Bugs were the price of eternal sunshine; gnat assaults were a regular thing and cockroaches roamed the dorms like prairie horses. The roots of the tree were enormous, stretching out of the ground like an octopus.

She looked up at its highest branches, long eyelashes sweeping her cheeks. I had a feeling that she spoke to this tree often—it was her friend. I had a relationship with a bottle of beer when I was ten . . . an empty bottle of beer.

My dad canceled a camping trip we'd been planning together for months. It was all I thought about for weeks. At the last minute he canceled, texting my mother to tell her he'd come down with a violent case of the flu, and he wouldn't be able to travel. I'd really been looking forward to it, my bag had been packed for weeks. My parents were divorced; I hardly got to see him as it was. It was crushing. I did the thing that kids do when they're mad at their parents; I ran away. Taking the backpack I'd so carefully packed I planned to go on a forever camping trip; make my dad sorry. I only made it a quarter mile when I saw it: a brown bottle, unremarkable except the label was peeled off and someone had taped a piece of duct tape across the middle of it. On it they'd written two words in what looked like black Sharpie: Fuck it.

"I'd love to stand around and feed into your ego with chitchattery, but I have to go."

"Good word."

She looked over at me with her dark, fervent gaze and I was suddenly pinned down by my need to impress her . . . make her smile . . . marry her . . .

"If you were born an animal, you'd be a llama," I said a bit too quickly. It was true. Her face flushed with color and her eyes widened like I'd insulted her. I happened to really like llamas, but I wasn't going to tell her that; I was enjoying her silent outrage. Besides, everyone knew llamas were awesome. When you pissed one off, which was usually by getting in its space, they spat at you. It happened to my brother at a petting zoo when he was six.

"Hey, I'll see you around," I said. As I watched her walk away I knew two things: I wanted her, and it was going to be a lot of work.

NO ONE KNEW who she was despite my inquiries. Dark hair, seething eyes, a waist small enough to wrap my hands around.

I had an ex-girlfriend named Emma who worked in the admissions office. We were still on good terms so I went to see her on Monday after my classes were over.

"What's up?" she said as soon as I walked through the door. "You have that look on your face . . ."

I dropped my backpack on the worn blue carpet next to her desk and sat down in a chair that looked like the carpet. Behind her was a short corridor with several office doors which were all closed. "What look?"

She pointed a long acrylic fingernail at my face. "That one."

"It's just my face, Emma Grace . . ." She always liked it when I called her by her full name.

"What do you want?"

I told her and she immediately shook her head.

"Emma Grace," I said leaning forward in my chair, "I'm not asking for her address, I just want to know her name so I can find her."

"Find her for what?" She crossed her arms over her chest like she meant business.

"Weed," I lie.

"Oh." Emma typed something into her computer.

She seemed to relax. Emma had such long nails she had to do everything with flexed fingers.

"Just this once, Emma . . . please."

"Fine," said, "But I want an ounce . . ."

"Deal," I said.

That's all it took. Fingers flexed she typed on her keyboard.

"You have to give me something, like a class or a building?"

"Conners," I said quickly.

She looks at me like I'm stupid. "There are over five hundred girls in Conners. You're going to have to be more specific."

She didn't wear the same deer in the headlights look that the freshmen had on their faces. "Sophomore," I decided.

She typed something into her keyboard and sighed. "Great, now we have two hundred."

I racked my brain for something else. I could take a guess at her major.

"Try prelaw . . ." She had one of those combative personalities that lawyers specialized in. She'd been staring up at a tree, deep in thought.

Emma quickly spun the monitor toward me. She tapped her nails on the screen like an influencer.

"These are the sophomores in Conners who are premed and prelaw . . ."

"You're an angel."

I glanced through the column of photographs. There were about thirty to a page. She scrolled and my eyes searched.

"Hurry up, lover boy. I could get fired for this."

"She's not there," I said after a few seconds.

"You're lying." She returned the monitor to its original position. "Don't forget our deal."

"Oh, I won't," I answered quickly.

I gave her a quick wave and jogged out. Her picture had been there, third from the top.

Olivia Kaspen. Her name backward was *Aivilo,* her animal was a llama, and her personality was as icy as her hands. I felt that we already knew each other. Familiarity . . . was that it? I couldn't stop thinking about her. I looked for her socials, but she didn't seem to have any.

The tree was my best bet. I walked past it at least twice a day. She didn't go to the gym. She was never in the cafeteria or at any of our home games. She was either a first-class hermit or I'd imagined the whole thing. Olivia Kaspen. A cross between Snow White and the Evil Queen. I had to find her.

I SPOTTED HER in the stands at one of our last games of the season. We'd made it to the playoffs and were leading the game by ten points. By halftime the game was neck and neck, tension buzzing through the gym. Exhaustion clung to every player's movements. The minute I saw her, I was distracted. I kept glancing up into the stands where she was sitting, clutching a Styrofoam cup between her hands like it was cold. One thing was clear: she wasn't looking at me. I don't know what possessed me to believe that I could impress her with my game play, but I tried. The visiting team went on a ten-nothing run. The game was tied. I stood at the free throw line, and to this day I don't know what possessed me to pull the little stunt that cost us the game. I jogged over to my coach. Normally a stunt like that would have gotten me kicked off the team, but I happened to be the BMOC and it helped that he was a family friend.

"I can't focus. I have to take care of something," I told him.

"Caleb, you have to be fucking with me right now."

"Coach," I said quietly. "Give me two minutes."

He narrowed his eyes and stared at me over his glasses. "Is this about that girl?"

My blood ran cold. My coach was an insightful guy, but—

"The one who's missing?" he finished.

I stared at him blankly. Laura? We'd dated, but not seriously. I wondered if my parents said something to him. Our mothers played tennis together and at some point, thought it would be fun to play matchmaker with their kids. Laura was pretty and she liked to go to the movies, so that's what we did. I doubt we ever had a meaningful conversation. Before I could correct him, he said, "Go. Hurry up."

As the whistle blew for a timeout coach put the team in a huddle.

I took the stairs two at a time. If I were hoping to fly under the radar it wasn't going to happen, people were turning around in their seats to see what I was doing. She didn't notice me at first, she was looking around the stands trying to figure out what was going on. The closer I got to Olivia, the paler she got, and she was already pretty pale. When I crouched down next to her, her eyes were wide and she looked ready to bolt.

"Olivia," I said. "Olivia Kaspen."

She looked momentarily shocked. She composed herself quickly. Her eyes danced around my face before she leaned toward me and said, "Bravo, you found out my name." Then in a lower voice, "What the hell are you doing?"

"You're quite the mystery on campus," I said, tracing the outline of her lips with my eyes. I'd never seen such sensual lips in all my life. How had it taken me this long to find those lips?

"Are you going to be making a point anytime soon, or are you holding up the game to brag about your detective skills?"

Oh my God. How could I not laugh at that? I wanted to tell her right then and there that she was going to marry me. "If I make this shot, will you go out with me?"

"If you . . . wait—what?"

She blinked rapidly as if struggling to believe what she'd heard. "What a little peacock you are."

"It took you all week to think up that one, didn't it?"

"Sure," she said, shrugging, but her cheeks colored.

"So then, it's fair to say that you were thinking about me all week?"

"No . . . and . . . no, I will not go out with you." Her

eyes widened in shock and a deep blush spread across her cheeks. She wasn't looking at me anymore. The pink on her cheeks deepened to crimson as her gaze darted nervously around. People were looking.

"Why not?"

That did it. Her nostrils flared, anger bubbling just beneath the surface. This was not going the way I'd imagined.

"Because I am a llama and you are a bird and WE are not compatible."

"Okay," I breathed. "Then, I'll fly to you—what will it take?"

She let out a rush of air through her nose. "Miss it."

"Miss it?"

"Yep."

I stared into her cold blue eyes, unwavering and expectant, and a trickle of excitement slid down my spine. "Olivia?"

"Miss it," she said again, "and I'll go out with you."

For a second I couldn't breathe. There was no way I heard that right. The look on her face told me that she wasn't joking. My mind was racing searching for a way out of this. Checkmate. I wanted to laugh at the sheer audacity of this tiny woman with tall demands. Her face was set as stone. I was out of time. I jogged back to the court; I wasn't going to do it.

There had been something in her eyes that I couldn't shake. A dare. She asked me to do the impossible: sell out my team, disappoint my coach . . . She set the bar high and she expected me to fail.

The ball felt good in my hands, just like always. *Trust the routine. Everyone is watching, just make the shot.* I dribbled once . . . twice. Simple mechanics, this was no big deal, I'd done this a thousand times before. *Just shoot. One. Smooth. Motion.*

I raised the ball, my palms curved around it like it was an extension of my body. If I made it, they'd talk about it for weeks, if I didn't make it they'd talk about it for weeks. All movement seemed to freeze as I took the final shot.

I could feel the entire gym holding its breath. The ball hit the rim and bounced off. I missed the shot. The whistle blew.

I looked for her face in the stands, but there were people everywhere.

I WANTED HER.

I missed the shot.

I was in way over my head.

4

The Past

My mother always told me that I didn't take anything seriously . . . enough. It was a joke in my family—my lack of dedication to any one thing. Just pick something! I tried everything: golf, tennis, sailing, piano, guitar, and my longest stint: basketball. The British have a mixed relationship with American sports. The closest my dad came to worship was Michael Jordan. His status as one of the greatest athletes of all time reached even the most dedicated football fans. His love for Jordan is what got me into basketball, that and my height. In America when you were tall everyone—and I mean everyone—asked you if you played ball. So I did. I was good at things, but I didn't love any of it. Not basketball, or finance, or boating, or the money that ran through my family like the Thames. The truth was that nothing *did feel* like enough. I wasn't sad or angry. I just didn't care. The problem was that there was no problem. Not one that I could identify anyway. Until Olivia asked me to miss the shot. In that moment I felt alive.

She asked me to do one thing: miss the shot; deny yourself for me. Sacrifice. Suddenly I knew what longing was. I wanted to give her something. So I missed the shot.

"Is it true?"

I looked up from my plate of pancakes. Emma slid into the seat opposite me. She was wearing her makeup from the night before and my buddy Kiel's jersey. Why did girls want to wear a guy's jersey?

"Is what true?"

"You missed the shot for a girl?"

"Where did you hear that?" I pushed my plate away my appetite suddenly gone.

"Come on, Caleb, everyone is talking about it."

"Oh yeah . . . ?"

I didn't care what people were saying. Let them talk. Let them have their small stories because I was after the bigger one. I took a sip of my coffee, bitter and lukewarm.

"Stop acting like you don't care what people are saying. Everyone cares."

I let my eyes wander, two tables over a group was sneaking glances at me.

"Who are they saying I did it for?" If people found out it was Olivia I'd missed the shot for, things would get very uncomfortable for her. Emma was examining me like she knew something. I should have been more careful when I asked her to find someone for me. Had I exited out of the screen before I turned it back to her? Had she gone through the names herself and somehow discovered it was Olivia?

"Oh, there are definitely rumors."

I shrugged, trying to be nonchalant, but my shoulders were tense. "Humor me."

She pursed her lips and leaned forward. "Where's my weed?"

"In my room."

She studied me like she was looking for the lie.

"Okay," she said with a sigh, leaning over to help herself to my pancakes. She pinched a chunk of dough with the tips of her fingers and ripped it off. "Some people say they saw you talking to her before you missed the shot. What were you doing up there anyway?"

It didn't matter what the story was; it was the same as all the others. The names changed, the details shifted, someone's reputation would take a hit.

"Maybe my game was just off," I said, setting my mug down and standing up.

Emma smiled up at me. "Maybe. But your game has never been off before. If you ask me, it's kind of romantic."

"Romantic?" I repeated.

"Yeah. She must be pretty hot."

I leaned down until both of my hands were flat on the table, and Emma and I were at eye level. "Does that really sound like something I would do, Emma Grace?"

She looked at me for a long minute before shaking her head. "No, actually."

"Well, there you have your answer."

I left, wiping my palms on my pant legs. How many people had seen me speaking to Olivia? It was stupid . . . careless, but then I could have never anticipated her challenge. If things had gone my way, she would have agreed to a date for *making* the shot. Everyone would have walked away a winner, i.e., I would have walked away the winner.

I couldn't help but smile as I jogged down the stairs in

front of the dining hall. Forget it. I would have missed that shot five hundred times for a date with her.

I'd never felt anything like her.

Bang, bang, she shot me down.

I TOOK HER to Jaxson's, my favorite ice cream place. The energy of Jaxson's was always high, families crammed around tables, the hum of conversation, and the smell of fresh waffle cones wafting through the air. The walls were a clutter of vintage tin memorabilia from long-forgotten brands: soda advertisements, quirky slogans, and old-timey license plates. But the real showstopper? The Kitchen Sink. Twelve scoops of ice cream drenched in rivers of fudge and whipped cream, served in an actual sink, delivered to your table with clapping and fanfare from the staff. The whole place invited lingering.

At the start of the evening, Olivia had been prickly—her body was rigid, tone clipped. She made it abundantly clear she was only there because she had to be. But as we settled into our table and ordered desert, her edge softened. Somewhere between the syrupy chaos of the ice cream and the easy rhythm of conversation, her opinion of me seemed to shift.

For the first time, I saw a glimmer of something I hadn't expected; she looked like she was actually enjoying herself. She was curious, snarky, and wickedly funny. Her quick wit kept me on my toes, but beneath all the fire there were rare, fleeting moments when I glimpsed something softer. She didn't trust love—not the way most people did. For her love was a losing game where the house always won, and she wasn't about to place any bets.

Then she opened up. I don't know what I said that cracked the armor, but it happened. She told me things about her past, and about her mother. I thought things had gone great. Hell, better than great. We'd texted back and forth all week—playful banter, little snippets of shared jokes. It felt like something was building. Until . . .

I just don't think we're compatible.

"That's not how it feels to me," I said, my voice steady, though my chest felt like it was caving in.

She blinked at me—fast little blinks, like a bird fluttering its wings before flight. "Um, well, I'm sorry. I guess we're just on two different wavelengths."

"I guess so."

What I wanted to say was: *I know you like me just as much as I like you. Give me a chance to show you instead of just tell you.* It felt so simple in my head. But the words got stuck in my throat.

"Okay, Olivia." Her name tasted bitter now.

Before I could grab her, before I could shake sense into her, I turned and walked away.

Don't walk away! Fight her on this!

That's what my brain screamed at me. But the last thing I wanted to do was chase after someone who didn't want me—or worse, someone who didn't know they wanted me.

I went back to my dorm room and cracked open a beer. Rejected for the first time—it wasn't pretty. It was ugly, actually. Fucked-up, even. I'd done everything she'd asked of me. My teammates were barely talking to me, my coach had put me on suspension, and my heart was in pieces over a girl I barely knew. How had it come to this?

I stared at the label of my beer, my statistics textbook

open in front of me. I spent thirty minutes trying to study without seeing a thing. No, that's not true, I saw her. Olivia Kaspen. Her eyes, her smirk, the way she looked when she frowned. I pretended not to. Pretended she was just another girl, not *the* girl.

My friends thought I was losing it. Months later I saw her with someone else. Not just anyone—an asshole. I hated him instantly. I hated them together. So I told myself she wasn't who I thought she was. She wasn't worth it.

And that's when I met Jessica. The first thing she ever said to me was, "Damn, I don't know if I want to lick you or marry you."

I laughed. "How about both?"

That was it. We were together. Jessica Alexander was everything Olivia wasn't. She was sexy, kind, and a little ditzy—exactly my type. She babbled endlessly about clothes and movies and campus gossip. And I loved it. She took away the edge I'd been living with. With Jessica, I felt normal again. Olivia faded into the background, just another blip in my past.

But life has a way of pulling the rug out from under you when you least expect it. Jessica got pregnant. And then she didn't tell me. She had an abortion without ever saying a word. It could have been a conversation instead of a revelation. The news hit me like a freight train. I didn't know what to do with the guilt and anger. I did what any other emotionally stunted man in his twenties would do: I punched a tree. Not my finest moment, especially since the tree won. I walked away with a sprained wrist and went into what I like to call a dating hibernation. No apps, no bars, no awkward first dates, absolutely no cheerleaders. Just me, my overthinking, and a lot of late nights pretending homework was my personality.

"YOU'RE COMING TO the party," Matt declared standing in my doorway like a human bulldozer. I groaned when I saw Chris behind him. This was an ambush.

"It smells like self-pity and ramen in here, man."

"I'm good," I said barely glancing up from my laptop.

"No, you're not," Chris said, opening my closet.

"What are you doing?"

"Getting you dressed, my man."

"Guys—" I started, but Matt cut me off.

"Dude, you punched a tree."

An hour later I found myself in the back seat of Matt's car, wedged between a six-pack of beer and a cooler of Jell-O shots. The ride was mostly Matt hyping up the night. The party was already chaos when we pulled up—music shaking the walls.

"This is a nightmare," I said to Matt as we walked in. "Nah, this is your comeback arc, bro. Go vibe."

Olivia was on the dance floor, spinning in circles. For a moment I forgot to breathe. The song's bass line pulsed through the floor, and she hit every beat like she owned it. The way her hips moved like she didn't give a single damn. It was impossible to look away, trust me I was trying. I leaned against the wall, my drink forgotten in my hand, watching her. And then, her eyes found mine. The smile stayed on her lips and my stomach tightened. As quickly as she'd looked at me, she turned away, throwing her head back. I couldn't stand to watch her anymore. I didn't hesitate, I went to her like she was calling me. When I was close enough to be in her orbit she opened her eyes and saw me. For the first time in a long time I felt like I was exactly where I needed to be.

AFTER MY PARENTS DIVORCED, my mother made the decision to move us to America. It wasn't just a spur-of-the-moment idea. She had been born in Michigan, after all. My grandfather met my grandmother studying abroad at Cambridge. Their story always seemed romantic in a distant, fairy-tale sort of way. Two worlds colliding, love bridging the gap. When they married, they moved back to the States for a while and had my mother. But fairy tales are never that simple. When my grandmother grew homesick, my grandfather sold their house and moved to England. A true prince charming.

My parent's story wasn't quite as poetic. They ran in the same social circles—privileged, tight-knit, and suffocating. Their union wasn't the story of star-crossed lovers, but one of convenience. They happened to happen. My mother, always the rebel, insisted on breaking tradition when it came to naming my brother and me. She vetoed all the "Alfreds and Charlies" of the world and gave us American-sounding names. It was her way of spiting my dad when he tried to mold her into something she didn't want to be. When she caught my father cheating for the third time, she'd had enough. She packed us up and moved us to America. My brother adapted faster than I did. I took the divorce personally. I blamed her for all of my problems after that— the uprooting, the culture shock, the fractured family. For a long time I refused to see her side of it. That all changed the summer I flew back to England for my dad's fourth wedding.

Each time the same vows, the same smiles, the same promises of forever that always fall apart. Yet here I was again, sitting in another rented venue, watching my father swear that this time, it would be different. Maybe he even believed it.

The bride is beautiful. They always were, each one younger than her predecessors. My dad loved big, but he didn't love long.

Despite everything I hoped he was right this time. I hoped she (Elisabeth?) was the one who proved me wrong. Fourth time was the charm? Or maybe I was just fooling myself because it was easier than admitting I'd given up on him. When you're the kid left behind, watching your family fall apart over and over, you learn the value of things your parents took for granted. You learn to want something better. To be better.

5

____

The Present

Pass the butter, please."
Damn.

I pass her the butter, but not before I assess the density of that request. When you're passing a woman butter across the table, you're in something serious. That's relationship territory. I kiss her tanned arm as she takes it from me, kissing the inside of her wrist. She smells like clean linen—like Sundays in the summertime. She gives smiles freely and frequently. Dimples, the kind that carve their way in deep when she's happy. Jessica doesn't just smile with her mouth; her whole face gets involved, like her body is incapable of containing the joy.

She butters her toast while scrolling her iPad. I watch her, trying to decipher what it is about this moment that feels both comforting and . . . off. A routine. Something resembling normalcy after my divorce. It's been a while since my world felt steady.

She looks up suddenly, catching me staring. "What?"

"Nothing."

Mostly we are here, but that's because I like my own bed.

I watch her butter her toast while she plays on her iPad. We have a nice little thing going on. I still feel like a barren wasteland on the inside, but she makes it better.

"Pass the salt, please." I test this out. See how it feels. She passes the saltshaker without looking up, and I frown. Everyone knows you don't pass the salt without the pepper. They're a pair. Even if someone only asks for one, you pass both. Now I'm going to have to break up with her.

Kidding.

We get ready for work and kiss at the bottom of the elevator.

"Caleb," she says, as I'm walking away.

"Yeah?"

"I love you."

Wow. Okay.

"Jess," I say. "I—"

"You don't have to say it back." She smiles. "I just want you to know."

"All right," I say, slowly. "I'll see you tonight, yeah?"

She nods.

Eight months, one week—that's how long it has been since she spent the night at my place for the first time. *Acissej*—it doesn't really roll off the tongue like some of them do. What she just said feels strange, but I can't pinpoint why. Maybe it's time to move in together. I climb into my car and crank the AC. She likes my facial hair. Leah wouldn't tolerate facial hair. She said it chaffed her face. When she used the word *chaffed* I wanted to divorce her. Or maybe I just always wanted to divorce her. When I think about Leah, I feel sick. Not because of her—she has very little power over me anymore. It's that little girl.

I pull my thoughts away from that. When I get to work, my mother is already there chatting with my stepfather, Steve, in the main office. The sight of her brings on a mix of emotions—love, exasperation, and a simmering guilt I've been carrying around for months. She spots me the moment I step inside and beams, arms outstretched.

"He's never home anymore, and you hardly come to visit," she says, pulling me into a tight hug.

Her perfume—a familiar floral blend—pulls me back to similar times.

"I have to come here to see my two boys." She looks between us with teary-eyed affection.

The guilt intensifies.

Her arms linger around me for a second longer than I expect, as if she's holding on to something unspoken. I pat her back awkwardly before stepping away. "Good to see you too, Mom."

She follows me to my office, her heels clicking softly on the floor. I know the look on her face—the one that says she's got something on her mind and she's not leaving until she gets it off her chest. I toss my keys on the desk and start shuffling papers, trying to act busy, it's no use.

"How's Jessica?" my mother asks.

She sits down, smoothing her skirt.

I half smile, but it's forced.

"She told me she loved me this morning."

Her eyes light up, but I cut her off before she can say anything.

"I didn't say it back," I admit, keeping my gaze on the stack of papers in front of me.

The room goes quiet. I can feel her eyes boring into me,

but I don't look up. She finally speaks, her voice softer now. "I really liked Leah," she says.

My hand freezes mid-sort. Of course she brings up Leah.

"When you lost your memory, she really just stuck with you. As a mother, I appreciated that." She sighs heavily, the weight of years behind it. "But I know you still love *that* girl."

My turn to sigh. I drop the papers and lean back in my chair. "I don't know what you're talking about. And even if I did, I wouldn't want to talk about it. So talk about something else. How are your roses?"

"Don't even . . ." She waves me off like I've said something offensive. "Jessica is great, Caleb. Really, she is. But she wants a commitment. You do know that, don't you?"

"Ugh . . . mom. Yes."

"Do you want to be married again? Have . . . children?"

I flinch.

"I don't really want to talk about this right now," I say, my voice tighter than I intend.

"You can't let Leah steal who you are," she says gently. Her words are meant to be comforting, but they're anything but.

She doesn't understand. She can't. My heart is still broken, splintered into pieces I'm not sure I can put back together. I'm trying to figure out how to live without what I really want. That includes letting go of old dreams and forcing myself to think about new ones. At least that's what I tell myself.

"I don't want those things anymore," I say firmly, hoping she'll hear the finality of my tone.

She doesn't. "I saw Estella."

I freeze. The words stop me cold. My heart lurches in my chest.

"What?"

"At the mall," she says. "I ran into Leah and she was with her."

The world tilts, just a little. My mind races with questions I'm too afraid to ask. How is she? Is she talking? What does she look like now?

I run a hand across the back of my neck and stare at the armrest on her chair. It's easier than looking at her. She doesn't say anything for a full minute.

"She was my granddaughter, Caleb. I love her." Her voice drops off at the end, and for the first time, I consider my mother's feelings in all of this. She lost Estella too.

"She's yours, Caleb. I feel it."

"Mother, stop it . . ." My voice cracks, betraying the control I'm trying so hard to maintain.

"No, I won't." Her voice is sharp now, cutting through my defense. "You get a paternity test. There is something not right."

I stop what I'm doing and sit down. My chest feels tight, like I can't get enough air. "Why would she lie to me about that? She loses child support, babysitting, and claim on me by lying."

"Oh, Caleb." My mother leans forward, her eyes pleading. "Leah is the type of girl who values revenge more than practicality."

Her words send a shiver down my spine. Honest to God, goose bumps. Could it be true? Could Leah be that vindictive?

I shake my head, more to myself than her. "You want

that to be true. I do too. But it's not. There's a good chance she's your grandchild. Talk to your son."

"Just think about it," she adds softly. "If she refuses you can get the court to order one." She leans forward, her voice dropping to a whisper. "Caleb, she has your nose."

"Fuck." The word slips out before I can stop it, and the look on her face makes me feel worse. "Okay, we're done here." I stand abruptly and walk her to the door, desperate to end the conversation.

Before I push her out, I kiss her on the cheek. "You're a good mother," I say, and I mean it. "But I'm an adult. Go meddle in Seth's life."

She smiles, but it's strained. Her worry hasn't lessened.

"Goodbye, my son."

As the door clicks shut behind her, I collapse into my chair, my head in my hands. Her words play on a loop in my mind, each one more unsettling than the last.

If Estella really is mine, what does that mean for the life I've been trying to build without her? And if she's not, can I handle losing her all over again?

6

The Past

I had her. It wasn't a firm grip, but I finally had her. We fell into a relationship easily. The day-to-day routine was light and airy. We played, we kissed, we talked for hours about things that mattered and things that didn't. I could never predict what she was going to say next. I liked that. She was so different from the girls I was used to. Even Jessica—who was the closest thing I'd come to falling in love with—had never elicited the feelings from me that Olivia did.

There was one day in particular when we were talking about how many kids we wanted—or maybe I was talking about it. Olivia shied away from the future.

"Five—I want five."

She raised an eyebrow and crinkled her nose. "That's too many. What if your wife doesn't want that many?"

We had taken a drive to the beach and were lying on a blanket pretending to look at the stars, but mostly we were looking at each other.

"I guess you and I can come to a compromise."

She started blinking rapidly as if something had flown in her eye. "I don't want children," she said, looking away.

"Yes, you do."

She hated when I did that—told her she was wrong about her own thoughts.

I leaned up on my elbows and looked at the water to avoid the dirty look she was giving me.

"You're not going to mess them up," I said. "You're not going to be like your father, and you will not end up like your mother because I will never leave you."

"I'll die of cancer, then."

"No, you won't. We'll have you checked regularly."

"How do you always fucking know what I'm thinking?"

I looked over at her. She was sitting up with her knees pulled to her chest and her head resting on her knees. Her hair was piled on top of her head in a large, almost comical knot. I wanted to pull it out and let it tumble down her back, but she looked so cute I left it.

"I see you, even when you think I'm not looking. I'm probably more obsessed with you than is healthy."

She tried to swallow her smile, but I saw it pinching the corners of her mouth. I tackled her to her back. She giggled. She hardly ever giggled . . . I could probably count the number of times I'd heard that sound on my two hands.

"You don't give an inch. That's why I like you, Olivia—no middle name—Kaspen. You make me work for every smile, every giggle . . ."

She shook her head. "I don't giggle."

"Really?" My fingers crept up her ribs. I tickled her. She giggled so hard I was laughing too.

When we sobered up, she lay with her head on my

chest. Her next words took me by surprise. I lay as still as I could, barely breathing, afraid that if I moved she would stop speaking her heart.

"My mom wanted six children. She only got me, and that sucks for her because I was a total weirdo."

"You were not," I said.

She twisted her head up to look at me. "I used to line my lips in black eyeliner and sit cross-legged on the kitchen table . . . meditating."

"Not that bad," I said. "Crying out for attention."

"Okay, when I was twelve I started writing letters to my birth mother because I wanted to be adopted."

I shook my head. "Your childhood sucked. You wanted a new reality."

She snorted air through her nose. "I thought a mermaid lived in my shower drain, and I used to call her Sarah and talk to her."

"Active imagination," I countered. She was becoming more insistent, her little body wriggling in my grip.

"I used to make paper out of dryer lint."

"Nerdy."

"I wanted to be one with nature, so I started boiling grass and drinking it with a little bit of dirt for sugar."

I paused. "Okay, that's weird."

"Thank you!" she said. Then, she got serious again. "My mom just loved me through all of it."

My arms tightened around her. I was afraid the wind, the water . . . life would take her away from me. I didn't want her to blow away.

"When she was in the hospital toward the end, she was

in a lot of pain, but all she did was worry about me." She
paused, laughed a little. "She had no hair. Her head looked
like a shiny egg and it was always cold. I tried to knit her a
hat, but it was terrible, full of holes, but of course she wore
it anyway."

I could hear her tears. My heart was aching like she had
it between her fist.

"She was always asking me, 'Are you hungry? Are you
tired? Are you sad?'" Her voice cracked. I ran my hand up
her back, trying to comfort her, knowing I couldn't.

"I would have switched places with her."

Her sob ripped me open, spilled everything out. I sat us
both up and held her in my lap as she cried.

Her pain was so jagged. You couldn't touch her without it slicing through you too. I wanted to fold myself
around her and absorb the rest of the blows life would
deliver.

That was the exact moment my heart threaded with
hers. It was as if someone reached down with a sewing nee-
dle and stitched my soul to hers. How could one woman
be so sharp and so vulnerable at the same time? Whatever
would happen to her would happen to me. Whatever pain
she would feel, I would feel it too. I wanted it—that was
the surprising part. Selfish, self-centered Caleb Drake loved
a girl so much he could already feel himself changing to
accommodate her needs.

I fell.

Hard.

For the rest of this life and probably the next.

I wanted her—every last inch of her stubborn, combative, catty heart.

A FEW MONTHS after that, I told her I loved her for the first time. I'd loved her for a while, but I knew she wasn't ready to hear it. The minute the words were out of my mouth, she looked like she wanted to stuff them back in. Her nostrils started flaring and her skin flushed. She couldn't say it back. I was disappointed but not surprised. I knew she loved me, but I wanted to hear it. The more she rejected me, the more aggressively I fought to tear down her walls. I pushed too far sometimes . . . like the camping trip. I tried to prove to her that she wasn't as autonomous as she thought. I wanted to show her that it was okay to be vulnerable and to want me. For someone like Olivia, sex was directly tied to her emotions. She tried to pretend that sex wasn't important to her—that she could have a healthy relationship without it. But her body was her playing card. The longer she held out with sex, the longer she held on to her power.

When I walked into that tent, I was determined to strip her of her power. "You are master of your own body, yes?"

She jutted her chin defiantly. "Yes."

"Then, you won't have a problem controlling it."

I could see the uncertainty in her eyes as I moved toward her. If she wanted to play games, I was going to play harder. She was out of her league. For the last year, I'd had to fight away every desire, every need I had. All I wanted was three words. Three words she wouldn't give me, and now she was going to pay.

She tried to walk away, but I grabbed her by the wrist and pulled her back.

The restraint I'd held back for a year sat precariously on the edge of a cliff. I let it dangle there for a minute before I shoved it off and kissed her. I kissed her like I would have kissed an experienced girl. I kissed her like I kissed her the first time, in the pool—before I knew she was so broken. She responded better than I thought. It was almost as if she'd been waiting for me to kiss her like that. She tried pushing me away a couple of times, but it was half-hearted. And even then, she never stopped kissing me. Her mind was at war with itself. I decided to give her a little help. Pulling away from her, I grabbed her flimsy T-shirt and ripped it off, neck to seam. It tore like paper. Her mouth dropped open as I drew the remaining fabric from her arms and tossed it aside. I pulled her toward me again and kissed her as my fingers found the clasp on her bra and flicked it off. She was against me now, skin to skin. I yanked her pants down and she keened into my mouth like it was the best and worst thing I'd ever done.

She was panting into my mouth—God I was so turned on. I slowed down a little. I wanted to take my time kissing all the places I'd always wanted to and had never been allowed—the space between her breasts, the insides of her thighs, the commas on her lower back.

She had a sweet spot right above her collarbone where her neck dipped. I listened to her intake of breath in satisfaction and worked my way down. I'd just reached her perfect nipples when she leaned into me like her lust was too heavy and she couldn't stand. I put her on the ground and lowered myself on top of her. I was sucking on her nipples and letting my hand slide up the inside of her thigh. She was wearing black lace panties; they stood out against her creamy skin. My hand stopped when it reached the junction of her thighs. I wanted her to want it. I let my thumb brush across the lace and she bucked underneath me. I wondered if anyone else had ever touched her there. I was having a hard time controlling myself. I breathed into her hair. It smelled like fresh laundry.

"Are you still in control?"

She nodded. I could feel her shaking and I wanted to call bullshit.

"Stop me," I said. "If you're in control, then stop me."

I pulled off the sweatpants that were still lingering around her ankles. She looked up at me with glassy eyes, like stopping me was the last thing she wanted to do.

That's when I snapped out of it. My game was turning toxic. I breathed in hard through my nose. I could take her now. She'd let me. But that wouldn't be fair. I was manipulating her. She'd be angry with me after—she'd fold in on herself and I'd lose her. I just needed her to acknowledge me. "Who owns you?"

She licked her lips. Her hands were locked on my arms. I could feel slight pressure as she pulled me toward her. She was silently asking me. I held back—she'd taught me how. She shook her head, not understanding.

I hunted her eyes down, forced her to see me.

I put a hand over her chest. I could feel her heart . . . pounding.

I want her. I want her. I want her. Please, Olivia. Please let me have you . . .

"Who owns you?"

Her eyes liquefied. She understood. Her body went limp.

"You," she said softly.

Her vulnerability, her body, her hair—it was all turning me on. I had never in my life wanted a woman more than I wanted her.

I threw my head back, closed my eyes, and rolled off her.

Don't look at her. If you look at her again you'll end up inside of her.

"Thank you."

And then I left as quickly as I could to take a cold, cold shower.

She wouldn't look at me for a week after.

7

The Present

My cell phone rings. The sound cuts through the still-ness of the night, dragging me from the kind of deep sleep that feels like sinking. I crack open an eye. There is no light filtering through the blinds, which means it's either too fucking late or too fucking early to be calling. I grope for my phone, squinting at the glowing screen before press-ing Answer and crushing it to my ear.

"Hello." My voice is rough, edged with irritation.

"Caleb?"

Her voice is familiar, but my brain is slow to catch up. I sit up, blinking at the darkness, and glance over at Jessica. She's sleeping on her stomach, her face obscured by a cas-cade of blond hair.

"Yeah?" I rub my eyes and pull my knees up.

"It's me."

There's a beat of silence before it clicks. I recognize the voice now—soft but tense, like a wire pulled too tight.

"Olivia?" Her name feels like a punch to the chest, a sudden jolt of adrenaline.

My glance shifts to the clock: 4:49 a.m.

"I'm sorry," she rushes, her voice shaky. "I didn't know who to call."

I'm already swinging my legs over the side of the bed, the phone wedged between my shoulder and ear. My hand is grabbing for my jeans before she's even finished her sentence.

"Don't say sorry. What's going on?" My tone is sharper now, fully awake.

"It's Dobson," she says. Her words tumbling out. "The police think he's coming here."

I break away from my phone to pull a shirt over my head.

"Where's Noah?" I ask, trying to keep my voice steady.

Silence. It stretches long enough that I think the line has gone dead.

"Olivia?"

"Not here."

"All right," I say. "I'll be there in thirty minutes."

Jessica stirs when I shake her shoulders gently. "Hey," I whisper. "I have to go. Olivia is in trouble."

Her eyes barely open but she murmurs, "Do you want me to come with you?"

"No, it's fine."

I kiss her temple and she sinks back into her pillow without another word.

The air in the parking garage is thick with salt, the kind of clean briny tang you can only smell before the city fully wakes up. I pull out and navigate the empty streets of Sunny Isles Beach. Her building looms like a reflective monolith against the inky sky, towering over its neighbors. I text her to let her know I've arrived. The lobby is eerily quiet. The night manager eyes me suspiciously.

"Caleb."

I turn, and she's walking toward me. She's dressed in white yoga pants and a matching hoodie, the hood pulled low over her head. Strands of dark hair escape, framing her face, which looks pale and drawn. Without thinking, I cross the room in four strides and pull her into me. She folds into my chest like she belongs there, her arms hooking upward instead of around, the way she always did. It was our thing.

"Are you okay?" I ask the top of her head.

She nods against my chest. "I deserve it, this is what I get for taking the case."

"You wanna go get some breakfrast?" She cracks a smile at my deliberate mispronunciation, a callback to a thousand mornings spent together.

She looks nervously toward the entrance of the building.

"Duchess," I say, squeezing her arms. "I got you."

"That's good—" she nods "—because if he gets me, I'm in a lot of fucking trouble."

When Cammie barrels into the picture—her energy a whirlwind of snark and loyalty.

"Let's take my car," I offer.

We take the elevator down to the parking garage and climb into my BMW.

"Well, look at us," Cammie says. "All together again, like ten fucking years of lies and bullshit never happened."

I glance at her in my rearview mirror. "Angry much?"

"Nope, nope—I'm fine. Are you fine? I'm fine." Cammie's tone laced with sarcasm makes me smile. She folds her arms across her chest and looks out the window.

I shift my attention to Olivia, who's sitting in the passenger seat, her fingers lightly tapping the armrest, trying not to engage.

"Can we just not fight tonight, Cam?" Olivia says, half-heartedly. "He's here because I asked him to be."

I frown. I know better than to ask what is happening between the two of them. It could result in a full-blown argument. I turn into the parking lot of a Waffle House. The glowing yellow sign buzzes faintly.

"Here we go, ladies," I say as we pile out of the car and head inside.

When we've settled into a booth Cammie kicks Olivia's shin to get her attention. Olivia shoots her a warning glare.

"So, did you tell him about Noah, O?" Her voice deceptively casual as she picks up the menu, not even bothering to look at Olivia.

"Shut up, Cammie." Her voice is low, dangerous.

"What?" Cammie shrugs, glancing up with a look that's almost too innocent to be believable. "He's sitting right here. Might as well get it all out in the open."

I look at her out of the corner of my eye, curiosity piqued. Olivia's lips are pressed together, clearly trying to keep her composure. "Tell me what?"

This is going to be a long day.

Cammie opens her mouth clearly to answer me, but Olivia spins in her seat, her finger pointed like a weapon. "I will destroy you."

"Why would you do that when you're so good at destroying yourself?" Cammie shoots back.

"Waffles. Mmm." I try to redirect the conversation to anything else, but they're locked in a snark-off. "You're both acting feral."

They glare at me. When the server finally comes to take our order there is a palpable tension at the table.

"Yesi," I say, reading her name tag. "Please save my life and get these women something to eat."

SLOWLY, FORKS SCRAPE against plates and coffee is sipped, the tension ebbs. I cut into my omelet and watch as they slowly come out of their funk. In a few minutes they're laughing and taking bites of each other's food.

"What are the police saying?" I ask quietly.

Olivia sets down her fork and wipes her mouth. "After I won the case, he was convinced it was because I loved him and we were supposed to be together."

"Seems like that happens a lot," Cammie says through a mouthful of waffle. "Your ex-clients becoming obsessed with you and self-destructing." She sucks syrup off the tip of her finger and stares pointedly at me.

I kick Cammie under the table.

"Ow!"

Olivia props her chin in her hands.

When I look at her, I can't seem to look away. It's been that way since the first day I saw her under the tree.

Our eyes meet. It's an intimate unspoken connection that lasts just long enough to make my stomach knot.

I pay the check and we climb back into my car. The girls don't want to go back to Olivia's. I thought about volunteering my place until I remember that Jessica is curled up in my bed.

"We can go to my place for a few hours," Cammie offers.

"My man gets back at noon to record his podcast, but we can hang there until then."

Olivia nods like she likes the idea.

"Cammie's boyfriend has a show called *Deep End with Derek*," Olivia explains.

"It's mostly just conspiracy ranting, but he has a pretty good audience," Cammie says. "His last episode was about the Bermuda Triangle. He's unhinged."

The three of us are sitting around Cammie's living room thirty minutes later, the TV on mute. Derek's recording equipment sits in the corner, the mic perched on a stand like it's watching us.

"How are you doing?" Cammie asks Olivia. "Are you blaming yourself again?"

Olivia stares at her hands, her fingers twisting her wedding ring. "My job wasn't to figure out whether he was guilty. My job was to defend him." Her voice cracked and she buried her face in her hands.

Olivia was always so composed, so certain of herself. Seeing her like this—broken, angry, and afraid—was like seeing a stranger.

Cammie, for once, didn't say anything. She just sat there, her face pale, her hands gripping the edge of the couch like she was bracing for something.

"He used to send me letters. After the trial. At first, they were just thank-yous. Telling me how much he appreciated my help. Then he started getting weird. Talking about fate. Things dropped off for a while. I was so relieved I tried to forget about it."

We leave Cammie's before her man gets home, climbing back into my car with even less enthusiasm than before.

"I have an idea," I say, the words slipping out before I can think them through. When they press me for details, I shake my head and smile.

"Not yet. I'm still figuring this out in my head. It may be reckless, but I like how it's developing."

Without hesitation I make a sharp U-turn, weaving through the early morning traffic with more confidence than I feel. I glance at her beside me.

"Do you want to grab some clothes from your place?"

She nods her face pale but determined. Cammie waits in my car while we go upstairs.

Her condo is quiet, almost too quiet. It feels like the place itself is holding its breath. Being in her home reminds me of her husband. I try not to let my eyes linger on the details that feel like him—like them.

I follow her into the master bedroom. It smells like her perfume. The bed is unmade, the comforter halfway on the floor like she left in a hurry. Olivia always teeters on the edge of control, never quite falling over.

Empty Coke cans litter the nightstand, artifacts from a life I'm no longer part of. Olivia disappears into the closet while I linger outside. I can hear her pulling open drawers and then the sound of a zipper. Directly across from Olivia's closet is the secondary closet I assume is Noah's. My hand moves before I can stop it. I push the door open and find it empty. I stare at the barren shelves. I glance back at Olivia's closet where the faint shuffle of movement continues.

"I think I have everything." She sees me looking in his closet. She can see the questions written all over my face. She looks away.

"Ready?"

WHEN I SLIDE back into the car I notice Cammie snoring softly in the back.

Olivia pats the duffel bag on her lap with a little sigh like she's relieved.

"You game for this adventure?" I ask.

"Say less . . ."

"Okie."

We pull out of the garage to a beautiful sunrise, a smile on my face.

8

The Past

Soap sprayed on my windshield, bubbles racing down the glass as the car vibrated under the rhythm of pounding jets. The world outside was blurred and distorted, a kaleidoscope of muted colors. It was just the two of us trapped in this fragile bubbling limbo. Olivia pulled away from my mouth, her breath warm against my cheek, and glanced over her shoulder like she expected someone to catch us. No one would, it was just us, the car and the relentless sound of water hammering the metal. My lips found the elegant curve of her neck, the spot where her perfume lingered. My fingers slid into the back of her hair, tangling in the strands as I steered her mouth back to mine.

She was grinding against my swollen dick, one tiny piece of cotton between us. All I could think about was being inside of her. It wasn't just physical. It was intoxicating, overwhelming. I was painfully conscious of the fact she'd never done this before.

Her weight shifted, pressing down in a way that made me suck in a sharp breath. Every nerve in my body felt like it was on fire. I didn't want to mess this up. It was impossible not to react.

I grabbed her by the waist, lifting her effortlessly, and replanted her in the passenger seat. The look on her face was equal parts confused and disappointed. My hands were gripping the steering wheel like a lifeline as I forced my thoughts elsewhere.

"I thought we were just messing around."

I groaned.

"The thing with messing around is—you slowly work your way toward sex. It starts with hands and then mouths and then before you know it you're doing all three . . . at the same time."

She blushed.

I opened the bottle of water that was sitting in my cup holder and took a sip. The dull ache of blue balls. Honestly, it wasn't unbearable—it's not like I was doubled over in pain—but it was definitely uncomfortable. The car wash rattled around us, strips of soapy rubber slapping the metal. I felt those slaps.

She climbed back into my lap as the dryers turned on, her hands framing my face as she pressed her nose against mine. Her breath was soft, tentative and I could feel her walls crumbling a little. This was the side of Olivia that wrecked me—the soft vulnerable side that made me want to shield her from the world.

"I'm sorry, Caleb. I'm sorry I'm so messed up."

My hands went back to her waist. "You're not messed up."

But then my eyes drifted downward—to the curve of her legs, the way her skirt rode up—I knew I was teetering on the edge of self-control. All I would have to do was unzip my pants. She was ready. She really had no idea what she did to me.

"You're going to have to go back to your seat." My voice was gruff. Mercifully she climbed off my lap and settled back into her seat. The loss of her warmth was immediate, but so was the relief. Kind of.

The dryers roared above, blasting air like the final push in some industrial birthing process. With a last jolt the car broke free from the clutches of the wash, emerging into sunlight.

She held my hand as I steered.

She studied me, her fingers squeezing mine, her icy blue eyes softening just enough to make my chest tighten. "You're a good man, Caleb Drake." The sincerity in her voice caught me off guard.

"But," she added, a sly smile tugging at the corners of her mouth. "I have to admit, I kind of like watching you squirm."

I let out a shaky laugh. "You're killing me, Duchess."

"I wish I knew what you were thinking," she said.

"There's always the option of asking me." I put the car in gear and pulled forward. "I feel like you're always trying to sneak into my mind. You're like Peter Pan."

She scrunched up her nose, her expression so endearing it made my stomach flip. "Did you really just call me Peter Pan?"

"I've called you worse."

"A llama," she smiled. "I loved that," she said with obvious sarcasm, though there was warmth in her voice.

She reached over and turned on the radio, scrolling through stations until she found a song we both knew. Without missing a beat she started rapping along, her voice half serious, half silly. I tried to keep up, but we were completely out of sync, tripping over lyrics and cracking up at each other's mistakes.

Later, we watched an episode of *The Bachelorette* sitting side by side on her bed, our backs propped against the wall. She suddenly turned off the TV.

"Peter Pan."

I glanced over at her, raising an eyebrow.

"You want to know what I'm thinking?"

She nodded.

"Are you sure, Olivia Kaspen?"

"Are you kidding me, Caleb Drake?" She put the remote down and climbed onto my lap until she was straddling me. "I want to know all of your thoughts."

"I was imagining what it would feel like to make you wet and then slowly push inside you."

Her breath hitched and her eyes grew glassy.

"How *would* you make me wet?"

"Is this show or tell?"

"Both."

Without the TV on the only light in the room comes from the LEDs strung across her ceiling. I was already hard.

Slow I reminded myself. I put one hand on her waist and with my free hand I cupped her breast and traced circles around her nipple with my thumb. She arched her back, her eyes rolling.

She ground against my dick as I kissed her neck, then her ears, then her mouth.

"Are you wet?" I pulled one side of her tank top down and sucked on her nipple.

Her fingers were in my hair, gripping as I sucked.

"You should check." Her voice was breathy and strained.

I reached between us, my hand moving under her skirt. I got the feeling she liked it like this: where I could feel her but not see her. I found the center of her body and stroked. She writhed against my touch, her hips jerking.

"I can't tell." I lied.

She gasped against my mouth, sucking on my bottom lip.

"Caleb . . . please . . ." Her mouth was warm and wet.

It took a second to push aside her underwear and slip my finger into her body.

Throbbing and hot, her muscles tightened around my finger. She was wet . . . soaked. I leaned my head back so it was resting against the wall, and closed my eyes, listening to the sounds she was making. This was slow death.

"You're wet . . . and tight."

Her body contracted around my finger and I groaned.

She rested her forehead on my collarbone and tilted her hips to give me better access.

"It feels really good . . ." She was breathless. Being inside of her without being inside her of her was making me lose my mind.

She'd be choking the truth out of my dick.

When my finger slid out of her she cried out in protest. I'd never heard anything sexier in my whole life.

She grabbed my hand and put it back. She didn't tense up, her body opened up and I slide two fingers inside of her this time. She said my name when she came.

A WEEK LATER we met up for dinner in the cafeteria. Olivia was wearing a Nirvana tee; it had been washed so many times the print on it was barely visible.

"My mom's," she said when she saw me looking at it. My sadness for Olivia was followed by guilt. I'd been avoiding my own mother's calls all week.

"Pizza or mystery meat?" Olivia asked, staring with resignation at the questionable stir-fry. It was globby and gelatinous. I eyed the square pieces of pizza, soggy crust and peperoni that looked like burnt rubber. "Looks like a cereal night for me!"

Olivia assembled a salad while I grabbed a bowl. I was staring at the dispensers trying to decide which generic cardboard I wanted: Cheerios, Raisin Bran, Frosted Flakes, or Mini-Wheats. I was pouring milk over my Frosted Flakes when a passing conversation caught my ear.

"Definitely don't want to end up like Laura Hilberson—" I looked over my shoulder to see two girls walk by, arm in arm, their heads together. Had they found her? My stomach sank.

I hadn't heard Laura's name spoken aloud in weeks. Or maybe I hadn't wanted to hear it. Guilt crept in. I'd completely forgotten about her. That would explain the calls from my mother. I wasn't sure how much attention I owed the situation being that our relationship was so short-lived, but I could at least call my mom back and ask how the Hilbersons were doing. Making a mental note to call her later, I glanced at Olivia, who was drizzling dressing on her salad. I felt a connection with her: deep and sure. I didn't know her, not in the way you knew someone you'd spent years with—but maybe someone you'd spent another life with. Olivia took up every spare second of my thoughts. I saw her standing under the tree that day and I knew her. It's not something I was prepared for, but then again, how could I have been? How could anyone be ready for the moment when everything inside of you suddenly aligns with someone else?

We went back to her room after dinner to do homework. There was a thunderstorm warning in the area, but it wasn't raining yet. I'd stretched out on her bed with my laptop when she came out of the bathroom, holding her phone out so I could see the screen.

"Laura is all over social media." I took the phone from her. A sick feeling bloomed in the pit of my stomach. *New leads in the Laura Hilberson case.*

Her credit card had been used at a gas station in Mississippi. There was no video footage since the security camera on-site was broken. The clerk, a teenager, had been high when the transaction took place. I read through the comments.

Was she seeing someone? Does
anyone know who?

I heard she was involved with a guy
from MS. She met him online.

We need to find her—this is so messed up.

The rumors, the speculation—they were everywhere. People were grasping at anything they could, creating stories that didn't fit the facts.

"What was she like?" Olivia's voice snapped me out of my thoughts.

"I don't know. Quiet. She was close with her family—she had two sisters and they did everything together. She liked ice cream and Jane Austen—honestly, that's all I remember." Olivia rolled onto her back and stared at the ceiling.

"I bet someone took her then, happy people don't run away . . ."

Did happy people run away? I thought about Jessica, funny and carefree. We'd been happy, or so I thought. We laughed a lot when we were together. She was goofy. She had a habit of trying on outfits and narrating them like she was on a runway. "And here we have Jessica sporting the 2010s classic: leggings and a hoodie. Perfect for binge-watching Netflix and avoiding responsibility." It always cracked me up. She had a ridiculous talent for impersonating animals. She could do cats, dogs, even a surprisingly accurate dolphin. It was great entertainment on road trips. She was happy and she'd run away. Not from everyone, but me.

Then there was Olivia.

Olivia was the opposite. Her smiles were hard-won and her moods were erratic. One day after class, I found her in my room lying on my bed, her face buried in the pillow like she was trying to disappear into the fabric. "What are you doing here? Why aren't you in class?"

I was surprised, I hadn't meant to sound harsh. My tone seemed to jar her. She bolted up, bleary-eyed like she'd been asleep. I reached out instinctively, but it was too late. The words hung in the air, too sharp, too clumsy.

She stood up, stiff and uncomfortable and shoved her feet into her sneakers.

"I . . . I don't know. I shouldn't have come."

"No, that's not what I meant—" I dropped my backpack on the floor next to my desk.

She wasn't buying my attempt to backtrack. She headed for the door.

"Olivia, where are you going? Talk to me—"

SHE GHOSTED ME for three days instead. When she finally texted me back her responses were cold.

Sry. Stayed in bed, felt awful.
Thnx for the concern.

I called her right away.

"Why are you being weird?" I asked when she answered.

She was quiet for so long I checked my phone screen to make sure she hadn't hung up.

"I invited myself over and I was embarrassed about that."

"You're my girlfriend, you can come to my room any-time you want."

Another long silence. "I can't come unless you invite me."

"Like a vampire?" I joked.

"I feel awkward about it now."

"I get it," I said. "I always felt unwelcome at my dad's house. It was a terrible feeling; the need to belong and not feeling like you actually did. But that's not the case here. I can't get through five minutes of my day without thinking about you."

"I don't believe you."

"Come here so I can say it to your face."

"To your room?"

"Yeah, I'm inviting you. I want you to be comfortable being here."

Her "okay" was reluctant, but she'd agreed to come over, that was a win. When she arrived thirty minutes later, she was carrying a giant bag of fries and my favorite milkshake. "Food apologies. I overreacted. It was the anniversary of my mom's death, and I was freaking out, so I came here. And then when I saw the look on your face, I felt needy, and clingy, and disgusted with myself for even having the audacity to be here . . ."

"You make me happy. I don't feel displaced when I'm with you. You're not clingy, we're falling for each other, this is what happens when people date." She looked unconvinced, but she let me lead her to the loveseat in front of my TV.

That was a lie. I'd never felt this way about anyone before, this was not what happened when people dated, this was what happened when they fell in love.

We ordered takeout and watched a comedy. She lay on my chest while I played with her hair.

"I'm happy when I'm with you too," she said before drifting off to sleep.

A FEW DAYS later I casually mentioned that I'd forgotten to call my mother back. It was a throwaway comment, something I didn't think twice about, but Olivia's head snapped up immediately. She looked genuinely upset.

Her tone was both sharp and shaky. Thinking of her mother made her cry. She cleared her throat, eyes filling with tears. Her reaction wasn't about me and my mother, she was hurting all while trying to tell me not to take my own mother for granted.

I never took it personally. Olivia's anger wasn't about the daily things, it was about trust, about effort, and being seen and valued in ways that mattered to her.

9

The Present

"**W**here are we?" Cammie sits up in her seat. Her hand instinctively reached for the seatbelt.

"Naples." I pull down a heavily wooded street, the trees arching above us, casting dappled shadows on the road. Cammie's eyes dart around, confused.

"What the hell?"

I glance over at Olivia who has not spoken a word since we started the drive. She's staring out the window. The road curves sharply, and I make a right turn onto a much smaller street. The houses are spaced farther apart, each sprawling over five acres, secluded by tall trees and hedges. Olivia is craning her neck to get a better look at the horses grazing peacefully in a field. We driver farther down the road, and the houses become fewer, the space between them growing wider.

I loved it here; it was the kind of quiet that made you feel peaceful.

"It's so pretty here," she finally says, her voice soft and almost reverent, like she's afraid to disturb the tranquility.

I smile to myself as I steal a glance at her.

"It's peaceful," I add. We reach a solid black gate. I roll down my window and warm humid air climbs into the car. Flipping open the lockbox I type in the code. A soft beep precedes the gentle whir of the motor followed by the scraping of metal against track.

There's a moment of hushed anticipation, as if the gate is a curtain drawing back to reveal the stage. The drive-way stretches ahead, curving gracefully, framed by towering royal palms that sway in the breeze. Solar lights embedded in the manicured landscape cast a soft, golden glow over the path, making it seem almost enchanted.

I can feel Olivia's gaze darting around, her neck craning as she tries to take it all in. Her curiosity is palpable, and I bite back the urge to study her every reaction. I want her to love it as much as I do.

I grab her hand before she can pull away and hold it right over my heart. She lets me hold it there.

"What are you doing?" she asks, her lips twitching with a hint of amusement.

"Feel that?" I ask, my voice low.

Her eyes meet mine, a playful spark flashes behind the blue.

"Feel what? A lot of muscles or a little ego?"

"Behind both of those," I say.

She presses her palm a little harder against my chest, and thinks, feeling the steady rapid thrum beneath.

"You really like this place," she finally says.

"Yes, but not as much as I like it when you touch me."

Throwing open my door, I step out and stretch, the tension in my shoulders easing. I lean the seat forward to let Cammie out, her excitement evident as she scrambles out of the car. I circle around to Olivia's side to open her door, but she's beat me to it.

She gets out and stretches her arms above her head, looking at the house.

I wait for her reaction.

"It's beautiful," she says. I grin and my heart, which had been hammering against my ribs, steadies. "Whose house is this?"

"Mine."

Her eyebrows shoot up, her expression a mix of surprise and curiosity. Without a word, she follows me up the stone steps. The house looms ahead, a grand three-story structure with brick facing that glows softly under the solar lights. A turret rises on one side, its windows catching the faint reflection of the lake behind the house. A widows walk stands silhouetted against the fading sky, a promise of breathtaking views.

The knocker is a masterpiece—solid brass molded into the intricate shape of a crown.

I pause at the door, turning to look at her.

"And yours," I say quietly.

Her lips part, and her brow furrows slightly. There's a flicker of something in her eyes—disbelief, perhaps, or maybe the weight of realization.

I turn the key in the lock, and the door swings open with a soft creak. The house greets us with cool air and the smell of polished wood and linen. We walk into our house.

"Like it?" I ask, my voice betraying the vulnerability I can't hide. She takes a moment, her gaze sweeping the space, her arms wrapping around her waist as though she's grounding herself. Then she meets my eyes, and for the first time in the evening her expression is unguarded.

The house is fully furnished, carefully curated. I've had someone come in once a month to dust and clean the pool—which has never been used. It's a house waiting to come alive.

I open the shades with the touch of a button, and flick on the lights. Olivia and Cammie follow behind me, their footsteps light, almost hesitant.

When we reach the kitchen, Olivia stops. Her arms wrap tightly around her body like she's taking it all in.

"Like it?" I ask, watching her face.

This wasn't how I imagined showing her the house.

The room feels soft, almost romantic. The cabinets are painted a muted blush tone, with delicate gold hardware that gleams under the soft glow of the overhead lights. The countertops are marble, pale with subtle swirls of pink and gray, catching the light inside of a seashell.

A crystal chandelier hangs above the island, its cascading prisms catching the light and scattering rainbows across the walls. Open shelves display soft pink dishes and glassware, while a few copper pots hang elegantly from a small rack, adding a touch of rustic charm to the space. It was the decorator's way of adding me to the kitchen.

On one wall is a refrigerator in a soft ivory shade, its vintage-style curves nostalgic of the fifties.

"This is a very cool fridge," Olivia says.

I can't hide my smile. I knew she'd like it.

"You two have a lot to work out," Cammie says, looking between us. She stretches her arms over her head dramatically. "I'm tired. Point me to the couch . . ."

I point.

Olivia and I watch her wander out of the room, her footsteps echoing against the tile. The silence between us feels fragile, like a thread pulled too tight. I shove my hands in my pockets, trying to ground myself. "Want me to show you the rest of your house?"

She nods and I lead her out of the kitchen, toward the staircase that spirals to the second floor.

"Leah—" she starts, but I cut her off before she can say more.

"No," I say firmly. "I don't want to talk about Leah."

Her lips press into a thin line. "Fine," she says, sharply.

We climb the stairs in silence. I focus on the faint creak of the stairs and the way the fading sunlight pours through the floor-to-ceiling windows. She pauses to look out the window. The view is spectacular.

"Where's Noah?"

"If I'm not allowed to ask, you're not allowed to ask."

"Let's make a truth trade."

Beyond the glass, the backyard is being touched by the sun's last rays. Emerald green grass stretches toward the water, flanked by flowerbeds brimming with passionflowers and clusters of fire bush.

Above it all the sky is a masterpiece in transition. Wisps of clouds are streaked with fiery orange that melts into soft purple.

"It's so beautiful, Caleb." She sighs, so wistfully my heart aches. It's a garden designed by both nature and care, but it feels wild enough to slow the world down when you look at it. We'd lost a lot of time together, but it wasn't too late. There was still time for us.

"What type of truth trade?"

"You're going to have to tell me what happened eventually don't you think?"

She turns away from the window to continue up the stairs, stopping to examine a painting at the top of the landing.

The Heart Feels More than the Eye Sees. Morpho butterflies flutter with tropical birds, blooming flowers, fiery dragons, snakes, all weaving into a living anatomical heart.

The piece seems alive, the elements feeding off the heart's energy. It's dark and heavy and joyful all at the same time. Like Olivia.

I look at her out of the corner of my eye. I can tell she likes it.

"Eventually, you'll tell me you're faking your amnesia. Eventually, I'll tell you that I'm pretending not to know you. Eventually, we'll come back together, fall apart, come back together again. Eventually, you'll tell me you built me a house . . ."

I watch her closely, captivated by her words. She has a way of cutting straight to the heart of things.

Every detail, every decision—it was her. She's been the ghost in every room for years.

She turns left and stops at the first doorway. I stand behind her resisting the urge to pull her against me and wrap my arms around her. Does her hair still smell like candy? Instead I reach around her to flip on the light switch.

"I was building it for you. I was going to bring you here the night I proposed. It was only an empty lot then, but I wanted to show you what we could build together."

She inhales sharply, and I see her shoulders tremble with her exhale. "You were going to ask me to marry you?"

"I'd ask you again now, but I heard you're taken . . ."

She rolls her eyes.

For a moment, I consider telling her about the night she walked in on me at the office—the night everything fell apart. But I hold back. This isn't the time. "This is the office, it faces the lake."

Curved floor-to-ceiling bookshelves line the walls, following the gentle arc of the circular space. At the center of the room is a statement desk that sits beneath a skylight.

"Oh my," she says. She steps inside, then glances over her shoulder. "I can't believe you did this . . ."

"Really?" I ask, crossing my arms and leaning on the door frame. "It's what you wanted."

"Caleb!" Her tone is scolding but her eyes are doing a happy dance around the room. "You're obsessed with me," she says. "I love it."

I laugh. I'm enjoying her reactions. She's cute when she's excited about something.

She examines the desk, the books, the flooring. "I can't believe you remember that conversation."

"Oh, you mean the one where you told me, 'I want a circular office with a skylight' and then spent twenty minutes doodling the idea on a napkin? You called it the church of Olivia," I remind her.

"I don't want to leave," she says.

"That was the point."

"But after things ended you kept building. Why?"

"A project, Duchess," I say softly. "I needed something to fix."

"Ah, the savior complex. You couldn't fix me—or Dirty Red. So . . . you built a house?"

I'm amused. "Dirty Red?"

"That's right. She's the slimiest redhead on the planet. Filthy little liar."

"Well, then, yes. I couldn't fix you or Dirty Red and I needed a project."

She rolls her eyes. "Show me the rest."

Olivia steps cautiously into the master bedroom, her movements hesitant, almost reverent.

I can practically hear the wheels turning in her head. The ceiling beams are rich mahogany. I chose mismatched nightstands because I like intentional imperfection. She walks to the closest one and flips the lamp on. The light makes the blue on the walls look green. I watch as her eyes land on the bed, and for a second, I wonder if she can feel the weight of everything this room represents.

We would have made our babies on this bed, five at least. I wouldn't be able to keep my hands off her. On Christmas morning they would have piled on the bed to wake us up.

"Have you ever slept here . . . with another woman?"

"No, Duchess, I've never slept here with another woman."

"This is not at all like your other place." It sounds like an accusation.

A corner of my mouth shoots up. "No shit, Sherlock. I intended on sharing this one with a woman. The love of my life."

She runs a finger along the plush white comforter then tentatively sits on the edge of the bed. "Did Leah know about it?"

I nod. "It caused a lot of fights when I refused to sell it."

"It's too beautiful to sell."

Before I can process that, she suddenly rolls. Not once, but twice, like she's a little kid testing the space she can cover. She lands on her feet on the opposite side of the bed. Her hair is mussed and her face triumphant.

I show her the rest of the bedrooms—four in total and then take her up the narrow flight of stairs to the third floor. It's spacious . . . empty. The floors are hardwood, the ceiling slanted.

"What was this going to be . . . ?"

"I was leaving that up to you."

"This is a lot to take in."

I hold out my hand. "Let's process in the kitchen with food."

She makes me show her the library/office one more time before I lead her back to the kitchen. She sits on one of the barstools around the island and drops her head into her hands. "I feel like I'm dreaming. Am I?"

I walk over and kiss the top of her head.

"I hope not."

WE SPEND THE next two days existing in a comfortable silence. Even Cammie is strangely quiet, her normally expressive face immobile. Occasionally she glances up from her phone to scowl at one or the other of us. Olivia sits between us, cross-legged, reading a book. She hasn't turned a page in fifteen minutes. Her eyes are distant, unfocused. I want to know what she's thinking. Is she reliving the past, the way I am? Or is she lost in Noah? Dobson? I suggest a dip in the pool, but neither of them is in the mood to swim.

The quiet stretches on. It's a truce of sorts, a moment

to catch our breath before the next inevitable storm. We watch the first season of *Schitt's Creek* while we eat from take-out containers. That night we all fall asleep on the sectional, covered in blankets and listening to the thunder as a storm rolls by.

They catch Dobson in Olivia's building two days later. He was incoherent and distraught when he approached the elevators. He made it all the way up to her floor before the police arrived. It took them fifteen minutes to subdue him. I can't stop thinking about how she'd been right about him coming for her.

The thought sends a wave of fury through me, so sharp and visceral my hands clench into fists. I want to kill Noah. What if she hadn't called me? What if I hadn't answered? My mind reels with the possibilities.

When we get the call that he's in custody, a strange mix of relief and dread settles over me. Relief because she's safe. Dread because I know what comes next. This was never meant to be a permanent escape, and the inevitability of returning to the real world looms over us.

Cammie takes my car to the beach to take a walk and clear her head. I don't blame her. It's starting to feel suffocating in here. We're all just marinating in constant anxiety.

I challenge Olivia to a game of checkers—which she wins. For a moment she's relaxed enough to fist pump.

She puts the pieces back in the ziplock bag, looking at me through her lashes. "Remember when I beat you every single time at *Mario Kart* and it would make you so mad?"

"I was the master before you. No one questioned my skills."

She giggled.

"Do you feel ready to go home?"

She sighs.

It's not like I want her to go home; it seems the logical thing to ask at this point. Cammie has a job and a boyfriend to get back to. I've been working from my phone, but they are going to need me back at the office in a few days.

She stands up and puts the game away, then despite all of the chairs in the house, goes to sit on the stairs. "I'm ready. Whenever you guys are. I feel bad about making you both—"

I interrupted her. "Don't. We both want to be here. You can stay at my condo until you're ready to go home."

Her eyes flick over my face. I can see the snarky comment making its way from her brain to her mouth.

"Would I sleep between you and Jessica?"

"If that's your thing," I shoot back. "How do you know I'm still seeing Jessica?"

She looks away, her gaze falling to the ground as she purses her lips. Guilty. "I keep tabs on you."

Her admission catches me off guard. "Do you?" I ask, my tone light, teasing. I like the idea of her typing my name into a search bar, thinking about me even when I thought she wasn't. "I thought you didn't do social media."

"Most people are lying when they say that. We all have secret accounts we use in case we need to creep on someone."

I lower myself onto the step beside her. There's just enough space between us to feel the tension.

"I have to make sure you're still alive." She bumps me with her shoulder.

"I'm alive. And I'm not sure where Jessica and I will be after this."

"What have you told her about being here with me?"

"She was at my place when you called me. She went home. She's texted a couple of times to ask how you are."

"That's nice of her."

The jealousy in her voice makes me smile.

"How do you feel about her?"

I raise my eyebrows. "Are you asking me if I'm in love with her?"

She dips her chin. "Does it sound like I'm asking you that?"

I tap her on the tip of her nose. "If you want to ask me personal and extremely uncomfortable questions, go ahead. I'll tell you anything you want to know. But for the love of God—just ask a direct question."

"Fine," she says. "Are you in love with Jessica?"

"No."

She looks surprised. "Were you before? In college, I mean?"

"No."

"Would you have married that girl if she'd kept the baby?"

"Yes."

She bites her bottom lip and her eyes get watery.

I know she takes culpability for that, but I don't see it that way and never have.

"She didn't want children," I say. "She had six siblings and said her parents made her raise the little ones."

"Oh. Well what's going on with you and Jessica?"

"It's a right now thing. We were just doing what felt good."

"But you're together. What's the point of your relationship if it isn't going anywhere?"

I laugh softly. "Fucking."

"Classy."

"You don't do anything without purpose. It's why you wouldn't give me a shot in the first place. You didn't see yourself marrying me, so you wouldn't even have a conversation with me."

"You won that round," she jokes, though there's a slight edge to her voice, like the words sting more than she wants them to.

"Jessica broke up with someone before she moved back here. I got a divorce. We are both a little messed up in the head, and we like being around each other."

"And you like fucking," she says.

I grin, shrugging. "It's what people do, Olivia."

She sucks in her cheeks, clear disapproval etched on her face.

"You know," I say, breaking the quiet, my voice lower now. "Nothing has ever felt as good as you in the orange grove that night."

Her reaction is instant. The flush that was faint before blooms into a full blush, spreading up her cheeks. Her lips part slightly, as if she wants to say something, but can't.

"Which part are you thinking of? My favorite part was—"

"Caleb—" she cuts me off. "I am not."

I can see the memories flooding into her eyes.

"Liar."

It wasn't just sex. It was something more, something I've never been able to replicate since.

And judging by the way she walked away just now, she knows it too.

10

The Past

"Let me see that one."

He reached into the spotless glass case and pulled out something a little more striking than the last. Engagement rings all started to look the same after a while.

"That's three carats, colorless with a VVS2 rating," Thomas said, placing it on a square of black velvet. *Samoht*.

I picked it up, held it up to the light. The diamond sparkled, pristine and cold. It didn't speak to me. "It's nice. I think I'm just looking for something more . . . unique."

"Tell me about her," he said. "Maybe I can get a better feel for the right ring."

I hesitated, the request catching me off guard. "The wrath of the most beautiful god."

When I looked at him, his eyebrows were slightly raised. We laughed at the same time.

"Well, you're definitely in love," he said.

"Yes, I am."

He walked a few steps away and came back with another ring. "What about this one?"

Surrounding the center stone was a halo of smaller diamonds, creating a blooming flower.

"This is it," I said. "It looks like a gardenia."

I LEFT THE store and walked into the overly warm humidity that clung to everything like a second skin. The ring in my pocket felt heavier than it should, as if it carried the weight of my decision. Olivia's ring. I slid my hand into my pocket, my fingers brushing the smooth edges of the velvet box. My chest swelled with something I could only describe as certainty.

The plans were in motion. In six weeks I would ask Olivia—no, tell Olivia—to marry me. She'd probably say no, at least the first time, but I wasn't worried about that. The thought of her saying no didn't scare me nearly as much as the thought of never asking.

She was it.

I hit her number and waited as it rang.

"Hi," she breathed, her voice soft and warm.

"Hey, baby."

I could almost see her—probably sitting cross-legged on her bed.

"You sound weird. Are you okay?" she asked, her tone dipping.

"Yeah I'm good. Just wanted to hear your voice. I'm making plans for a few weeks from now. I thought we could go away for a couple of days—the Keys . . . Daytona."

She sounded excited. "I've never been there."

"You've never been to which place?"

"Either. Caleb," she said softly, "I'd love that."

"Okay," I said, smiling.

"Okay," she repeated.

"Hey," she said after a few seconds. "Don't get separate rooms."

"What?"

She laughed, light and musical.

"Byyye, Caleb," she said, dragging out the word with playful finality.

"Bye, Duchess."

The call ended, and I stood on the sidewalk, staring at my phone.

I was grinning from ear to ear.

I headed to my mother's house.

"CALEB, IT'S A MISTAKE," my mother said, her voice trembling. Her face was pale, her lips pressed into a thin line as she tugged on the locket around her neck.

I leaned back against the edge of her kitchen counter, crossing my arms. "A mistake," I repeated, my tone flat. Her eyes darted to the black box I'd set on the counter between us, its significance impossible to miss.

"Yes," she said, her voice firmer now. "She's not right for you. She's volatile. You're obsessed . . ."

I laughed, a sharp humorless sound that echoed through the kitchen. I didn't want to be disrespectful—I never did— but something about hearing those words, *she's not right for you*, made my blood boil.

"I'm not here for your opinion. I'm here because you're my mother and I want to keep you involved in my life. However, that is subject to change."

"You can't be serious."

She was my mother, the woman who raised me, who I owed so much to. But Olivia was my future, and in that moment, I realized I couldn't cater to them both, emotionally. My mother's disapproval could create a wedge I couldn't repair. I would have to choose.

My mother stared at me blankly, her lips tightening as if she was carefully considering her next move.

"Have you told your father?" she asked. Her sharp features were framed by shoulder-length hair, not a strand out of place.

The question caught me off guard.

"No. Why would I do that?" My voice is clipped.

She tilted her head slightly, her eyes narrowing. "Your brother?"

I shook my head.

"Are we—your family—not even a consideration to you anymore? She's taking you away from us. Talk to your brother. He'll confirm what I'm saying. You're too young to make such a huge life decision."

I almost laughed. Too young. As if I were still a kid, fumbling through life without any idea of what I wanted or who I was.

"Caleb."

Her voice softened, and I glanced down at her, really looked at her for the first time in what felt like years. She had been a good mother; she left my father when she saw how damaging his influence was to her boys.

I never expected her to embrace Olivia, not really. But I had hoped for something less . . . predictable. Maybe even forced happiness for my sake. Instead I was met with this:

her thinly veiled disapproval, her quiet but pronounced cat-tiness. And I was growing weary of it.

She placed her hands on my arm again, her grip firm. There was desperation in the gesture. "I know you think that I'm shallow . . . superficial." It wasn't an accusation. It wasn't defensive. It was just a quiet acknowledgement, as if she rehearsed saying it in her head.

And she wasn't wrong. I did think she was superficial.

"I probably appear that way. Back then we were taught not to dwell on our feelings. What mattered was doing what needed to be done—keeping things together, maintaining order, preserving the image of a perfect life. I learned to survive in that world, Caleb, but survival doesn't always leave room for depth."

She sighed, her hand loosening its grip on my arm. "I see more than you think I do. And I see her, Caleb. I see what she could do to you." She paused. "She'll break you. She'll ruin you."

I stared at her, my chest tightening under the weight of her words. Then, gently but deliberately, I reached up and removed her hand from my arm. "Then let her destroy me."

I didn't wait for a response. I slipped the ring box into my pocket and turned toward the door, leaving her stand-ing in silence.

11

The Present

We left the following morning. Olivia wanted to leave before the sun came up and I didn't argue. The early hour suited her mood—quiet and subdued. The rest of the ride was quiet. It reminded me of our drive back from the camping trip, when there was so much to say and no courage to say it. We're so much older now, so much has happened since then, but somehow, it still felt hard.

I glance at her once or twice, catching the way her eyes stayed fixed on the horizon, her profile soft in the dim light of the early morning. Cammie doesn't say much when we drop her off. She gives me a look that conveys a thousand warning messages.

"Goodbye, Drake. Whatever you do next, make sure it doesn't piss me off."

"Love you too, Cam!" I grin.

When we reach Olivia's building, I carry her bag upstairs without a word. She puts her keys on the console table by the door and glances around like she's not sure where to go.

Setting her bag down in the kitchen, I do a quick search

of her condo while she waits at the sink, an anxious look on her face.

"All clear," I say.

When she emerges from the bedroom she's wearing a pair of black leggings and an oversized gray sweater.

She opens a cabinet, her movements precise, and pulls out two mugs.

"Tea?" she asks, glancing over her shoulder at me.

"Please," I say, leaning against the island watching her as she fills the kettle with water and sets it on the stove.

I sit at her table, study the view. Even now, with her back to me her presence fills the room. The slight arch of her spine as she leans forward, the graceful curve of her neck as she tilts her head, it was so familiar it hurt. Her unit overlooks the water, a vast shimmering expanse that stretched out toward the horizon. The beach is dotted with early risers—joggers, walkers, and the occasional paddleboarder carving slow lines through the still water. Beyond the beach, a collection of sleek high-rises dot the coastline, their glass exteriors reflecting the sun. I turn to see her leaning casually against the counter, a steaming mug of tea in her hand.

"This is my favorite time," she says. "Before the world wakes up."

She sips her tea her fingers brushing the rim of the mug as her eyes drift back to the view.

There is a storm brewing between us. Maybe that's why we are savoring the calm.

"I love you, Olivia. I still want you. I want to be with you," I say, my voice steady.

She laughs, a low, throaty sound that makes my chest tighten. "Fuck you, Caleb Drake."

"Because I love you?" I ask, refusing to flinch.

"You're a fool. Nostalgic, rose-colored glasses—all of that."

I shake my head, leaning forward slightly. "Uh-uh. This time you found me, remember?"

She licks her lips. "Let go."

"First, tell me why you called me when you could have gone to your husband."

"Fine," she says after a long pause. "You were the first person I thought to call. Actually, that's not true—I wanted to call my mom—you were the first alive person I thought to call."

"Because . . ."

Her jaw tightens. "Goddammit, Caleb!"

"Because . . ." I say again, pushing.

"You're always wanting to overtalk everything."

"There is no such thing, stop changing the subject."

She bites her thumbnail.

"Because you're my hiding place. That's what it feels like. When I'm scared, I want you. I hate that it's like that, but it is."

My tongue knots itself, my brain freezes. I just sit there staring at her with a dumb smile on my face.

"Ugh," she covers her face with her hands.

"Do you still love me?" I ask her.

"Yes."

"Leave him," I say. "If you don't leave him this is the end of the road for us."

Her eyes snap to mine, and they're blazing, a searing blue heat.

"The. End. Of. WHAT?" Her words came out like

punches, each syllable a jab to the chest. "We've never had a beginning, or a middle, or a fucking *minute* to be in love."

"Then let's have our minute," I shoot back, my voice rising to match hers.

"Why are you always fighting me?"

"Because Noah doesn't deserve this. He hasn't done anything wrong."

"He married you when he knew you were in love with me. I'd say that was pretty fucking stupid."

"I love him." The words land like a slap, but they don't ring true. Not in the way she says them. Not with the fire still burning in her eyes, directed entirely at me.

There is so much pressure building in my chest it feels like my ribs might snap. I shove back my chair, the legs shrieking against the floor, a sharp, ugly sound that mirrors the crackling in my head. I don't look at her. I can't.

I stalk toward the bathroom, each step heavier than the last, and slam the door harder than necessary. I'm angry. I catch sight of myself in the mirror and freeze. Eyes bloodshot, jaw locked, a line etched between my eyebrows. I grip the edge of the sink, fingers curling hard around the porcelain.

When I finally drag the door open, the hallway feels cold and heavy. I walk back to her living room and she's there.

Arms folded tight across her chest, shoulders squared.

She draws back slightly when she sees me, her confidence faltering for a moment. She doesn't say a word. Just looks at me.

"Do you love him more than you love me?" I ask, my voice cracking.

She flinches. Just barely. A blink. A shift of her weight from one foot to the other. I feel as if I've just punched a hole through both of us.

"I don't love anything more than I love you," she says finally. "I hate that, but it's true."

I'm afraid if I so much as breathe, this whole thing will split open and we'll never be able to get it back. My jaw is clenched so hard it feels like my teeth are going to crack.

"Then why are you looking at me like we're over, Olivia?"

She shakes her head like she can't believe what I'm saying. "I came to Rome to tell you how I felt, and you walked away from me. I had to get over you—us. Your choice."

"I know that," I grind out, and the words taste like iron and regret. My hands are balled into fists at my sides. "It was a mistake. Leah was falling apart, and thought that I could fix it—her."

My words hang there, thick and ugly. I shake my head, a bitter laugh catching in my throat.

"You are a fucking coward." Her voice shakes. "If you had just talked to me that day in the record store, without the lies, we wouldn't be here."

It's like pressing a bruise—the pain is immediate. "Duchess, I don't know how to take it back. I wish I could."

Her shoulders—which just a moment ago had been tensed in battle stance—go slack. A single sob escapes her lips. She reaches a hand up to catch it, but it's too late.

"You got married . . . you had a baby . . ." Her tears are flowing freely now, mingling with her mascara and tracking black streak down her cheeks. "You were supposed to marry me. That was supposed to be my baby." She drops to the sofa behind her and wraps her arms around herself.

Her tiny frame is racked with sobs. Her hair has cascaded over her face and she bends her head with the purpose of veiling her face.

I can't just stand there, I go to her, scooping her up without hesitation, and carry her to the counter. Setting her down so we're eye to eye, I brush the hair away from her wet cheeks, but she ducks her head. She is trying to hide behind her hair. It's almost to her waist again, like it was when I met her. I pull the hair tie from her wrist and stand behind her dividing her hair into three pieces. I braid her hair, then tie it off.

"Now I can see you."

Her voice is raspy when she speaks. "I hate that you always make jokes when I'm trying to feel sorry for myself."

"I hate that I always make you cry." I rub little circles on her wrist with my thumb. I want to touch her more, but I know I shouldn't.

"Duchess, it wasn't your fault. It was mine. I thought that if we had a clean slate . . ." My voice trails off because there is no such thing as a clean slate. I know that now. You just embrace your dirty slate and build over it. I kiss her wrist. "Let me carry you. I'll never let you touch the ground. I was made to carry you, Olivia. You're fucking heavy with all of your guilt and self-loathing. But I can do it. Because I love you."

She has her pinky pressed against her lips as if she's trying to hold everything in. This is a new Oliviaism. I like it. I pull her pinky away from her lips, and instead of dropping her hand I lace my fingers through hers. *God, how long has it been since I've held her hand?* I feel like a little boy. I fight back the smile that is trying to take over my face.

"Tell me," I say. "Peter Pan . . ."

"Noah is in Munich right now. Last week, Stockholm, the week before that, Amsterdam." She looks away. "We're not . . . we're taking a break."

I shake my head. "A break from what? Marriage or each other?"

"We like each other. Marriage, I guess."

"Fuck, that doesn't even make sense," I say. "If we were married, I wouldn't let you out of my bed, never mind my sight."

"What is that supposed to mean?"

"I'm here. He's not."

She's quiet for a long time. "He doesn't want children." Estella's face blurs my vision.

"Why not?"

She shrugs, but the tension in her body gives her away. "His sister has cystic fibrosis. He's a carrier. He saw how much she suffered before she died and he doesn't want to bring children into the world with the risk of them having it."

I can see how much it bothers her. Her mouth is pinched and her eyes are darting around.

I swallow. This is a touchy subject for me too. "Was he up-front about it before you got married?"

She nods. "I didn't want children. I . . . changed my mind."

"You're allowed to do that."

She changed but not for me or with me. She changed with him, she let him see parts she never gave me.

"I'm jealous," I admit.

She nods slowly, no hesitation, her gaze locked on mine. "I know the feeling," she says. "It wasn't about you. It wasn't about Noah. It was about me and what I thought I deserved. And I didn't think I deserved that kind of happiness with you."

"Why not?"

"Because you expected me to be the perfect version of myself. I was barely functioning when I met you, my grief was large."

I stare at her, the words sinking like stones. Is that what I did? Did I love her so much I turned her into something unreachable, even for myself?

"I never wanted you to be perfect," I say softly. "I just wanted you."

She closes her eyes for a moment, as if trying to hold back her tears. "I wasn't ready."

I look at her trying to strike the balance between saying too much and saying too little. I don't want to say too much or too little. "You are worth fighting for. I haven't given up yet."

My gaze falls to her lips, and the familiar ache returns. God, I want to kiss her. To close the space between us. The pull toward her is relentless. I turn, grabbing my keys off the counter, the cool metal grounding me as I force myself to walk away. Fighting or kissing—either one could happen if I stay, and both would leave us in pieces. She doesn't move, doesn't speak. She stays by the window her figure framed by the ocean.

But just as I step toward the door, I stop. Her name escapes my lips. "Olivia."

She turns her head just enough for me to see the tension in her jaw.

"Your marriage won't last. Tell Noah the truth. Be fair to him and to yourself."

Her eyes narrow slightly, but she doesn't argue. She doesn't deny it.

"When you do," I add, stepping back into the doorway, "come find me." She turns just enough for me to catch the faintest flicker of vulnerability in her expression. "And I'll give you that baby."

The door clicks shut behind me.

The silence in the hallway feels deafening, and for a moment, I lean back against the wall, exhaling. I glance at the keys in my hand, then back at her door. I should leave. I have to leave. But even as I take the first step away, I know I'll be back. I always come back.

THE GUILT HITS me hard as I leave Olivia's building. I can't stop thinking about what I just said—offering her a baby when I know Jessica is probably at my house right now. Jessica, who's been patient, who deserves more from me than I've been willing to give. She's waiting for me—maybe not consciously waiting for a proposal, but something close to it. A promise, at least. But instead, I spent the morning telling my ex-girlfriend I'd give her a baby.

The guilt follows me like a shadow, growing heavier with every step. By the time I get in my car, it feels like it's pressing against my chest. By the time I slide into the driver's seat and yank the door shut, it feels hard to breathe. Ending things with someone was never a good time. Never painless. I rest my forehead against the steering wheel while I run through all of the usual bullshit:

Jessica deserves better.

She deserves a man who doesn't hold back pieces of himself that he'd rationed for someone else.

By the time I pull up to her house, it's like the guilt has metastasized, sinking all the way to my marrow. The headlights cut through her front yard—tidy flowerbeds, huge monstera climbing the side of the single-story—and the whole thing looks so normal. My normal for the last few months. I kill the engine and just sit there, hand still curled around the steering wheel. All of my noble words are gone, scattered like ash. I'm not the man she thinks I am. And I'm about to break her heart to prove it.

Letting myself in, I walk toward the kitchen, and there she is. She's standing at the stove, her hair loose around her shoulders.

"Hey stranger," she says, turning back toward the stove.

I stand in the doorway to the kitchen and watch her for a moment, trying to figure out what I'm going to say.

"Hungry?"

"Always," I reply.

She plates the food and sets the bowl in front of me. I can't bring myself to pick up the fork. Jessica notices.

"Olivia?" she asks.

The way she says her name—like it's both a question and an answer.

Jessica exhales softly, setting her fork down. "Look," she says. "I'm not going to pretend I don't know how you feel about her. But I can't be the woman who sits here, waiting for you to figure it out."

"I'm still in love with Olivia," I admit, the words coming out heavy and raw. "It's never going to be fair to anyone I'm with. I don't want to give you pieces of me. I'm so sorry, Jessica."

"You should go," she says quietly.

There's nothing I can say that will make this better.

12

The Past

Four o'clock, five o'clock, six o'clock, seven. The hours dragged, each one louder and heavier than the last. I was still at my desk, drowning in paper and frustration. A day that should have ended hours ago stretched into eternity.

I glanced at the clock. Seven fifteen. I was late.

The faint hum of voices filtered in from the hallway. Laughter, clinking glasses, the distant hum of office small talk. My stepfather, ever the pragmatist, decided that hosting in the office building made more sense than renting a venue.

"Caleb." Neil popped his head into my office, his tie slightly loosened like he was gearing up for an all-night networking marathon. "You sticking around for the party?"

I grinned. "No, I have somewhere to be tonight."

He raised his eyebrows. "You have somewhere better to be than a dinner your boss is throwing for potential clients?"

"Much better," I said, typing into my keyboard without looking up.

"Well, I hate to break it to you pal, but Sydney is here."

"Send her in," I said, standing so quickly that my chair rolled back and bumped the wall.

Neil raised his eyebrows, "Sydney, huh?" he said, pushing off the door frame. "This should be fun."

"Neil," I said, my voice carrying a warning. "I need to get out of here, don't hold her up."

He didn't leave, he leaned against the door frame, settling in to enjoy the show.

"Caleb!" Sydney squealed, yanking me into an overly enthusiastic hug. "Oh, my gosh, it's been like, what? Three years? Four? Crazy how time flies. Anyway, I brought iced oat milk lattes because I figured you're a flat-white guy, but I took the liberty of adding a splash of lavender syrup. You're welcome."

"Listen, Sydney, I'm kind of in a rush tonight. Do you think—?"

"Well, duh, everyone is in a hurry nowadays. No offense, but it looks like you could use some relaxation, you've literally been this uptight since you were, like, twelve."

"I'm fine, thanks."

"Are you nervous?"

"About which part?"

"Building a house is not for the weak, my friend."

With that she produced the forms in a flurry of paper and enthusiasm.

We spread everything across my desk, and Sydney talked me through each form. I'd just about signed half of them when Steve wandered into my office in his tux. As soon as Steve walked in, Neil removed himself.

"Sydney!" I watched as he hugged her. "You lost all of your freckles, and what happened to all of that metal you used to wear on your teeth?" They saw each other regularly enough, but this was their game—old jokes, recycled banter, and awkward small talk.

"You're a riot."

"Please tell me you're staying for a drink . . ."

I checked my phone, nothing from Olivia. I was worried. The empty screen gnawed at my nerves, a reminder of how much tonight mattered.

"I'm staying," she said. "I was hoping I could get Caleb to have a drink with me before he speeds off on his steed."

"I can't tonight."

Sydney's head popped up, her expression halfway between guilt and amusement. "You're going to hate me," she said, her voice a singsong.

I froze, narrowing my eyes. "What did you forget?"

Her cheeks flushed. "It's not a big deal! I can just run back to the office and grab it, give me, like, fifteen."

Steve, who had been quietly observing the exchange, suddenly stood, brushing invisible lint from his jacket. "Let her go get it, Caleb. Fifteen minutes won't kill anyone. Meanwhile you can make those rounds."

I slammed my laptop closed and stared at him. "I'm proposing to my girlfriend tonight. You can't be serious."

Sydney flushed.

I shook my head, trying to keep my tone neutral. "Can I live without it?"

She hesitated, her shoulders slumping. "It's the key fob to the property, it's gated."

She looked genuinely sorry. I couldn't bring myself to press her further.

By the time Sydney got back, the evening had officially

derailed. I paced the office trying to think of how to explain the situation to Olivia without giving too much away. My text hovered unsent on the screen, a jumble of excuses and vague reassurances.

The door opened suddenly and Sydney rushed in, her face flushed. "Traffic, Caleb. I'm so sorry." Her eyes were wide and earnest. "You look great by the way—she's going to love this whole vibe . . ." She pointed at my suit.

"It's fine, let's just get back on track, okay?"

"Can I see the ring?"

I hesitated. The ring box was sitting on my desk.

Before I could respond she picked it up, cracking open the lid.

"Wow . . ." She perched herself on the edge of my desk, leaning back so it could catch the light. I didn't like her holding Olivia's ring. I reached for it and Sydney put her arms around my neck, pulling me in for a hug.

I opened my mouth to say something, but my words died on my tongue as I caught sight of movement behind her.

Olivia stood in the doorway, her waist-length black hair spilling over her shoulders, glacial eyes locked on mine. She was wearing one of my gray hoodies over leggings, her feet hastily stuffed into Nikes. She looked like a storm in human form. The blood drained from my face as I took in her expression—her lips parted slightly. Moving between me and Sydney.

"Caleb."

She said my name like it was a curse, a question, and a punch to the gut all at once. My stomach did a little freefall. Behind me Sydney made her exit, but Olivia's gaze didn't flicker. Her focus was all on me.

Slowly, painfully it dawned on me what she saw when she walked in. How it must have looked. My pulse hammering in my ears. I was irrationally angry with the situation. I was going to have to tell her everything, the ring, the house . . .

"I loved you," Olivia said, her voice trembling.

"Loved?"

She wasn't just angry. She was done. Something in me cracked, but I refused to let it show. I clenched my jaw, forcing myself to meet her gaze. *So that's how it's going to be?*

She was wielding love as a weapon.

"I didn't do anything," I said, my voice low and flat. I wanted to explain. To tell her that this was all a misunderstanding. But I didn't. I couldn't. She'd wounded my pride.

I heard my mother's words, about her being too broken. Everything shifted in that moment. I wish it hadn't, but it did. I couldn't fix her. I couldn't love her enough to chip away at the calcified hurt that was affecting everything she did. My thoughts about our life together went from a house in the sunshine and a yard full of children to Olivia crying in a corner, blaming me for rushing her into something she wasn't ready for.

I could see the accusation in her eyes. She was comparing me to her father.

"You're just like him . . ."

"Right," I said, my voice cold. "Of course I am, because that's easier isn't it? Easier to make me the bad guy. Easier to push me away than admit this was never going to work."

Her face twisted. "What is that supposed to mean?"

"It means," I said, gesturing between us. "This was all

temporary wasn't it? You've been looking for a way out since day one."

"That's not fair," she said, her voice cracking.

My office door opened, Neil stuck his head in. His eyes darted between us, taking in Olivia's rigid posture and my tightly clenched fists. He muttered something and closed the door.

The hurt was profound. Especially since I'd spent the last year and a half trying to show her that I was nothing like him. When she ran out of my office, thinking that I'd cheated on her, I didn't stop her.

I stood frozen, the ring box pressing against my thigh, the room swinging around me.

I leaned both hands on my desk and squeezed my eyes closed, breathing through my mouth. Five minutes. My whole life had changed in just five minutes.

She only wanted to see the bad. Maybe it was for the best. Maybe all I saw was my love and I hadn't weighed the consequences of that love.

Steve walked into my office stopping short when he saw me. His eyebrows furrowed. "Did I just see Olivia?"

I looked up at him, my vision blurring. He must have seen something on my face.

"What happened?"

"She saw me with Sydney. She assumed . . ."

"Caleb," Steve said, his tone firm but not unkind. "Caleb, go after her."

My head snapped up. That's the last thing I expected him to say, especially considering how much my mother had probably poisoned his perceptions of Olivia.

"She wants out," I said. "Since we first got together. She's always finding a reason for us not to be together. What kind of life can we have if she does that?"

Steve shook his head. "Some people take more work than others. You fell in love with a really complicated woman. You can weigh how hard things can and will be for the two of you, but what you really need to consider is if you can live without her."

I stared at him, his word sinking in.

Could I live without her?

No.

I was out the door a second later, my feet moving before my brain caught up. I took the stars, my heart pounding in my chest. How had I let this day get away from me? If I'd just left when I was supposed to . . .

Her car was gone. I stood there for a moment, frozen under the harsh glow of the streetlights. I went back for my car keys not making eye contact with anyone in the office. I grabbed my phone; when it unlocked the first thing I saw was my unsent text to her.

Cammie.

"She's with me," Cammie said, when I called her.

"Let me talk to her, Cammie. Please."

"She doesn't want to talk to you. You need to let her cool off."

"Cammie," I started, my voice cracking. "You know me. You know I wouldn't—"

"No," she said, her tone turning sharp. "I don't know you."

"Cammie, I'm not trying to bulldoze anything, I just want to explain—"

"She doesn't want anything from you right now."

The line went dead.

By the time I got in my car, my hands were shaking. I kept replaying everything that happened over and over. When I got to Cammie's, the first thing I noticed was the empty driveway. No Olivia. No car.

Cammie lied. I didn't bother calling her back. I just drove.

13

The Present

I t's been a month since I left her condo, the night she told me about Noah. A month of silence. A month of trying not to think about her decision. But I know what *I've* decided.

I pull out my phone and send her a text.

Divorced?

Her reply comes back almost immediately.

O: Fuck off.

I smirk, my fingers flying across the screen.

You at work?

O: Yes

I'll be there in ten.

O: No!

I turn my phone off and wait. I was already in the parking lot when I sent the first text. Sitting here, staring at the sleek glass doors of her building. I linger in my car for a minute, running my finger over my bottom lip. I know what she's going to do next, so when I see her walking quickly out of the building, I smirk. She's trying to leave before I show up. I jump out of the car and walk toward her. She doesn't see me until the last second, too focused on her car keys.

"Going somewhere?"

Her shoulders jerk and she spins around. "Are you trying to give me a heart attack?"

"I'm trying to do something to your heart, but not that." I hold out my hand, palm up. "Come on, Duchess."

She bites her bottom lip. After a quick glance over her shoulder—probably to check if anyone is watching—she places her hand in mine. I don't let go and she doesn't take it back.

"You look terrified," I say.

"I am."

I lead her to my car. "Of what?"

"Bob the Builder, a gluten-less world, sharks . . ."

I squeeze her hand and she squeezes back.

Her hair is piled on top of her head, secured by a claw clip. I open the passenger side door for her. She doesn't get in right away. She looks up at me and I put my hand on the back of her neck. I can see her throat convulsing as I massage her neck gently. She doesn't protest when I reach behind her, undoing her hair from the clip. It tumbles down thick and heavy. I smell her shampoo and her skin and I get hard. Her lips part and she makes a noise that almost sends me over the edge.

My mouth is dry. My throat clear is a dead giveaway. Her brow lifts and I drop my hand. We're still close. She brushes her knuckles against the scruff on my chin.

"You . . ." she says.

"What has Bob the Builder ever done to you?"

She laughs a throaty laugh.

When I get in the driver's side she sighs. "Why are you always so goddamn early?"

I turn the car on. "Why are you trying to run away?"

"I'm good at it." She glances at me out of the corner of her eye. I want to hold her hand again.

She doesn't ask where we are going. I drive to the beach. I get a spot close to the water and pay the meter. She watches me through the windshield, her face serious but soft. I walk around to her side of the car and open the door. She's wearing heels. We make eye contact as she swings her legs outside the car without standing up. This is a language only we know. I crouch in front of her and undo the ankle strap on her right foot, holding her calf in one hand. Her skin is soft and warm. I do the left side and stand up, grinning. She leaves her shoes in the car. She jumps on my back and I carry her to the sand. It's windy and her hair whips around her face. She laughs grabbing my hand first this time.

It's considered winter in Florida. Only a handful of brave sunbathers. There are canvas-covered gazebos with lawn chairs underneath them. We find an empty one and I sink down, stretching my legs out and taking a deep breath of the salty air. Olivia hesitates, glancing at the chair next to me like she's debating whether or not to put that extra distance between us. But I don't give her the chance. I reach out, grab her wrist, and pull her down to my chair. She settles against me, leaning back against my chest. I loop one arm around her waist while the other rests behind my head. It's been so long since I've had her like this, so close, so warm. It feels natural and forbidden.

"Olivia."

"Don't do that."

"Do what?" I say, leaning closer, my breath brushing her ear.

"That," she says, flustered.

I can see the goose bumps on her exposed skin. "You're doing the romance audio book voice."

"Let me switch to thriller-narrator Caleb," I joke changing my voice.

I gather her hair and swipe it over her left shoulder. I kiss the exposed skin on her neck, and she shivers. I kiss an inch above it and her head tilts to give me better access.

My lips hover near her ear. "I love you."

"Don't, Caleb . . ."

"Why not?"

"Because it's not right."

"It's not right for me to love you? Or it's not right for you to love me back?"

"Neither." The sadness in her voice cracks my reserve, cracks my game, cracks my heart.

I glance away, staring at the water as I gather myself. "I can't stay away from you. I don't want to."

She wriggles her shoulders. "Do that thing to my hair that you used to do."

I thread my fingers through her hair until I'm clutching a fistful of it. I pull back gently while tugging. She sighs in contentment.

I imagine her like this, letting me have control, trusting me enough to fall apart. The love of my life deserves so much more than words. She deserves the feel of everything I've been trying to tell her.

I kiss her temple, which is the only thing I can reach, and entwine our fingers, wrapping my arms around her. She snuggles against me and that familiar ache starts in my chest.

"Peter Pan," I say.

There are five seconds of silence before she speaks. "When I'm with you, every emotion I can possibly feel comes spilling out. I drown in them. I want to run to you, and I want to run away from you. Does that make sense?"

"Yes, but don't run away. We can do this."

She snorts. "We don't know how to love each other the right way."

"Bullshit," I say against her ear. "You're full of love that you can't get out. You can't say some things. I'm okay with that now. I know it's there. We've hurt each other. But we're not kids anymore, Olivia. I want you." I let her go and spin her around so she's kneeling between my spread legs.

I cup her face with my hands, threading my fingers into her hair and laying them flat behind her head, massaging her scalp with my fingers.

"I want you." I've said it before, but she's not getting it. She still thinks I'll leave her. Like I did.

Her bottom lip quivers.

"I want your babies, and your anger, and your cold blue

eyes . . ." I choke on my words and I am the one to look away. I bring my gaze back to her face and realize that if I can't convince her now, I'm never going to be able to. "I want to go on anniversary dinners with you; I want to wrap Christmas presents with you. I want to fight with you about stupid things and then hold you down in my bed and make it up to you. I want to have more cake batter fights and camping trips. I want your future, Olivia. Please come back to me."

Her whole body is shaking. A tear spills down her cheek and I catch it with my thumb.

I grab the back of her neck and pull her toward me so that our foreheads are touching. I run my hands up and down her back.

Her lips are moving, she's trying to formulate words—and by the look on her face I can't tell if I want to hear them. Our noses are parallel: if I bump my head half an inch forward, we'd be kissing. I wait for her.

Our breath mingles. She has my shirt in a vise grip between her fists. I understand her need to clutch something. It is taking every ounce of my self-control to keep from crushing us together.

Both of our chests are rising and falling like the waves. I nudge her nose with mine, and that seems to break her reserve. She wraps her arms around my neck, opens her mouth, and kisses me.

I haven't kissed my girl in months. It feels like the first time. She's up on her knees, leaning over me so that I have to tilt my head back to reach her lips. My hands are under her dress on the back of her thighs. I can feel the material of her panties on my fingertips, but I keep my hands still.

We kiss slowly, just with our lips. We keep pulling back to look each other in the eye. Her hair creates a curtain between us and the world. We kiss behind it, as it falls around our faces, blocking everything out but each other.

"I love you," she says into my mouth. I smile so big I have to pause in our kissing to recompose my lips. When we start using our tongues, things get heated fast. Olivia likes to bite when she kisses. It really, *really* does something for me.

My heart is in my throat, my brain is in my pants, my hands are up her dress. She pushes away from me and stands up.

"Not until the divorce is finalized," she says. "Take me back."

I stand up and pull her toward me. "All I heard was *Take me.*"

She laces her arms around my neck, her teeth latching onto her bottom lip.

I kiss the tip of her nose.

WE MAKE OUR way back to my car. As soon as we shut our doors, Olivia's phone pings. She lifts it out of her purse, and immediately her face darkens.

"What is it?" I ask.

She looks away from me, her hand frozen midair, still clutching the phone. "It's Noah. He wants to talk."

14

Noah

I spin my wedding band on the sticky countertop, watching as it becomes a blur of gold before doing its inevitable dance and landing flat. I pick it up and do it again. The bartender gives me a look. The "man wrestling with his choices and losing" look. I pick up the band, rub it between my fingers like it's a worry stone, and shove it back into my pocket.

She doesn't know I'm back in town. I don't know if I'm ready to tell her. I checked into a hotel near the airport four days ago and have been slumming around at the local bars since.

Caleb is back. Of course he's back. That's his whole thing. You know, the charming, devil-may-care attitude. He never sticks around to put out the fire. He's spontaneous, reckless, emotional.

It's like he can sniff out when she's vulnerable.

I take a sip of warm beer, grimacing. I work for one of the largest consulting firms in the US. My job is to analyze complex systems. I traveled, made good money. It was smart money, but also the fastest way to ruin a marriage. I missed her birthday. Our first anniversary. Thanksgiving. The trifecta of husband failure.

I didn't realize how it was affecting Olivia until it was too late. Instead of making it a fight, she adjusted to my absence. I'd made her a partner on the sidelines.

I told myself lies, mostly the kind you tell yourself to sleep at night. Lies like, absence makes the heart grow fonder. In hindsight it was only healthy for me. The part that gets me: she stopped expecting anything of me. I didn't see it at first. In reality absence plants doubts. It builds walls.

It was like watching someone slowly learn to live without you while you're still in the room.

I stare at my phone. Enough hiding.

Can we talk?

It takes three hours for her to respond with:

O: About what?

You and me

O: Haven't we done enough of that?

I have something new to put on the table.

Twenty minutes tick by before her response.

O: okay

Here's the thing: I'm not going to let Caleb take her from me.

As far as I'm concerned he had his chance in Rome, and he let her go. Broke her heart.

THAT NIGHT, WHEN Olivia and I parted after dinner, I went back to my hotel and thought about my life. How empty it was. I think I'd already made the decision to change it by the time she called my room, crying. I caught a cab to her hotel and sat with her while she mourned him. She told me it was the last time, that she could only bend and break so many times before the damage was irreparable. She hadn't wanted me to touch her. I wanted to. I wanted to hold her and let her cry on me. But she'd sat on the edge of her bed with her back straight and her eyes closed, and cried silent tears that flowed like rivers down her cheeks. I'd never seen anyone deal with their pain with so much restraint. It was heartbreaking—the way she wouldn't make a sound. Finally, I'd turned on the television and we'd sat with our backs against her headboard and watched *Dirty Dancing*. It was dubbed in Italian. I wasn't sure about Olivia, but I had a sister and I'd seen the movie enough to know the dialogue by heart. I was still there when the sun came up. I canceled my appointments, made her get dressed, and took her to see Rome. She fought me at first, saying she'd rather stay at the hotel, but then I'd ripped open the drapes in her room and made her stand in front of them.

"Look. Look where you are," I said. She'd stood beside me and the mist seemed to lift from her eyes.

"Okay," she laughed. "I get it. I'll work on my attitude."

First the Colosseum, then we ate pizza at a little shop near the Vatican. She cried when she stood in the Vatican beneath Da Vinci's handiwork. She'd turned to me and firmly said, "These are not tears for him. These are because I'm here and I've always wanted to be." Then she'd hugged me and thanked me for taking her.

A year into our marriage, back when I thought being practical was a personality trait to be proud of, Liv started talking about getting a puppy.

I shut her down with one sentence. Classic me. Always ready to be the responsible one, the grounded one, the guy who kills the fun before it has a chance to breathe. We didn't have a yard. I wasn't home enough. Dogs live for ten to fifteen years, did we really want to commit to that?

If I could go back, I'd get her a wolf pack.

You know, I should come with a warning label: highly skilled at overthinking, under-communicating, and making a mess of good things.

15

The Past

Six months before I saw Olivia at the music store on the corner of Butts and Glade, I bought an engagement ring for Leah.

It sat next to Olivia's ring in my sock drawer for a week. I don't know why I put them together in the first place. It wasn't some poetic gesture; it was laziness, really. But every time I opened the drawer it felt wrong. I found myself standing at the edge of my bed, both rings in my hands, weighing the differences like they held some hidden answer. Olivia's ring was a solitaire, nestled in a filigree setting. It was strong and delicate. I hadn't known what to do with it. Sell it? Pawn it? Keep it forfuckingever? In the end, I couldn't part with the past and it had stayed exactly where it was. Leah's ring on the other hand, sat heavy in my palm, big and bold and trying too hard. It's what she wanted.

I planned to propose to Leah while we were on our ski trip to Colorado. Romantic, wasn't it? Or at least as romantic as one can be while wearing thermal underwear and trying not to break a leg.

We skied there twice a year with her friends—"The

squad," as they called themselves. They looked like extras from a high-budget ski resort ad. She looked genuinely baffled when I suggested we go without them.

"But we always go with the crew, it's tradition . . ."

It took three days for me to convince her to go without them, and by then I think she sensed the possibility of a ring.

The trip was weeks away when the panic hit. Running four miles a day wasn't enough to outrun it, and scotch wasn't enough to drown it out.

It was the kind of spiral you don't come back from without some collateral damage.

THE ACCIDENT WASN'T DRAMATIC. No cinematic explosions, no slow-motion spinning through the air. Just a patch of black ice, overconfidence, and a stop sign I missed. The last thing I heard was the crunch of metal. When I woke up I felt blinding pain.

"Hey there, buddy, stay with me."

He was shining a flashlight in my eyes. "What's your name?"

My name?

"I don't know . . ."

"Okay," he said, nodding like it was perfectly normal. "Don't worry about it. We're going to take care of you. Just focus on your breathing for me, okay?"

His tone was steady, unhurried. I followed his instructions, taking slow shallow breaths.

"What day is it?" His face was square and open, with wind-chapped cheeks.

"I . . . no," I managed. "I don't know."

"You're doing great," he said.

"What happened?"

He glanced over his shoulder at the wreckage. "You got into a car accident." I turned my head slightly, wincing at the sharp pain in my neck. The twisted remains of my car were wrapped around the guardrail. "Looks like you have a head injury, we'll let the docs sort it out. You're in one piece that's what matters. What should I call you?"

I said the first thing that came to my head.

"Joshua."

"Let's get you to the hospital, Joshua. Might even get a popsicle if you're nice to the nurses."

By the time we reached the hospital, the fog in my head started to clear. My name, my job, Leah—it all came rushing back. And when it came the sinking realization that forgetting everything for a while hadn't been a bad thing after all.

It started as a split-second decision—one part panic, two parts avoidance—and somehow it snowballed into a full-fledged reality. I didn't wake up one day thinking *You know what would fix everything? Amnesia.*

What was the alternative? Admitting I didn't lose my memory—that I lost my nerve.

Had she not walked into the Music Mushroom that day I don't know how long I would have kept up the facade. Weeks? Months? Years? I'm a guy who's too scared to fix anything. Too scared to face her. And then, just like that, there she was.

The sight of her nearly knocked the air out of my lungs. Olivia.

She was wearing a white shirt, splattered with rain.

Her hair was longer now, a dark cascade that framed her face and fell past her waist.

It had been three years, but in that moment, it felt like no time had passed at all. She looked like the person who used to steal my hoodies and give unsolicited critiques of my Spotify playlists. Except . . . she was different.

I wanted to tell her everything—every messy painful detail. How I'd lied to my friends and family rather than facing the truth. How Leah had been crying for months because of me. But then I remember why I started this charade in the first place. I wasn't trying to escape the truth, I wanted to buy myself more time. I opened my mouth but the words wouldn't come. All I could do was stand there, a coward cloaked in regret.

The things about pretending that you don't remember is that no one expects you to explain yourself. No one bothers to pry deeper when they believe your memory has failed. It's as if you've hung a giant out of order sign on yourself. I'm the guy who knows exactly what he should do but chooses not to.

"They any good?"

Olivia's eyes widened, briefly, her lips parting in surprise. But almost instantly she schooled her expression, smoothing it into an unreadable mask.

All I could think was: this is either going to be very bad, or worse than bad; a situation with no plan, no exit, and no dignity.

She looked at the record she was holding like she didn't know how it got there. "They're not your style . . ."

"They're not my style?" I repeated. My tone was playful. "What exactly do you think my style is?"

She paused, her eyes flicking up to meet mine. "You're a classic rock kind of guy . . . but I could be wrong."

"Are you stereotyping me? Maybe I'll surprise you."

Her eyes were bright and amused. "Maybe you will . . ." She flipped the record around so I could see the cover. "Shakira."

It was harder to lie to Olivia than it had been to lie to everyone else. But I did. "I don't remember what I like . . ."

I gave her the short story not the full novel.

"Wait, what? Like actual amnesia? Are you serious?"

She studied me with a sharpness that made me feel like I was under a microscope. She was dismantling me with her eyes.

"It's complicated," I started, forcing myself to meet her gaze. "Car accident a few months ago. It's like someone hit a reset button in my head. I've got bits and pieces, random flashes, but most of it? Gone. That's the short version of it."

Her expression stayed cool, the practiced neutrality of a seasoned negotiator.

For a moment the silence stretched so far I thought it was going to snap. I felt like I was standing on the edge of a cliff, waiting to see if she'd push me off or extend a hand to pull me back.

"So you have no idea what type of music you like?"

She was wearing a woven bracelet on her wrist, and a cluster of gold bangles that tinkled when she moved.

"My life is a silent film right now. No soundtrack."

"That's kind of sad," she said. She looked thoughtful for a minute, then she said, "I have a soundtrack for you."

I exhaled. Hand extended.

My heart was beating fast when she came back. She had

a record in her hand. I glanced at it: Pink Floyd's *The Dark Side of the Moon*. Arguably, their magnus opus. It was my favorite of their albums. The cacophony of clocks. It's not just a song, it's a wakeup call. It's Roger Waters showing up to say, *Hey, remember all the time you thought you had? Yeah you don't.*

A piece of her hair was caught in her lip gloss, she pulled it away. "You'll like this," she said. She tossed it to me. I caught it without breaking eye contact. She smirked, her lips teasing. Behind her the door opened and a man walked in flanked by a dog that looked like it had been bench pressing boulders for fun.

"Well, I guess I'll see you around," she said. It looked like she wanted to say more, but at the last minute she turned and walked out the door. The dog gave me a dirty look. I stood there for a moment unsure of what just happened.

I went home and put the record on, turning the volume all the way up. I thought about her—the way she ate pizza, backward because she thought the crust was the star. How she would ask me to explain the rules of football and start giggling every time I said *tight end*. How her laughter was the most satisfying sound in the universe. I brushed my teeth and got into bed. Her face kept drifting through my thoughts.

I ventured out for groceries two days later. Fluorescent lights hammered overhead flickering in rhythm to the music still echoing in my ears. Every year *was* getting shorter.

I was walking through the frozen food aisle in Whole Foods, trying to convince myself that microwavable dinners counted as a real meal. I picked up a few boxes and stared at them blankly. That's when I heard the crash.

Cardboard boxes of sugar cones were scattered across the floor. I helped her pick them up.

"Thanks," she said.

"Are you . . . okay?" I asked. "We met the other day . . . in the record store?"

She tucked her hair behind her ears, nodding. "Yeah, I remember. And I'm just clumsy as usual . . ." She was having trouble looking at me this time.

"Hey, you want to grab a coffee . . . ?"

I KNEW WHAT I had to do. The brake lights ahead glowed in a relentless red parade, stretching into the horizon. A truck rumbled on my left, to the right a sedan full of kids jostling around, their parents looking increasingly frazzled. I was stuck in rush hour traffic. When I pulled into Leah's driveway, I had my speech all worked out.

"Caleb, I know you feel lost right now, but when your memory comes back everything will make sense," she said.

"What if it doesn't?" I asked. "What if I don't come back to who I was?"

Her eyes glistened with tears, but she didn't look away. "You will," she said with conviction.

"Leah, I'm sorry." My voice caught. "I know this is a mess. I don't want to hurt you, but I need to take care of some things."

16

The Present

It's drizzling when we pull into the parking lot. She opens the door and gets out without a backward glance. I sit there a moment gripping the steering wheel, watching her walk away. I throw my car in Reverse backing into an empty spot. The door slams open. I don't even bother closing it. The air is thick with the smell of wet asphalt, the drizzle now a mist that clings to everything. Her hand hovers on the door handle, poised to leave. My feet move faster than my thoughts.

Before she can react, I'm there, pressing her against the side of her car. The metal is cold beneath my palms as I cage her in, my body flush against hers. Her breath mingles with mine, shallow and quick. I cradle the back of her head in one hand, my fingers tangling in her damp hair as I pull her closer.

I kiss her—hungrily, desperately—as though this moment is all we have. It's not a gentle kiss; it's raw, consuming, the kind of kiss that you feel all the way in your toes.

When I finally pull away, her chest rises and falls with unsteady breaths. Her lips are parted, her cheeks flushed.

My hands remain planted on either side of her head, anchoring us in the moment. "Do you remember the orange grove?"

She nods, slowly, almost hesitantly. Her eyes are wide, glimmering with recognition.

Her lips part as though she wants to say something, but no sound comes out.

"Good," I say, letting the word linger, my voice rough with an edge of vulnerability. My thumb brushes along her bottom lip, the touch tender. Her breath catches, and for a moment the air between us feels electric. "I do too . . . all the time. Just so I can feel something."

"Wow. That's a lot of pressure to put on a citrus grove."

I crack up, the laughter escaping my chest raw and unexpected. The tension between us dissolves. The door to her office building cracks open. Both of us freeze, the moment suspended in time like a deer caught in the headlights. A man in a navy suit steps out, holding a briefcase in one hand and a half-eaten granola bar in the other. He stops mid-bite, his gaze darting between us, eyebrows shooting up as he takes in the scene—me standing way too close to Olivia, her back pressed against her car. Olivia doesn't miss a beat. She straightens up.

"Morning, Zach," she says. As soon as he's gone, Olivia lets out a long sigh, rubbing a hand over her face. "Great," she mutters, her voice laced with resignation. "He's the office gossip."

"Tell them we were discussing citrus farming strategies."

Her lips curve into a reluctant smile, and she shakes her head. "Bye, Caleb."

My competition is good. Undoubtedly he's never lied to

her, broken her heart, or married another woman to spite her. But she's mine, and I'm not giving her up without a fight this time.

As I pull away, my rearview mirror gives me one last glimpse of Olivia. She's still standing there, hand pressed to her chest, looking like she's trying to piece together what just happened. My pulse is still racing, the taste of her still on my lips, and I wonder—no, hope—that she's feeling the same chaos I am.

I almost laugh at myself. I didn't plan any of that. Not the kiss, not the orange grove comment, none of it. But the second I saw her walking away, something snapped. And now I can't stop thinking about what she's going to say the next time I see her. Because Olivia? She's never been one to let things slide.

It doesn't take long. That night as I'm lying in bed staring at the ceiling, my phone buzzes. It's a text from her.

O: We need to talk about your Caleb moment.

I can't help but grin. My intensity and need to take control of a situation and express myself in a way that complicates things further.

Did it feel like just a "Caleb moment" to you?

Three dots appear, then disappear. She's typing, then rethinking. I can picture her pacing her kitchen, working through exactly how to come at me.

Finally her response comes through.

O: You kissed me in a parking lot, Caleb.

And you kissed me back.

There's a pause. I can practically feel her frustration bleeding through the phone, like she's pacing faster now.

O: You're exhausting, you know that?

And yet here you are.

O: Whatever you're trying to do . . .
it's not going to work.

If it's not going to work, why are we still talking?

No response. The dots appear and vanish again, but this time she doesn't send anything.

She's rattled. I got under her skin.

Olivia can pretend all she wants, but she can't erase the way she looked at me in that parking lot. Like I wasn't the man who broke her heart. Like for a moment, I was the man she still loved.

I WAIT A few days and then I text her while I'm at work.

What did he want?

I close the door to my office, loosen the top button of

my dress shirt. With a heavy sigh, I prop my legs up on the desk, my phone balanced in one hand as the other rubs the tension building in my neck.

O: He wants to work things out.

I stare at the screen, the words blurring. I knew it was coming. I knew. But knowing it doesn't make it any easier. Fuck that.

What did you tell him?

There's a longer pause this time, and with each passing second my anxiety ratches up a notch. Finally the message appears.

O: That I need time to think.
Same thing I'm telling you.

No

O: No?

No

I rub a hand over my face, willing myself to calm down, to think before I respond. But my emotions have a mind of their own, and I find myself typing again.

You've had ten years to think.

O: It's not that easy. He's my husband.

The words feel like a slap. They echo in my head, louder than they have any right to be.

He filed for divorce! He doesn't want
to have children with you.

O: He said he'd be willing to adopt.

A hundred retorts run through my mind, each more pointed and desperate than the last. What I'm doing is wrong. I know it's wrong. I should let them be together. I should step back, let her try to fix things with the man she vowed her life to.

But I can't.

O: Please, Caleb, give me time. I'm
trying not to be the person you used to
know. I need to do the right thing.

Then stay with him. That's the right thing
to do. But I am the right thing for you.

The message hangs there, stark and final, a challenge I know she won't answer.

I sit at my desk for what feels like an eternity, my mind racing in circles.

The door to my office creaks open, and I glance up startled. My stepfather steps in, his sharp blue eyes immediately taking in the scene. "There are only two things that can put that expression on your face." He takes a seat opposite me and folds his hands in his lap.

"And what's that?" I love my stepfather. He's the most perceptive man I know.

"Leah," he says watching me carefully, "and Olivia."

I grimace at the first name, frown at the second.

"Ah," he says, smiling.

I run my thumbnail across my bottom lip, back and forth, back and forth.

"You know, Caleb . . . I am very aware of what your mother thinks about her. But I couldn't disagree with her more."

I look up at him, surprise evident on my face. He very rarely disagrees with my mother, but when he does, it's usually because he's right. He also never shares his personal thoughts unless asked. The fact that he's doing it now makes me sit up straighter in my chair.

"I remember the way she looked at you, like you hung the moon and stars."

"Your mother," he says, grinning. "She's terrible—truly. I've never seen someone as ruthless. But she's good too. The two sides balance each other out." He leans back, folding his arms across his chest as his grin softens. "I think the first time she met Olivia, she recognized a like soul and wanted to protect you."

My stomach twists at the memory of that first dinner. I'd brought Olivia home to meet them, full of nervous excitement. My mother had, of course, made her as un-comfortable as possible. By the time the main course was served, Olivia's face was pale, her smile forced. I couldn't take it anymore. We left in the middle of dinner, the door slamming behind us as I fumed with rage. I never wanted to speak to my mother again. But Olivia . . . laughed once we were in the car, her head falling back against the seat. "She's like a queen cobra but in pearls."

It had made me laugh too, despite everything.

"Most men like danger. There is nothing sweeter than a dangerous woman," he says. "Makes us feel a little manlier to be able to call them ours."

He's right . . . possibly. I lost interest in uncomplicated women after meeting Olivia. It's almost like a curse—once you've been drawn into something that raw, that real, everything else feels watered down. She's real and raw and completely unpredictable.

"Is she still married?"

I sigh and rub my forehead. "It's complicated."

"Isn't it always?" he laughs.

He's the only one in my family who knows what I did. He saw me through my spiral. He didn't tell my mother—not even when I confessed everything to him, the whole ugly truth about Olivia, about the amnesia, about the mistakes I kept making. Not once did he judge me.

"What do I do, Steve?"

"I can't tell you what to do, son. She brings out the worst in you and the best in you."

It's true and it's hard to hear.

"Did you tell her how you feel?"

I nod. "I told her and I showed her."

"Then, all you can do is wait."

"What if she doesn't choose me?"

He grins and leans forward in his seat. "Well, there's always Leah . . ."

My laugh starts in my chest and works its way out. "Worst joke ever, Steve . . . worst joke ever."

JUST LIKE THAT, as soon as it began again, she's back with Noah. I know because she doesn't call me. She doesn't text. She moves on with her life and leaves me in the balance.

17

The Past

The way she said my name that night. Three years later. Small. Shaky. Like the words hurt on the way out. Olivia never asked for help. Not even when she had every reason to. The night she called, her voice was trembling and afraid. I didn't hesitate. I wanted to get to her. Whatever it was, it was bad enough to break through the walls she'd built. Bad enough that she still thought I was the one who would come. And God help me, I would have burned the world down to get to her. By the time I pulled up to her place, she looked like she already regretted calling. She opened the door, eyes red from crying. She looked so small. I pulled her against my chest without saying hello. She melted into me.

"What happened?"

She shifts against me, arms crossed tight over her chest. Her voice is low and steady. The kind of steady you get when you're clinging to it by your fingernails.

"Jim's in town," she said. "He wanted to hang out, but he got drunk. Started saying all of these things about how I was just pretending I didn't want him. And then he accused me of leading him on."

Her jaw locked like she was daring herself not to cry again. She showed me her wrists, red from where he'd held them. The rage comes fast, hot, blinding.

"Did he—" I could barely get the words out. I have to dig my nails into my palms just to keep from moving.

She shook her head. "No. I scared him off. He went back to his hotel, I think."

The dam broke and tears came spilling out of her eyes. I unclench my hands, one finger at a time. She needed me.

Jim almost took something from her. Inside I'm already hunting him down. Already dragging him into the dark corners of my mind, where no one gets out clean.

"I don't want you to do anything. Please. I just . . . I can't be alone."

I nodded, hugging her tighter.

She fell asleep against my chest, clinging to me like I was the only thing holding her together.

Three years she spent fighting battles I should have been there for. Three years of drying her own tears, fending off assholes, and getting her own oil changes, and without me. She could take care of herself. But she shouldn't have had to.

THE NEXT MORNING, I left Olivia's apartment calmly because she was watching me. I could feel her eyes on me— the last thing she needed was more anxiety. The second I pulled out of her development, I hit the gas, my calm facade shattering. I wasn't calm. I was furious. I gripped the steering wheel so hard my knuckles ached. The urge to hit him wasn't clean or righteous. It was one of the ugliest angers I've ever felt. I wanted him to feel it—the terror he almost made her live with. I wanted him to carry something broken the way she would've had to. I told myself that violence doesn't fix anything. That Olivia would hate me for it. I didn't want to be the villain in her story, but all I could think about was my hands around his neck, making him understand. Making him bleed if that's what it took. She'd survived without me. That was her strength. But protecting her? That was supposed to be mine.

The Motel 6 was a rundown relic clinging to relevance on the edge of town. The parking lot was a patchwork of cracked asphalt and oil stains, scattered with rusted cars and the occasional motorcycle. I spotted his car. He was still driving the same 1969 Mustang that he had in college. I remembered him from college. Skinny kid with too much confidence and nothing to back it up. I never understood what Olivia saw in him. She could have had anyone. I heard a muffled voice and the sounds of something being knocked over. Jim swung open the door. He reeked of alcohol. I could smell it from two feet away. When he saw my face, his expression transitioned from surprise to curiosity . . . then landed soundly on fear.

"What the—"

I shoved him inside and kicked the door closed. The lock clicked, sealing us inside. The smell of beer, cigarettes, and sweat.

I hit him.

He fell back, crashing into the dresser and knocking over

a lamp. I was on him before he could stand up. I yanked him to his feet by his shirt, his legs flailing beneath him trying to find ground.

His face registered surprise. "Caleb?"

I ground my teeth together until I was sure they'd turn to dust.

"You lied to her about the amnesia." He was laughing so hard he could barely speak. I shoved him.

He staggered back, but he was still laughing. "You're just as bad as me, man. The two of you pretending not to know each other, it's like a fucking—"

Before he could finish, I grabbed the front of his shirt and flung him sideways. He landed on the bed, laughing so hard he was holding his stomach.

"You don't know anything about us. You look at her again, you speak to her again, you breathe in her direction, I will kill you."

"You've been killing her since the day you met her," he spat at me. "You're not better than me."

I stepped out of the motel room, slamming the door hard enough to rattle the walls.

18

The Present

Bar hopping," Deserae repeats. "The place where fun single people go to hang out on Friday night."

"I'm not into fun. I enjoy long walks with my depression."

"This is perfect for you then! We're walking from bar to bar. You can trail the group and feel sorry for yourself, nothing about your life will change."

Her reasoning was sound. Still, I hesitate. A bar crawl sounds exhausting.

"You're overthinking," Aja—pronounced Asia—piped in. "You need this."

"Do I?" I ask, raising an eyebrow. The question isn't rhetorical, but I don't want the answer either.

"Yes," they both say in unison, their synchronized certainty grating against my better judgement.

I consider them. Deserae, the ringleader, practically vibrating with the energy of someone who thrives on organized chaos. Aja, quiet but sharp, watching me like she knows exactly what's going on in my head.

"Fine," I say, "I'll go."

Deserae's grin stretches wide, victorious. "Knew it."

Aja doesn't gloat, but there's the flicker of satisfaction in her eyes. "Don't make us regret inviting you."

I let out a humorless laugh. "Oh, I'll definitely regret it enough for all of us."

"A word of advice," Steve says, when I stop in his office to say goodbye. "When you're in love with a woman, you shouldn't get involved with other women."

"Noted," I say. "Though, I would like to offer that she is probably sleeping with another man as we speak, likely by the name of husband."

He finally looks up, giving me one of those expressions that's half pity, half amusement. "You still think she's coming back to you?"

"No."

He nods, as if that's the most logical thing he's heard all day. "Carry on then."

THE NIGHT STARTS in the kind of bar that makes you question your life choices as soon as you walk in. It's a Fort Lauderdale classic—halfway between gritty dive bar and Instagram influencer paradise.

Deserae and Aja lead the charge, weaving through a bachelorette party. The bride-to-be is wearing a sash that says Almost Wifey and her friends are waving inflatable penises in the air like battle flags. Deserae joins them for a second shouting "Woo!" at the top of her lungs. I follow at a distance feeling like a reluctant bodyguard to their chaos. I make it to the bar just as Des orders a round of shots.

"Tequila?" I ask, raising an eyebrow.

"Obviously," she replies, sliding one toward me. I down the shot without a word, the burn of the alcohol a welcome distraction.

"See? You're already having fun."

"Sure," I say, my voice dripping with sarcasm.

The second bar is even more crowded. It's a rooftop with string lights crisscrossing overhead. The air is warm and sticky, the kind of humidity that clings.

Des and Aja dive into the crowd, leaving me to find a spot at the edge of the rooftop to wait. Below, cars are crawling down Las Olas Boulevard, groups of tourists spilling out of the other bars. It's almost peaceful for a moment, then Des appears out of the chaos with a pink shot for me. "You're dancing," she says, pointing to my hips.

"No, I'm not. I'm too sad to dance."

She wags a finger at me like she caught me in the act. "You're dancing, I can tell. Don't fight it, baby." She grabs my hand and pulls me toward the center of the rooftop where a makeshift dance floor has formed. Aja is already there grinding on some guy who looks like he just won the lottery.

"Show me what you got," Des says, pulling me to a stop.

I channel my inner twenty-two-year-old.

"Wait," she says, holding up her hands. "You can actually dance."

The crowd shifts, the music changes, and Des grabs my hand again, pulling me toward the bar. "All right, dancer boy," she says. "You've earned another round."

Women hold all the power. They should use it like a whip, not offer it up like a sacrifice.

A whip, I mentally tell her. *Use it like a whip.*

I am weaving through the suddenly packed bar, when something flashes in the corner of my eye. An emerald green dress curved around a truly magnificent ass. Her hair is up, coiled like black snakes and falling down in places. I'm watching her. Transfixed. Frozen. If what just happened to me is happening to the other men in the room. I need to get her before I kill someone. Where is Noah?

Then, I see it. A guy—some overconfident idiot—is trying to climb onto the speaker where's she's dancing. Olivia is up there alone, her hands in the air, her hips moving like sin. Cammie is yelling something at Olivia, who bends down to hear her. Her dress gapes.

I should walk away, call a cab. Pretend I never saw her here, that I don't care what she does or who she does it with. But my feet won't move, and my jaw tightens every time she moves, every time another guy's gaze lingers too long.

I have no right to feel this way. I turn ready to disappear into the crowd, when something stops me. A guy—tall, cocky steps forward. His hand curling around Olivia's thigh, his fingers pressing into her skin.

Olivia freezes, her movements coming to a halt. By the look on her face it's not Noah.

That's it. I'm already moving.

I shoulder my way through the crowd. He's still standing there, hovering like a mosquito.

"Nope," I say grabbing his wrist. Cammie turns around to see what's happening, her eyes growing wide when she sees me.

He startles, his grin faltering, then he pulls free and stumbles into the crowd. Olivia is frozen, her expression unreadable as she watches the scene unfolding beneath her.

I reach up, my hands steady as they settle on her waist.

"What are you doing?" she yells over the music.

"Getting you down."

She lets me. Her breath hitches as I lift her down, setting her on her feet. She points to an area less populated by gyrating bodies and we all move toward it. "You can't just swoop in and take over like that."

"I wasn't taking over," I reply, keeping my tone steady.

"Unbelievable."

She doesn't look angry.

"I have to pee," Cammie says, dancing on the spot. "How long are you going to argue?"

"Ten minutes," Olivia tells her. "I'll wait here." Cammie nods disappearing toward the bathroom.

"Can I buy you a drink?"

"No, but I'll buy you one."

"I'll let you do that because I saved your life back there."

"You're endearingly predictable." She pats me on the arm and then walks past me headed for the bar. It's impossible not to watch her. She doesn't seem to notice or care that heads turn as she passes.

I pass Aja who looks amused when she sees us.

At the bar Olivia leans forward, catching the bartender's attention. Her hair clings to her neck in sweaty tendrils, sweat glistening on her collarbone. She's electric, her cheeks flushed and her lips parted. He has bleached hair in a choppy mullet. When he sees her a flicker of appreciation crosses his face.

"Two shots," she says. She glances over her shoulder at me, "Would you like a Mind Eraser or a Snake Bite?"

I lean against the counter as I consider it. "Neither. I'll take a Cherry Bomb," I tell the bartender. He lines up the glasses, his eyes darting between us.

"Ex on the Beach," she says to the bartender without looking away, her voice light but deliberate. She turns fully toward me, her body brushing mine as she shifts.

She is facing me, our bodies pressed close enough that I get hard right away.

"You've got jokes tonight, Duchess."

The heat builds in my chest. I am hyperfocused on her. I can't think straight. I want to be the only thing she can think about.

I lean in slightly, close enough that she has to tilt her chin up to keep looking at me.

The bartender sets the shots down. She hands me mine.

"To your impeccable taste," she says, tilting her glass toward me.

We throw back the shots.

"You're not where you said you'd be," Cammie shouts materializing out of the crowd. "You've both betrayed my trust and now I must leave!"

Her exaggerated betrayal makes us both laugh, or maybe we're drunk on each other.

She leans in to kiss Olivia on the cheek and mouths *good night*. She doesn't say goodbye to me—she gives me a look that says everything.

"You're a good friend, Cammie!" I call after her.

"Where's your car?" I ask. The street is lined with swaying palm trees, string lights crisscrossing above. Cars inch through the boulevard, their engines rumbling like background music to the nightlife.

"At the office," she says, brushing the hair out of her face. "I drove with Cammie. You?"

"Same, I was with friends."

I glance at my phone, swiping to the ride share app. "Ten minutes for an Uber."

"Let's walk a bit," she suggests.

We walk two blocks before her feet start hurting. A neon-lit corner store has a display of beach hats and flip-flops. I run in to buy her a pair.

Once outside, I bend down in front of her and unstrap her shoes. They come off easily and I set them aside. She steadies herself on my back, her fingers curling into the fabric of my shirt.

When I straighten up she's so much shorter than me that I grin.

"Oh how the mighty have fallen," I tease.

There's fondness in her eyes. She pushes her bottom lip out with her tongue, attempting to look annoyed, but it doesn't quite land. A car crawls past us playing "Despacito."

"I got these!" I say holding up a bag of mini bottles of Titos. She loves Titos.

"Can you just not flirt with me for five seconds?"

She twists off the cap and lifts the bottle to her mouth, all without taking her eyes from mine. Her lips look like candy when she licks them. She flinches at the burn.

We start walking again.

"Thanks for being you."

"Anytime . . ."

"I know you want to ask," she says after a beat, "so just ask."

I look at her out of the corner of my eye. We move farther away from the main strip, but I don't want an Uber. I want to keep walking with her, the smell of the ocean all around us. She's carrying her heels on the tips of her fingers. I take them from her.

"Fine," I say. "What happened to Pickles?"

She lets out a sharp laugh. "Totally out of pocket."

We've drifted farther down the main strip, the chaos of Las Olas fading into the background, replaced by the rhythmic slapping of her flip-flops.

"Pickles crossed the rainbow bridge many years ago," she says, her tone softening. "She had heart disease."

"To Pickles," I say raising my own bottle of Titos.

"To Pickles," she echoes.

We toss our bottles in the trash and high-five for no reason at all.

We near the central business district, a cluster of office buildings, law firms, and corporate spaces, eerily silent like they're waiting for something to happen. We round a corner, and I catch sight of a woman walking a greyhound. She's the first person we've seen in five minutes.

"We had a fight. A pretty big one," she says breaking the silence. "Do you remember the fight we had when you followed your ex on Instagram?"

"Oh yes, how could I forget? You didn't talk to me for three days, and when you finally did, you accused me of being in love with her because I liked a post about her dog. I think you called me a thirsty simp."

"Minor overreaction, and I haven't been on Instagram since."

"Another overreaction . . ."

She nudges me with her shoulder.

"It was a golden retriever wearing a birthday hat . . ."

She laughs, a real one this time, and it echoes in the quiet street.

"Okay, so what was your fight with Noah about?"

We cross the street to avoid a tangle of construction barriers.

"You."

"You told him that you saw me?"

She nods.

"I can't imagine he liked that."

She lets out a resigned laugh. "He knows everything about us. I never tried to hide things from him. I thought you and I were over, and I wanted to be honest with him."

"I'm processing. Trying to figure out how I feel about being the subject of your domestic disputes."

All I can see are the outlines of her face. "I am in love with him, Caleb. I am."

I grind my teeth so hard I can feel the pressure in my temples. When I was a senior in high school I ground my teeth so much I had to get two crowns. I rub my jaw as I think of the dental bills this conversation alone could rack up. We walk in silence for a few minutes.

"It feels like time is running out. Is that dramatic?"

"Nope."

"I called an Uber," she says holding up her phone. "Time is literally running out."

I look over at her screen "Two minutes away," I note.

"Stop trying to avoid saying what you want to say. Spill your guts."

The Uber pulls up to the curb, its headlights lighting up the uncertainty on her face. "I love you."

I watch as she disappears into the back seat of the car, leaving me alone on the sidewalk, her words ringing in my ears.

And just like that I feel sober, the embellishment of the night has flaked off. I shove my hands into my pockets, my fingers curling around nothing the way my mind is curling around her words.

ON MONDAY AJA and Des appear in my doorway like a coordinated ambush.

"No," I say. "Not happening."

Des clutches her chest like I've mortally wounded her. "It's only decent to give an explanation after the scene you two created."

"And suddenly it's not just office gossip," Aja says dryly.

I look between them, a privacy nightmare. "How do you even know what she looks like?"

"Instagram," they say in unison, not even remotely ashamed.

"Thanks for the reminder about how creepy social media is."

"Everyone has been talking about this since I started working here," Aja says. "You're basically the protagonist of an office fanfic at this point."

"Who told you all of this—? Belen or Ruth?"

They exchange a look that makes me want to uproot my life and move to the woods.

"It's all very dramatic," Des cuts in. "The scorned ex-wife, the mysterious angsty love of your life, who's like, super unavailable."

"Okay," I say. "I'm done here."

They exchange a look. "Fine," Aja says, pushing off my desk, heading for the door. "But we're not done here."

"Noted."

THE CHURCH SMELLS like candles and dust, with an undertone of incense that makes my throat itch. We slide into the third row. Not too close to the altar—my mother is devout not fanatical. Being in church is strange and comforting, like standing in your childhood bedroom after you've outgrown it. The colors are the same, the walls are the same, but you're different now. A little too big and restless. My mother still wears the same perfume she wore to Mass when I was a kid—Chanel No. 5. Only the best for God, she always said. Now the scent wraps around me, cloying and nostalgic.

When the priest begins his homily, I force myself to pay attention, letting the words wash over me without really sinking in. After church I kiss my mother on the cheek and we head to our own cars. No lectures. No lingering looks of disappointment. That feels like a win. I drive aimlessly for a while, windows down, warm air sticky against my skin. Somehow I end up turning off the highway and into Topeekeegee Yugnee Park, which everyone calls T.Y. Park because no one has the energy to pronounce it right.

I park under the shade of a giant oak and kill the engine. I step out, yanking off my blazer like it's suffocating me. I toss it back in the car. The parking lot is busy, little kids are everywhere. It's prime birthday–party hour. They're sprinting across the grass, their faces covered in frosting, shrieking like sirens. Parents hover nearby half watching, half scrolling on their phones. Everything is bright and fast. I watch a little girl trip over her own feet, and a man, probably her dad, swoop in from nowhere to catch her. He spins her once and sets her down. Something inside me twists hard. I get back in the car, my soul sunburned.

On my way home I stop at Publix and buy a rotisserie chicken, a loaf of Cuban bread, a carton of Publix sweet tea, and a pint of rocky road ice cream.

At my condo I put the TV on for background noise and unpack the groceries.

Distraction, distraction, distraction. An idle mind is the devil's workshop.

"Hey, Alexa, tell me a joke . . ."

I tell myself it's just another Sunday, another routine, but it doesn't feel like it. I take the jug of tea, the bread, and the chicken into the living room with me. I watch *Shameless* because it's the kind of show that makes you feel better about your own life. I pick up the chicken not bothering with a plate. By the time the episode is over it is 7:00 p.m., and I have gone twelve hours without thinking about Olivia.

19

The Past

The scent of orange blossoms clung to my memory, sweet and delicate, curling through the air until it became something tangible. That night, the smell had wrapped around us, thick in the humid air, sinking into Olivia's skin until she became it. Until she smelled of something forbidden, something I'd never be able to wash off.

Moonlight sifted through the branches, shifting, uneven, painting soft lines of silver along the curve of her shoulder. The ache in my chest deepened, tightening, as the world around us blurred, shrinking until nothing existed beyond the quickening of our breathing.

A hum of cicadas pulsed in the distance. The sticky heat clinging to our skin.

And then—her.

She yielded, pressing into me, her body answering in a way that made my pulse stutter.

Had I ever really been inside of a woman?

I knew I had. There'd been bodies beneath mine.

But this?

This was different.

And then she came clamping down on me so hard it made my pulse roar in my ears.

Nothing else existed.

It was just me and her and pleasure.

The pink and beige stucco buildings of Harbor Cove looked the same, but the place felt different.

Olivia's apartment was on the second floor overlooking the retention pond. I could still see her leaning against the railing, hair damp from the shower, eyes watching the water like she was waiting for something to surface.

The door was slightly ajar when I arrived.

I hesitated, hand raised to knock. Before I could, it swung open. A man stepped out, a black garbage bag slung over his shoulder. His boots scuff heavy on the concrete. He gave me a once-over, eyes narrowing like he was trying to decide if I belonged there. "You lost or something?"

I wasn't looking at him. My gaze had already locked on the open doorway behind him.

The apartment was empty. Bare.

The art, the blankets, the candles—gone.

I swallowed the tightness in my throat.

"When did they move out?"

"This one's been open about twenty-four hours, but we got a waitlist, bro. You gotta go down to the leasing office—"

Twenty-four hours.

So she hadn't even hesitated.

I exhaled sharply, pressing my hands in my hair. "Did she leave anything behind?"

The dude looked annoyed. "Shit, I dunno. I just fix stuff, bro."

Right. Of course.

"Can I check?"

He sighed, lifting his shoulders in indifference. Tattoos peaked out from under his sleeves, arms dusted with dry-wall residue.

I already knew what I'd find. Nothing. That was the point.

"Are these units on a month-to-month lease?"

"Yep, furnished. Bed, couch, table, you need your own TV though . . ."

He followed me as I walked through the open plan kitchen/dining/living room, and into the bedroom.

Had she left something, telling me where she'd gone? Had Jim come back and scared her? Had he told her? There was nothing there. The cleaners had already worked their way through, probably tossing any last items they found into the trash.

"Hey, thanks man." I said to him. "I'll see my way out."

Outside the apartment I scooped up the trash bag he'd dropped earlier, carrying it down the stairs and to my car. I was sweating, my hands damp as I sifted through the trash. What was I looking for?

The trash held empty lightbulb boxes, a couple of out-dated yellowing appliance manuals, an empty shampoo bottle and . . .

The slight tinkling of something hitting the concrete. My eyes scanned the ground, desperate for anything. And then I saw it. Lying between my feet. A pressed penny that I once traded for a kiss.

Had she left it for me? Or had she just left it?

I picked it up and held it between my fingers. The once shiny surface had that greenish tint of aging copper.

This was her goodbye? Anger flared hot and sharp. But more than anger I felt confusion. What had I done?

I walked to the edge of the parking lot, the penny pressed tight against my palm.

Toss it, I told myself. Let her go. My muscles tensed, my fingers curled to throw it—

I couldn't.

Had I really thought I could anchor her in place with my dick? Maybe I'd been fooling myself this whole time. Maybe Olivia had given me her body, but not her heart. What I felt had stretched beyond lust, beyond the heat of her skin and the way she said my name. Low. Wrecked. Like it had been dragged from her throat.

But maybe that's all it had ever been—a moment.

A moment for me.

A way out for her.

I didn't just touch her that night, I memorized her. Now I was standing in front of her empty apartment.

Two days ago we'd danced in a parking lot. I had left Olivia and driven straight to Leah's townhouse. The second she opened the door, she knew. She looked at me, really looked at me, and in that moment, I hated that she could still read me so well.

It took me thirty minutes to break her heart. It wasn't just guilt that made my chest ache. It was her.

I loved her.

Maybe not in the way she wanted, but I did.

She never hesitated, never second-guessed herself, never ran from me.

I watched her eyes darken as she swallowed whatever words she wanted to say. She let the moment stretch. Like she was giving me one last chance to change my mind. Like she was already planning how to make me regret it.

"You'll be back."

I closed my eyes, just for a second.

Then I walked away.

Olivia was gone—again. Leaving nothing behind but a ghost of her scent in my lungs and a pressed penny burning a hole in my pocket.

I went to my condo. As I stood under the shower, I thought of our week together. I thought of the orange grove, the way she tasted, the way her skin felt like cold satin beneath my fingers. When my mind went to that first moment of being inside her, the way her eyes had widened and her lips had parted, I had to blast myself with cold water.

She'd given me everything—everything she'd held back before. She was different. She was also the same. Stubborn, defiant . . . full of lies.

I tried to break her before. Now I just wanted her as she was. I wanted every last beautiful flaw. I wanted the witty one-liners and the coldness that only I knew how to warm. I wanted the fight and the friction and the makeup sex. I wanted her to wake up in my bed every morning, rumpled hair and pillow marks on her face. I wanted her shitty cooking and her beautiful, complex mind. By the time I got out of the shower I was decided on what I needed to do. I could drown in the memory of her—or I could go find her.

20

The Present

The gym was emptying out, the late-night crowd thinning as I step into the humid air. I roll my shoulders, trying to shake the tension that hasn't left me since I walked in.

The workout had been pointless, every punch I threw at the bag, every mile on the treadmill—wasn't enough. My knuckles throbbed, raw from hitting the bag too many times. So far, my efforts at distraction were failing. I lean against my car, my breathing still heavy, the aftershocks of adrenaline buzzing under my skin.

Shower. Sleep. Forget.

But my hand is in my pocket pulling out my phone. I decide to call her instead of texting.

She answers on the third ring. "Caleb," she says, and it's different this time. A warning. A reminder. A whole history in my name.

I close my eyes my jaw tightening.

"Hey, Duchess."

There's a pause—long enough to make me second-guess

everything. Then she exhales, and it's . . . soft. "It's nice to hear your voice."

That's worse than if she hung up.

"Where are you?"

"I'm at the office."

I open my car door and get in. "Can I come see you?"

I hear the sound of movement, like she's debating.

I turn the car on, pull out of the spot.

"Okay," she says.

"I'll be there in twenty minutes."

When I get there the parking lot is empty. I park next to her car and leave my phone in the console.

The law office sits tucked between a designer boutique and a high-end café. The street is quiet this late, save for the distant hum of traffic and the occasional sports car flying down Collins Avenue.

The door is locked, but the light inside is still on. I cup my hands against the glass and peer in.

She's walking toward the door, no hesitation, no rush. She unlocks it, and steps back waiting for me to come in.

I step inside letting the door click shut behind me.

"Nice office," I say, not taking my eyes from her.

"Nice gym shorts . . ."

She exhales, pressing her fingers to her temple. "I have a headache. Come on . . ."

I follow her to her office and she closes the door. The space is neat . . . professional. Two chairs, a desk, a humidifier. A handful of essential oils are lined up on the windowsill. I take my time, hands in my pockets, eyes scanning the prints on her walls.

"Working late."

"Always." She walks around the desk and sits in her chair. Opening a drawer, she shuffles around until she finds a bottle of Tylenol.

She loved Thomas Barbèy, she had this print over her bed when we were in college—*Shortcut to China*. An ocean liner disappearing down a funnel-type hole, old New York looming in the background.

I sit.

"Why are you here?" Her voice is even but her eyes give her away.

"I missed you," I say.

She tilts her head, considering me, her lips curving into something wry. "Where was that energy ten years ago?"

"Ha!" I smile. And then, "You look good. I like your shoes."

She's wearing a dark blue sheath dress with black stilettos. The dress hits above the knee. No nonsense.

"Do you have any of those little bottles of vodka on you?"

I laugh. "Not this time."

"Ugh, okay. I'll bareback this conversation."

I raise an eyebrow. "That's kind of hot. Did you tell Noah you saw me?"

"Yeah . . . he thinks we're dysfunctional and toxic."

"We *were* dysfunctional and toxic," I correct her.

"I'm not so sure of that."

"How's your head?" I say changing the subject.

"I can't decide if it's from work or you."

"It's from dehydration."

She took another sip of her water, her eyes sliding down my arms. "You're super unfit. You should go to the gym."

"I could bench press you and your attitude at the same time—" I point at Alexa. "Is this song playing on repeat . . . ?"

"It helps me concentrate."

"Our song helps you concentrate?"

She raises an eyebrow. "How is this our song?"

"It reminds me of us."

I see a flicker in her eyes, then she shakes her head. "We weren't together when this song came out."

I shrug, "I didn't say we were . . ."

Neither of us speaks. The song keeps playing soft and insistent.

"We should dance," I say, getting to my feet.

"Don't you dare." She holds up a finger to ward me off. I brush it aside and take her hands, pulling her out of the chair.

I slide her arms around my shoulders, my fingers finding her waist. The warmth of her body presses against mine.

I dip my head down, my breath warm against her ear. "Let me do whatever I want to you for one night, and you'll have all the proof you need."

Her eyes glaze over and I laugh, bending my head down to touch our lips together. It's a soft kiss. When I pull back, her eyes are dark, but she looks disappointed.

"I make you feel vulnerable because you love me."

I feel the shift, the tension coiling.

I back her up until the backs of her thighs are flush against the desk. "How often do you think about the orange grove?" I ask.

"Every day."

"You know why?" I kiss the spot of skin below her ear. She reaches between us, her hand cupping me and I groan.

I grab the backs of her thighs and lift her onto the desk.

I stand between her legs and slide the dress over her head. I kiss one shoulder, then the other.

"Because."

Unstrapping her bra, I lower my head and take a nipple in my mouth. Her whole body arches backward and her thighs clench around my waist.

"Everything you do is sexy. Have I ever told you that?" I move to the other side . . . repeat until she squirms.

She latches her hands in my hair.

"Still the silent lover," I say, moving back to her mouth. Her eyes are closed, but her lips are parted. I trail a finger down her neck.

I kiss her neck softly. One of her arms is looped around my neck, and the other is clutching my bicep. I run my hands down her sides and hook my fingers around the waistband of her panties. As I pull down, she lifts her hips so I can get them off. Now she's naked, perched on the edge of her desk in nothing but three-inch black heels.

"We're going to keep the heels on . . ." I yank her thighs farther apart and trace a hand up the inside of her thigh.

She folds her lips in and her eyes close. I play with her, teasing, rubbing, sliding. I could do this every day. I *want* to do this every day. Our foreheads are pressed together, our lips touching but not moving. She has her hand wrapped around the back of my head. I can feel her need in the way her body is tightening. I like that I'm the cause of her untidy breathing and the jerking of her muscles. I like how her body responds to my hands. I still have one finger pressed inside of her when I speak.

"I'm not going to make love to you this time." My voice is husky. She's pushing my pants down, her tongue pressed against her top lip. I bite her tongue and move my mouth to her ear. "I'm going to fuck you." She stills—or freezes is more like it. I push my shorts down and step out of them. She's eyeing me with wildly glazed eyes.

She lies back, her hair draping over the side of the desk.

"Hard and fast, Drake—and make it last longer than last time."

AFTERWARD, WE LIE on the floor of her office. Me on my back, one arm behind my head, the other wrapped around her waist. She's lying on my chest in the picturesque post-coital position. About halfway through our tangle of hard sex, we started making love. We can't avoid it. Everything with us eventually becomes emotional—even when we try not to make it that way. I am replaying every warm second of it in my head. "I think I'm sexually addicted to you."

"It's just the newness of it," she says, "because we never did it before."

"Why do you always try to downplay my feelings for you?"

"I don't trust them," she says after a minute. "You claim that you love me, but you've loved other women in between."

"You pushed me away, Duchess. I'm a human being. I was trying to find someone to replace you."

"What about Leah? You married her."

I sigh. "Guilt. I dragged her into something, she fell in love with me, and then I lied to her about the amnesia. I felt like the only way to make up for everything I did was to marry her."

She's very still in my arms. I wish I could see her face, but I want to give her privacy to deal with my words.

My heart. If my heart had knees that's where it would be—doubled over, throbbing from the pain. I pull my arm from behind my head and rub my eyes, trying to push the ache away.

"Olivia . . ." My voice catches. Her name feels heavy on my tongue.

I want her to demand the whole story, make her force me to relive the seconds that changed both of our lives. But she doesn't. She doesn't say a word. Instead, she pulls her fingers away from my jaw, pressing her lips to mine. Sliding on top of me, she reaches a hand between us, and I forget everything—everything except us. Everything we're avoiding fades until there is nothing left but her touch.

We reach the parking lot just as the sky is lightening, a soft pink creeping across the horizon. She stands there, keys in hand, looking at me with a mixture of hesitation and sadness.

"This is about you and me, not you and Noah. Just take a few weeks. Spend some time with me. No decisions until it's a fair decision."

"The fair decision would be to do what's right—"

I cut her off before she can turn this into something noble. "For you," I say. "Yes, do what's right for you. Give me some time to show you."

She opens her mouth, pink lips parting, ready to fire something sharp.

"Hush," I say. "Pack an overnight bag. There's somewhere I want to take you."

I grab her wrist and pull her into a hug, pressing a kiss to the top of her head.

She buries her face in my chest like she's trying to

burrow herself into me. I rewrap her in a hug, trying not to laugh.

"Come on, Duchess. It'll be like the camping trip."

She lets out a dry laugh. "Yeah, it'll be just like that." Her voice is muffled against my chest. "Except you won't be lying about having amnesia, and I won't be lying about not knowing you, and your bitch of a girlfriend won't be trashing my apartment while we're gone."

My grip tightens around her. I pull away so I can see her face. "What do you say? Yes?"

"How long will we be gone?"

I think about it. "Four days."

She shakes her head immediately. "Two."

"Three," I counter. "To make up for the time we spend traveling."

She taps her fingers on my chest, considering. "You're in lawyer mode," I note. She pretends not to hear me.

"No camping."

"No camping. Pack something nice to wear, a couple bathing suits maybe. Or you can be nude for all three days, I'd like that too . . ."

I take a step back giving her space, but not too much. "I'll pick you up tomorrow at 8:00 a.m."

"Okay."

She tries to act nonchalant, but I can tell she's excited.

I kiss her forehead. "Bye, Duchess. See you soon."

She needed something to remind her how good we were together, not about the games we played. I pull out my phone as I climb into my car. I know the perfect place and it's only a few hours away.

I KNOCK ON her door at seven forty-five, just as the hallway light flickers overhead.

"Always early," she complains when she opens it. Her bag is in her hand, and I take it without asking. The strap is warm from her grip. My eyes flicker over her—wet hair clinging to her skin.

She sees me eyeing her Marlins shirt and she shrugs. "I went to a game," she says. I catch the defensiveness in her voice and I smirk.

"What?" she says. "I like sport."

"First of all, I'm the British one, not you. It's *sports*. Second, you hate it all. I recall you once told me that professional athletes were a waste of space."

Her mouth tightens, the corners dipping as she frowns. "Noah likes baseball. I was being supportive."

Ah.

I was jealous.

We ride the elevator in silence, standing so close the sides of our hands touch. The elevator dings. The doors slide open. Neither of us moves.

For a moment, we just stand there, suspended in that space between past and present, between what we were and what we might still be.

"HOW LONG WILL the drive take?" She looks at me over the top of the car as she tosses her shoulder bag into the back seat.

"Do you not like surprises anymore?"

"Not since your amnesia, no . . ."

I slide into the driver's side, gripping the wheel loosely. "We're not driving," I say casually, buckling my seatbelt. "You'll see. Just sit back and relax. We'll be there soon."

The drive takes twenty minutes. When I pull up at the dock she looks around, brows drawn together. I kill the engine and step out grabbing her bags from the trunk.

"Where are we?"

"A marina. It's where I keep my boat."

"Whaaat? You have a boat?"

I fight a grin. "Yes, love."

I have a 48-foot Viking convertible. Clean, sharp and built for speed.

When we reach my slip, I climb on first, setting our bags down in the small galley before turning back to her.

"*Peter Pan*," she says, humor in her voice. "You named it *Peter Pan*."

"Well, when I first bought it I named it *Great Expectations*, but Pip doesn't land up with Estella in the end. So I had it changed to *Peter Pan*."

The words hang between us, heavier than I meant them to be.

I don't look at Olivia right away, but I can feel her watching me. Measuring my words, weighing the silence that follows. She never asks about Estella. Never pushes, never pries.

I appreciate that.

We let the moment sit, the quiet lapping of the water filling the space. She reaches for my hand, squeezes it. A quiet acknowledgment. She lets go too soon.

I hold out my hand and help her on.

When we are bouncing forward, the helm of the boat

cutting into the waves, she scoots closer to me on the bench. It's subtle at first, but then I feel it—the press of her against my side, the way she tucks into me.

I lift my arm up and around her, instinctive, and she snuggles into me.

At one point, when we are in the middle of nothing but open water, I cut the engine. "Dolphins," I tell her.

Olivia's head snaps toward the water. "Oh my God."

A sleek body arcs out of the ocean, cutting through the surface before vanishing beneath the water again.

"I feel so mortal," she says.

"That's what the ocean will do to you."

"What's the ocean like in England?"

I glance out at the water, at the way the sun reflects off the swells. Endless deep blue. "Colder," I say after a moment. "Darker, rougher. The waves feel heavier."

"Sounds poetic. Sounds like my kind of ocean . . ." Of course, she'd like that kind of ocean—the kind that doesn't pretend to be soft, that demands to be understood on its own terms. "Which do you like better?"

"I prefer this, but if that's what you were I'd go sailing on it every day."

"Good answer," she says.

"I'm the only one who knows you."

"How is it that you always let me go so easily, then? Why don't you know that I want you to fight for me?"

I sigh. Here it is. The truth.

"It took me a long time to figure out that's what you were saying. And it seemed that every time one of us came back for the other, we weren't ready. But ten years later, here I am. Fighting. I'd like to think I've learned from my mistakes. I'd also like to think we've finally made it to the point where we are ready for each other."

She doesn't respond, but I know what she's thinking. Maybe this is finally our time. Maybe.

I start the engine.

We reach Key West around one o'clock. I ease *Peter Pan* into the marina. Rows of boats, from small fishing skiffs to yachts, bob in the turquoise water. The smell of diesel and fresh ocean is interrupted by the sweetness of coconut sunscreen. I love it here.

"Let's go find lunch," I say.

The restaurant sits on the edge of the marina, perched over the water on stilts that have weathered decades of sun, storms, and salt. A wooden plank walkway, slightly warped from the heat, leads to the entrance where a hand-painted sign swings in the breeze. Olivia's nose is sunburned and I see a scattering of freckles across the bridge of her nose and her cheeks.

Our server wears cutoffs and a tank top. Her nametag, slightly crooked, reads Maria.

"You tourists or trouble?" she asks, as she stops at our table.

When Olivia's margarita arrives, she takes one sip, closing her eyes like she's just had a religious experience. Maria looks happy.

"You ever make her eyes roll back in her head like that?"

I glance at Olivia, "Not today." I say keeping my face neutral.

Maria cackles before she walks off, a tray balanced on her shoulder.

Olivia licks the salt from the rim of her glass. "I like her."

The smell of grilled fish, citrus, and butter lingers in the air, mixing with the briny tang of the ocean. A guitarist plays something slow in the corner.

"Do you want to sleep on the boat or get a hotel?"

"Boat," she says.

"So you're okay with water camping?"

"About that," she puts her glass down, folding her hands on the tabletop. "I know I said camping was awful, but I was thinking about it more, and it wasn't that bad. It was kind of fun aside from the bugs, and the debilitating anxiety."

WE WALK THROUGH the little seaside shops after lunch. She points out a ridiculous cowboy hat. She plucks it from the stand, setting on her head. The oversized brim dips low over her eyes, casting a shadow across her smirk.

"Thoughts?"

I tilt my head pretending to consider. "You look like you're about to start a bar fight."

She tips the hat like she's greeting a saloon full of outlaws. "I almost got into a bar fight once."

"In Texas?"

"I didn't start it." She puts the hat back and joins me on the sidewalk.

For the first time in a long time I don't want to be anywhere else.

21

The Past

After graduation Cammie moved back to Texas. It wasn't hard to find her—all I had to do was follow the brightly lit social media trail she left behind.

I sent her a message on Facebook. The first message went unanswered. I poked her every day for a week.

WTF, Caleb.
She wants to be left alone.
BACK THE FUCK OFF!

In other words, Cammie wasn't going to help me. I considered flying to Texas, just showing up and figuring it out once I got there. Then Cammie changed her profile to Private and blocked me. I went through my other options: I could hire a private detective . . . or I could leave her alone. That's what she wanted.

One fake Instagram profile later and I was part of Cammie's extensive network of pretend friends, or *Priends* as they called them. Her entire cache of photos was a click away.

I was afraid to see Olivia's life—how easy it was for her to move on without me.

Cammie was living in Grapevine.

Olivia hated having her photo taken, but she's always in the background just out of reach of the lens. A hand resting on the edge of a table, a delicate gold bracelet on the wrist. I scroll down to the comments.

Who's the mystery guest?

Iconic as always.

That bracelet looks familiar, is it Olivia?

I stopped myself from liking the last comment, thumb hovering over the heart a little too long. I checked the date the photo was posted. A month after Olivia moved out of her apartment. I was too slow and too stupid to stop it. I scrolled back, heart hammering harder with every swipe. Looking for patterns. Looking for proof. Something that would make the pieces fit together and didn't leave me feeling like I was in the dark. New faces. New places. A blurry face at a concert. A cityscape at night. String of lights along a balcony railing. In the background blurred out but unmistakable—a woman. White dress. Bare shoulders, her hair loose.

That was all I needed. Olivia was with Cammie. I would go there. Talk to her.

The next morning, I asked Steve for the time off.

No real plan.

Steve looked at me over the top of his glasses.

"You good?"

No, I'm not good. I'm barely holding it together. I'm one scroll away from losing it completely.

"I just need a couple of days to take care of some things."

Steve scratched the back of his neck. "Is this something I'm going to have to answer to your mother for later?"

I didn't say anything.

Finally he sighed.

"Go."

"Thanks," I said, relieved.

"Don't come back worse than you left," he called after me.

I nodded, even though I had no way of guaranteeing that.

I DROVE. ONE thousand two hundred and ninety miles of podcasts and playlists and regret. I crossed over the Texas state line tired to my bones. The motel itself was a single story, L-shaped stretch of rooms, their doors painted in mismatched shades of turquoise and red. I needed to shave, shower, and sleep. Instead I sat on the bed pulling out my phone.

Several missed calls. Texts from my mother. I didn't open them. I tapped on the group chat with four of my friends instead.

Someone explain why Ben just Venmo
requested me $23.99 with no context.
I'm at a gas station in the middle of nowhere
and they have a petting zoo. Do I buy the goat?

There were three replies all saying, Buy the goat!

The contrast was too much. My world felt like it was about to implode. I stared at the messages before setting my phone face down. Sleep, then maybe I could formulate a clear thought.

CAMMIE OPENED THE door wearing nothing but an oversized T-shirt with a faded picture of Lady Gaga on the front. Her hair was sticking up in places like she'd just rolled out of bed—or hadn't been there at all. She clutched a coffee mug in one hand, steam curling from the rim. "Oh. My. God."

I lifted the mug from her limp hand. I took a sip.

"Bitter and strong," I said giving it back to her.

She stepped outside, pulling the door closed behind her.

"I want to see her," I said.

"You have lot of nerve coming here after all the stunts you pulled."

"Go get her," I pleaded.

Cammie didn't move. "No," she said finally. "I'm not letting you do this to her again."

"Do what?"

"Play games with her head," she snapped. "She's fine. She's happy. She needs to be left alone."

I swallowed hard. That was mostly true. Mostly. "I want to talk it out with her, not you."

"Uh-uh. You're a lying, cheating scumbag. She needs something better than you."

I mentally backed up a step. That was true too, mostly. But I could be better for her. I could be what she needed because I loved her.

"You're not wrong Cammie, but she should still be the one to hear what I have to say and make her own decisions."

She considered this for a moment before stepping aside. "Fine," she said. "Go . . ."

I opened the door, took my first step into the foyer.

To the left was the kitchen and what looked like the living room, to the right were the stairs.

"She was pregnant, you know."

Her voice stopped me cold. My skin tingled, burned, went numb all at once. "What?"

"After your little rendezvous under the moonlight."

I looked back at her, my heart suddenly pounding wildly in my chest. My mind went to that night. I hadn't used a condom. I hadn't pulled out. I felt tingling all over my body. *She was pregnant. Was . . . was . . . was . . .*

The word looped in my head, each repetition landing heavier. Why would she? How could she? Did she think I wouldn't step up? Maybe she thought I wouldn't support her decision. Or maybe . . . she just didn't want me to know. That was her choice.

"It's better that you leave her alone," she said. "There isn't just water under your bridge, there's maggots and shit and dead bodies. Now get the fuck out of my house before I call the police."

22

The Present

She has not lost her childlike awe. When she sees something that has never crossed her vision before, she becomes entranced: parted lips, wide eyes.

I bend down to her ear. "Okay, love?"

She nods. "I love it so much, am I supposed to love it this much?"

A rooster steps right over her toe to get to a piece of corn. She thinks the ragged-looking thing is cute.

At night Duval reminds me of a tropical version of Bourbon Street. It's a rum-soaked adventure. Live bands, loud crowds, and zero regrets. I take her to The Blue Anchor. The place has a weird energy, but I like it. When we walk in the band is playing "Summertime Sadness." There's no cocktail list—just a bartender who can read you well enough to know whether you need a mojito, bourbon neat, or something that doesn't even have a name. She slides onto a stool, fingers tapping. A gray-haired woman in an oversized sweater lines up tarot cards at a table near us, completely distracted. At the bar, four guys in Hawaiian shirts are sipping from rocks glasses. She shifts her weight and her wrap skirt rides up her thigh. Her sandal dangles from her foot like she's barely aware of it.

The bartender gives her one look and, then smirks, "First time?"

She nods. He's in his early fifties, with slicked-back salt-and-pepper hair. His face shows the evidence of too many cigarettes and too many late nights.

He reaches for a bottle without another word, pouring something rich and amber into a short glass, adds a dash of this and that. He slides it toward her. A silent offering, a flex.

She takes a slow sip, and hums in approval. "What's it called?"

"Widow's Mercy."

"I can taste the whiskey . . . but what else."

He leans his forearms on the bar, muscles flexing just enough to let me know he's there. "Chicory-infused whiskey. You taste how it's sweet at first then lingers with that little bite on the end of your tongue?"

"Yeah, what is that?"

"Orange bitters."

"I like it," she says.

"The other thing you're tasting is the pecan bitters . . ."

She looks mildly interested in what he's saying. Her shoulders are relaxed, fingers lightly wrapped around the glass. She takes another slow sip, and I swear to God, she even licks a drop from her lip—probably without realizing it, but I realize it.

And this guy? He definitely realizes it.

And that's when I decide we're done here. I roll my shoulders, shifting in my seat, forcing my presence back into the conversation.

He glances at me. Finally, like he's just remembered I exist. I hold his gaze, no hostility, just a clear understanding.

"I love it here," she says again.

A group walks in, pushing through the wooden doors and dragging the humid night air in with them. It gives him a reason to exit the conversation.

"He didn't make you a drink," she says.

"Yeah, somehow I think that was intentional . . ."

Olivia offers me a sip of her Widow's Mercy, but I don't want to drink tonight, I want to remember everything: the way her stool is pulled close to mine, the fish tank stretching across the back wall with the airport blue lights, the maritime relics, her bare face, the drink in her hand, her wrap skirt paired with one of my button-down shirts. It's too loud to talk, so after a few songs I pay the tab and head outside.

"You're different here," Olivia says.

"Yeah? What's that mean?"

"You're just . . . lighter."

"Yea, well . . . I think my brooding has a range limit. Once you hit a certain temperature, all the existential dread sweats right out of you."

"Is that why you go to the gym so much?"

"How do you know I go to the gym *so much*," I mimic her tone, tilting my head.

"You never miss an opportunity to roll up your sleeves."

"When you have a skill set you use it. Michelangelo painted the Sistine Chapel. I happen to be very good at rolling sleeves."

"I'm going to be completely honest with you," she says once we're out of the noise. "I was manic last night so I baked. I have cookies, brownies, and banana bread in my bag. Let's skip dinner and eat that."

I don't need to be asked twice.

My mind flashes to first time we baked together. It ended in a food fight. By the time we called a truce the kitchen was wrecked. Olivia was laughing so hard she could barely stand.

Beside me, Olivia gathers her hair into a topknot as she walks, twisting it up and securing it with a hair tie she wears on her wrist.

When we reach the dock I offer to give her a piggyback ride. She's warm, legs hooked loosely around my waist. "You sure you want to sleep here tonight?"

"There's a bed isn't there?"

"Yes, a small one. And a bathroom."

"We'll manage."

I don't argue because I don't care where we sleep . . .

While Olivia changes, I untie the lines. The dock creaks beneath my feet as I give the boat a gentle push away from the slip. The engine hums to life, blending with the rhythmic lapping of the waves. The marina recedes in the distance as I guide the boat past the cluster of fishing vessels moored in their slips. Olivia appears from the cabin, having changed into her bikini.

It's nude colored, simple, but devastating, at a glance it looks like she's naked. I slow the boat and stop in the middle of the vastness, cutting the engine. Olivia stretches out on the cushion bench. One leg rests against the railing, her knee bent, while the other stretches long. I sit down and she shifts her head to lay it in my lap. The boat rocks gently beneath us. She feeds me pieces of dessert from the foil packages open on her belly.

"This is a core memory," she says, gazing up at the stars.

"I'm eating cake off your body. Peak existence right here," I agree.

She hums, pleased, then adds casually, "I feel really bad about this but . . . I poisoned the cookies."

"It was worth it. I had four, how soon will I die?"

She lifts herself up, brushing crumbs from her stomach, some of them stubbornly cling to her skin. "An hour . . . maybe."

I lean back against the seat, stretching out like a man who's accepted my fate.

She climbs onto my lap straddling me. My hands automatically circle her waist. The weight of her makes me hard right away.

"What's your last wish?" she asks.

I shift so she can feel me. My hands move to her upper thighs, squeezing.

She unbuttons my shirt then runs her hands over my chest and stomach. I close my eyes and wait patiently while she touches me. Then she leans over to kiss me, pieces of her hair tickling my face.

I let out an audible moan when she starts moving her hips, grinding against me in slow circles. She lifts herself to her knees and unties the waistband of my shorts. They come off easily and she climbs back on top of me in a hurry. I untie the sides of her bikini bottoms and toss them aside. She lowers herself onto me.

23

The Past

Four months after Leah was acquitted, I filed for divorce. The minute—the very minute—I made the decision, I felt a huge weight lifted from my shoulders. I didn't necessarily believe in divorce, but you couldn't stay in something that was killing you either. Sometimes you fucked up enough in life that you had to bow to your mistakes. They won. Be humble . . . move on. Leah thought she was happy with me, but how could I make someone happy when I was so dead inside? She didn't even know the real me. It was like sleepwalking, being married to someone you didn't love. You tried to fill yourself with positives—buying houses and going on vacations and taking cooking classes—anything to try to bond with this person you should already have bonded with before you said *I do*. It was all empty, fighting for something that never was. Let it be my fault for marrying her in the first place; I'd made plenty of mistakes. It was time to move on. I filed the papers.

Olivia.

—That was my first thought. She was engaged to Turner. A filler fiancé. He was barely a blip on the radar. A name to write on wedding invitations. Lies were the real obstacle course between Olivia and me.

How long did I have to convince her? Did she still love me? Could she forgive me? If I could wrestle her away from that fucking tool, could we actually build something together?

We'd both told so many lies, sinned against each other—against everyone who got in our way. I'd tried to tell her once about what I'd done. It was during Leah's trial. I'd come to the courthouse early to try to catch her alone. She was wearing my favorite shade of blue: airport blue. It was her birthday.

"Happy birthday."

She looked up. My heart pounded out my feelings, like they did every time she looked at me. "I'm surprised you remember."

"Why is that?"

"Oh, you've just been forgetting an awful lot of things over the years."

I half smiled at her jab.

"I never forgot you . . ."

I felt a rush of adrenaline. This was it: I was going to come clean. Then the prosecutor walked in. Truth was put on hold.

I MOVED OUT of the house I shared with Leah and back into my condo. I paced the halls. I drank scotch. I waited.

Waited for what? For her to come to me? For me to go to her? I waited because I was a coward. That was the truth.

I walked to my sock drawer—infamous protector of engagement rings and other mementos—and ran my fingers along the bottom. The minute my fingers found it, I felt a surge of something. I rubbed the pad of my thumb across the slightly green surface of the kissing penny. I looked at it for a full minute, conjuring up images of the many times it had been traded for kisses. It was a trinket, a cheap trick that had once worked, but it had evolved into so much more than that.

I put on my sweats and went for a run. I turned toward the beach, dodging a little girl and her mother as they walked along hand in hand. I smiled. The little girl had long black hair and startling blue eyes—she looked like Olivia. Was that what our daughter would have looked like? I stopped jogging and bent over, hands on my knees. It didn't have to be a *would have* situation. We could still have our daughter. I slipped my hand in my pocket and pulled out the kissing penny. I started jogging to my car.

There was no time like the present. If Turner got in the way, I'd just toss him off the balcony. I was soaked in sweat and determined when I turned on the ignition.

I was one mile from Olivia's condo when I got the call.

It was a number I didn't recognize. I hit Talk.

"Caleb Drake?"

"Yes?" My words were clipped. I made a left onto Ocean and pressed down on the gas.

"There's been an . . . incident with your wife."

"My wife?" *God, what has she done now?* I thought about the feud she was currently having with the neighbors about their dog and wondered if she'd done something stupid.

"My name is Dr. Letcher. I'm calling from West Boca Medical Center. Mr. Drake, your wife was admitted here a few hours ago."

I hit the brakes, swung the wheel around until my tires made a screeching sound, and gunned the car in the opposite direction. An SUV swerved around me and lay on the horn.

"Is she all right?"

The doctor cleared his throat. "Your housekeeper found her and dialed 911. She's stable right now, but we'd like for you to come in."

I stopped at a light and ran my hand through my hair. This was my fault. I knew she took the separation hard, but suicide? It didn't even seem like her.

"Of course. I'm on my way."

I hung up. I hung up and I punched the steering wheel. Some things were not meant to be.

WHEN I ARRIVED at the hospital, Leah was awake and asking for me. I walked into her room, and my heart stopped. She was lying propped up by pillows, her hair a rat's nest and her skin so pale it almost looked translucent. Her eyes were closed, so I had a moment to rearrange my face before she saw me.

When I took a few steps into the room, she opened her eyes. As soon as she saw me, she started crying. I sat on the edge of her bed and she latched onto me, sobbing with such passion I could feel her tears soak through my shirt. I held her like that for a long time. I'd like to say I was thinking deep thoughts during those minutes, but I wasn't.

I was numb, distracted. Something was agitating me and I couldn't place it. It's cold in here, I told myself.

"Leah," I said finally, pulling her from my chest and settling her back onto the pillows. "Why?"

Her face was slimy and red. Dark half-moons camped around her eyes. She looked away. "You left me."

Three words. I felt so much guilt I could barely swallow. It was true.

"Leah," I said, "I'm not good for you. I—"

She cut me off, waving my comment away in the frigid hospital air. "Caleb, please come home. I'm pregnant."

I closed my eyes.

No!

No!

No . . .

"You swallowed a bottle of sleeping pills and tried to kill yourself and my baby?"

She wouldn't look at me. "I thought you left me. I didn't want to live. Please, Caleb—it was so stupid. I'm sorry."

I couldn't name the emotion I felt. I was somewhere between wanting to walk out on her forever and wanting to stay and protect that baby.

"I can't forgive you for that," I said. "You have a responsibility to protect something you gave life to. You could have talked to me about it. I'll always be around to help you."

I saw some color come back into her cheeks.

"You mean . . . help me while we're divorced?" She lowered her head and looked up at me. I thought I saw some fire in her irises.

I didn't say anything. We were locked in a staring contest. That's exactly what I meant.

"If you don't stay with me, I'm not keeping this baby. I have no intention of being a single mother."

"You can't be serious?"

Never did I think she would threaten me with something of this nature. It seemed beneath her. I opened my mouth to threaten her—to say something I'd probably regret, but I heard footsteps. The brisk kind that said *doctor*.

"I'd like some privacy to talk to my doctor about my options," she said quietly.

"Leah—"

Her head snapped up. "Get out."

I looked from her to who I presumed was Dr. Letcher. Her face was pale again, all the anger gone.

Before the doctor could say anything, Leah announced that I was leaving.

I stopped in the doorway and without turning around, I said, "Okay, Leah. We'll do it together."

I didn't need to look at her face to know it held triumph.

24

The Present

I have a decision to make. I'm pacing it off. That's what my mother would call it: *pacing it off*. I did it as a kid, across my bedroom. I guess I never grew out of it.

Olivia is making her decision, whether she knows it or not. Noah is going to come back for her, because she's that girl, the one you come back to again and again and again. So I fight. That's it. That's my only option. And if I don't get her, if she doesn't choose me, I'm going to be *that* guy—the one who spends his life alone and pining. Because I sure as hell am not going to try to replace her. *Fuck it.* It's Olivia or nothing. I grab my wallet and keys and jog down the stairs instead of taking the elevator. I go directly to her office. Her secretary holds Olivia's door open for me as I step in. I smile at her and mouth my thanks.

"Hi," I say.

She's in the middle of sorting through a mound of papers, but when she sees me, she smiles—all the way to her eyes. Almost as quickly, the smile sinks out of her eyes and the lines of her mouth firm into a straight line. Something's up. I walk around her desk and pull her against me.

"What's wrong?" I kiss the corner of her lips. She doesn't move. When I let her go, she drops into her swivel chair and looks at the floor.

Okay.

I grab a chair and pull it up to hers so that we're facing each other. When she spins her chair away from me to look at the wall, I know some type of shit has hit the fan.

Please God, no more shit. I've had about all the shit I can handle.

"Why are you being so cold with me?"

"I don't think I can do this."

"What?"

"This," she says, motioning between us. "It's so wrong."

I rub my fingers over my jaw and start grinding my teeth. "We are kind of experts on doing what's wrong, no?"

"Ugh, Caleb. Stop it. I'm supposed to be thinking of ways to make my marriage work. Not building a new relationship with someone else."

"Building a new relationship with someone else?" I am confounded. "We're not building anything. We've been in a relationship since before we were actually in a relationship." In actual fact, I tell people we were together for three years, even though it was only one and a half, because I was emotionally *with* her from the moment we met. "Why are you saying this now?" I say.

She opens a bottle of water that is sitting on her desk and takes a sip. I'm pretty damn sure my non-girlfriend is trying to end our non-relationship, so I stay still and quiet.

"Because it's better for everyone if we're not together."

I can't keep the sneer off my face. "Better for whom?"

Olivia closes her eyes and takes a deep breath. "Estella," she says.

It feels like someone has reached a hand into my belly and grabbed hold of my organs.

Olivia is chugging her water, her free hand limp in her lap.

"What the hell are you talking about?" I haven't heard her name in a long time. I've thought it plenty, but Olivia's voice wrapping around the syllables is jarring.

Her nostrils are flaring as she breathes. She still won't look at me.

"Olivia . . ."

"Estella is yours." It's a blurt. I blink at her, not sure where that came from, or why she's saying it.

Being told I had twenty-four hours to live would have been less painful than that statement. I don't say anything. I stare at her nostrils, which are working like fish gills.

She spins in her chair until her knees bump into mine, and she's looking me straight in the face.

"Caleb." Her voice is gentle, yet it makes me flinch. "Leah came to see me. She told me she's yours. She'll take the paternity test to prove it. But only if we're not together."

My head and my heart are in a battle for who can host the most pain. I shake my head. *Leah? Was here?* "She's lying."

Olivia shakes her head. "She's not. And you can get a court-issued paternity test. She can't keep Estella from you if you are her father. But Caleb, think about it."

I stand up. Walk to the window. How could something like this be true and I not know it?

"She was pregnant before Estella. We were separated, but we had sex once during that time. Anyway, she lost the baby after she swallowed a bottle of sleeping pills and had to have her stomach pumped. That's why we went to Rome. She said that she wanted to reconcile, and I felt so guilty about her sister and the miscarriage."

I look at Olivia when I say that. Her lips turn white as she presses them together.

"Caleb, she wasn't pregnant in the hospital. She lied to you. She told me that too."

I always wondered what Olivia felt when I told her I faked my amnesia. Painful truth is ineffable. It swings you around a couple times until you're dizzy, and then punches you hard in the stomach. You don't want to believe it, but it wouldn't hurt so badly if on some level you didn't know it was true. I run with denial for a few more minutes.

"She bled. I saw her bleed." Denial is such a friendly companion. It's normally Olivia's best friend. Suddenly, I want in on the party.

Olivia looks so distraught.

"Oh, Caleb. It wasn't from a miscarriage. She probably just got her period and passed it off as that."

Dammit. Fuck. Olivia is looking at me like the naive, gullible fool I am.

I remember how Leah chased me out of the room before I could speak to the doctor. How I stood in the doorway and told her I'd stay She was clearly trying to get me out of there before the doctor revealed the truth.

"How did Estella come to be?"

"After Rome we made it another month. She was angry with me. She accused me of not being present, and she was right. So I moved out again. I was at a conference in Denver and she was on a trip with her friends. We ran into each other at a restaurant. I was friendly but kind of kept my distance. She showed up at my hotel that night. I was pretty drunk and landed up sleeping with her. A few weeks later she called and told me she was pregnant. I never even questioned it. I just went back to her. I wanted a baby. I was lonely. I was stupid."

I don't tell Olivia that I found out she was seeing someone during that time. That when Leah came to me, I fell into her because I was trying to fill that Olivia hole in my chest again.

"So she told you Estella wasn't yours? That night you told her you wanted a divorce?"

"Yes. She said she'd slept with someone else before the ski trip. She also told me she only went because she knew I'd be there and she wanted to make me think she got pregnant that night."

"It was all a lie," Olivia says. "Estella is yours."

I see the tear in the corner of her eye. She doesn't swipe it away and it rains down her face.

"She's going to keep hurting you and Estella as long as I'm in your life. I have a husband," she says softly. "I should work things out with him. We've been playing house, Caleb. But this isn't real. You have a responsibility to your daughter . . ."

All of it—Olivia, Leah, Estella—ignites a fury in me. I spin and walk to her chair, leaning down and placing both hands on her armrests, and get right in her face. All I want to do is go find my daughter, but first things first. I'll deal with them one at a time. We are breathing each other's air when I speak.

"This is the last time I'm going to say this, so listen carefully." I can smell her skin. "You and I are happening. No one is keeping us apart again. Not Noah or Cammie or, least of all, fucking Leah. You are mine. Do you understand me?"

She nods.

I kiss her. Deep. Then I walk out.

25

The Past

What's the matter with you?"

She rubbed her hand down my chest. I caught it before it reached the top of my pants.

"Jet lag," I said, standing up.

Olivia.

She puckered her mouth sympathetically.

I'd been lying on the hotel bed for about ten minutes while Leah spoke to her mother on the phone. Now that her phone call was over, she was making her intentions known. I wandered over to the window so I could be out of her reach.

"I'm gonna take a shower," I said. Before she could ask if I wanted company, I closed the bathroom door and locked it behind me. I needed to run to clear my head, but how could I explain a midnight run in a foreign country to my suicidal, overly emotional wife? God, if I started running, I might never come back. I stepped into the shower and stood under the scalding hot water, letting it fill my nose and my eyes and my mouth. I wanted to let it drown me. How was I supposed to do life after what just happened?

Leah knocked on the door. I heard her say something, but her voice was muffled. I couldn't look at her right now. I couldn't look at myself. *How did I just do that?* Walked away from the only thing that made sense. I almost had her and I just gave up. I used *had her* loosely, because you can never really have Olivia. She floated around like a vapor, causing friction and then running away. But I'd always wanted to play the game. I wanted the friction.

You had to do it, I tell myself. It was a you-made-the-bed situation. And I was taking responsibility for my actions. Counseling, the endless marriage counseling. The guilt. The need to fix things. The confusion about whether or not I'm doing the right thing. The faking of my amnesia was my one rogue moment, when I stepped away from myself and did what I wanted to do without thought to consequences. I was a coward. I was raised to do what was socially acceptable.

I stood under the water until it turned cold, then I dried myself off and stepped out of the bathroom. My wife—thank God—had fallen asleep on top of the covers. I felt instant relief. I wouldn't have to act tonight. Her red hair was spread out around her like a fiery halo. I tossed a blanket over her, grabbed my bottle of wine, and retreated to the balcony to get drunk. It was still raining when I sat in one of the chairs and propped my feet up on the railing. I never had to "act" with Olivia. We just fit—our moods, our thoughts . . . even our hands.

ONCE, DURING HER senior year, she bought a gardenia bush to put outside her apartment. She fawned over that thing like it was a dog—Googled ways to take care of it and then made notes in one of those spiral notebooks. She even named it. Patricia, I think. Every day she'd squat on her haunches outside her front door and examine Patricia to see if a flower had bloomed. I watched her face when she came back inside—she always wore this look of hopeful determination. "Not yet," she'd say to me, as if all of her hope for life was tied into that gardenia plant blooming a flower. That's what I loved about her, that grim determination to survive even though the odds seemed to always be against her. Despite all of Olivia's plant nurturing, Patricia slowly started to fade away, her leaves curling at the tips and turning brown. Olivia would stare at that plant, a crease forming between her eyebrows and her little mouth puckered in a frown worth kissing. Florida had an especially cold winter that year. One morning when I got to her apartment, Patricia was clearly dead. I jumped into my car and sped off to Home Depot where I'd seen them selling the same bushes. Before my little love cracked her eyes open, I replaced her dead plant with a healthy one, repotting it over the grass in front of her building. I threw the old one in the dumpster and washed my hands in the pool before knocking on her door. She checked on it when she opened the door for me that morning, and her eyes lit up when she saw the healthy green leaves. I don't know if she ever suspected what I'd done: she never said anything. I took care of it without her knowing, sticking plant food into the pot before I knocked on her door. My mother always put used tea bags in the soil around her rose bushes. I did that a couple times too. Right before we broke up, that damn plant bloomed a flower. I'd never seen her so excited. The look on her face was the same as when I'd missed the shot for her.

If she came back and stood in that same spot beneath my hotel room, I'd probably jump right off the balcony to get to her. It's not too late, I told myself. You can find out where she's staying. Go to her.

I loved Olivia. I loved her with every fiber of my being, but I was married to Leah. I'd made a commitment to Leah—no matter how stupid that was. I was in. For better or worse. I had a brief moment when I thought I couldn't do it anymore, but that was in the past. Before she'd gotten pregnant with my baby and swallowed a bottle of sleeping pills.

Right?

Right.

I shook the bottle of wine. I was halfway through.

When a woman carried your baby in her body, you started seeing everything a little differently. The impossible became slightly less fucked. The ugly picked up a pretty glow. The unforgivable woman looked a little less stained. Kind of like when you'd been drinking. I finished the bottle and set it on its side on the floor. It rolled away and hit the balcony railing with a ting. I was in a baby coma. And I needed to wake the fuck up.

I closed my eyes and I saw her face. I opened my eyes and I saw her face. I stood up, tried to focus on the rain, the city lights, the fucking Spanish Steps—and I saw her face. I had to stop seeing her face so I could be a good husband to Leah. She deserved that.

Right?

Right.

WE FLEW OUT four days later. We barely had time to recover from the jet lag before it was time to leave again. It's not like I could focus on the trip with my ex floating somewhere around the city. I looked for Olivia at the airport, in restaurants, in cabs that splashed water on my ankles as they drove past. She was everywhere and nowhere. What were the chances that she'd be on our flight? If she was, I'd . . .

She wasn't on our flight. But I thought about her for the nine hours it took to fly across the Atlantic. My favorite memories—the tree, Jaxson's, the orange grove, the cake batter fight. Then I thought about the bad ones—mostly things she made me feel, the constant thought that she was going to leave me, the blatant way she refused to admit that she loved me. It was all so childish and tragic. I glanced at my wife. She was reading magazines and drinking cheap airplane wine. She took a sip and grimaced when she swallowed.

"Why do you order it if you don't like it?"

"It's better than nothing, I suppose," she said, looking out the window. Telling, I thought. I opened the book I brought with me and stared at the ink. For nine gracious hours, Leah left me alone. I'd never been so grateful for cheap wine. When we landed in Miami, she dashed to the bathroom to reapply her makeup while I waited in line at Starbucks. By the time we made it to baggage claim, I was in one of the worst moods of my life.

"What's wrong with you now?" she said. "You've been distracted this whole trip. It's really annoying."

I glared at her from behind my sunglasses and grabbed one of her bags off the belt. I flung it down so hard it wobbled on its fancy fucking rotating wheels. Who traveled with two large suitcases when they went away for five days?

"You're supposed to be working on this with me. You're not even mentally with me right now."

She was right.

"Let's go home," I said, kissing the top of her head. "I want to sleep for twelve hours straight and eat three meals in bed."

She stood on her tiptoes and kissed me on the mouth. It took effort to kiss her back so she wouldn't suspect anything was wrong. When she keened into my mouth, I knew I was every bit as good at lying to her as I was at lying to myself.

26

The Present

My car tires kick up gravel as I speed out of the parking lot. How could she? I run my hand through my hair. All I can think, as I speed on the 95 toward Leah, is of the little girl that still bears my name. The one she told me I was not a parent to. Was that a lie? If Leah lied about Estella's paternity, I would kill her myself.

Estella, with her beautiful red curls and her blue eyes—but she had my nose. I'd been so sure of it until Leah told me that she was someone else's. Then her nose had shifted. I thought that I was seeing things because I wanted so badly for her to be mine.

My mouth feels dry as I pull into her driveway. A million years ago it had been *my* driveway. *My* wife had been in that house. I broke it all apart because of the love I had for a ghost—a married ghost.

God. I think of Olivia now and a peace settles over me. She might not be mine, but I'm hers. It's no use even fighting it anymore. I just keep falling flat on my face and then rolling toward her. If I can't have Olivia Kaspen, then I'll be alone. She is a disease I have. After ten years, I am finally realizing that I can't cure it with other women.

I push the door to the car open and step out. Leah's SUV is parked in her usual spot. I walk past it and up the stairs to the front door. It's open. Walking into the foyer, I close the door behind me. Glancing around, I see that the living room is a mess of toys—a Cabbage Patch doll lies on its head next to a pile of naked Barbies. I step over a tricycle, heading toward the kitchen. I hear my name.

"Caleb?"

Leah stands in the doorway to the kitchen, a dish towel in her hand. I blink a few times. I've rarely seen Leah hold anything but a martini glass. She dries her hands with the towel and tosses it on the counter, walking toward me.

"Are you okay? What are you doing here?"

My chest heaves with everything that wants to come out. I grind my teeth so hard I'm surprised they don't crumble beneath the pressure. Leah notices what I'm doing and raises her eyebrows.

"Oh," she says. She beckons me to the kitchen. I follow her and watch as she pulls a bottle of tequila from the cabinet. She pours two shots, takes one of them, and refills the glass.

"We fight better with tequila," she says, handing one to me.

I don't want to drink the liquor. Adding it to the fire that is already coursing through me can only mean danger. I look at the clear liquid and bring it to my lips. If Leah wants fire, I'm going to give it to her.

"Where's Estella?"

"Asleep."

I set my glass on the counter.

Good.

I walk toward my ex-wife. She backs up, her nostrils flaring. "Tell me what you did."

"I've done a lot of things." She shrugs, trying to play it cool. "You'll have to be more specific."

"Olivia."

Her name pings between us, ripping open old wounds and spraying blood across the room. Leah is furious. "Don't say that name in my house."

"It's my house," I say calmly. Leah's face is pale. She runs her tongue along her teeth, blinking slowly.

"Did you know Turner?"

"Yes."

"And you had him ask Olivia out . . . to keep her away from me?"

"Yes."

I nod. My heart is aching. I lean over the counter to gather my rising anger before it explodes. I push it down, swallow my contempt, and look her in the eyes. Olivia and I never had a chance. The whole time we were destroying ourselves, someone else was having a go at it too.

"Leah," I say, closing my eyes. "The hospital . . . after you took those pills—" My voice cracks. I rub a hand across my face. I am so tired. "Were you pregnant?"

She raises her chin and I already know the answer.

Oh God. She lied. If she lied about that baby, what else has she lied about? I remember the blood. All the blood on the bed sheets. She said she was losing that baby and I believed her. It was probably just her period. How long after that had Estella been conceived?

I pace the length of the kitchen, my hands behind my neck. I say her name again; this time it's a plea.

"Is she mine, Leah? Oh fuck." I drop my hands. "Is she mine?"

I watch her face as she takes her time answering. She looks conflicted as to whether or not to tell the truth. Finally, she shrugs.

"Yeah."

The whole world goes quiet. My heart crashes. Rises. Crashes.

Grief cleaves me in two. Two years, I haven't seen her in two years. My daughter. *My* daughter.

The empty glass I drank tequila from sits to the right of my hand. I let my anger come, swiping the glass to the floor. It shatters and Leah flinches. I want to shake her; I want to throw her like that glass and watch her shatter for all the things she's done. I head for the stairs.

"Caleb." She comes after me, grabbing my arm. I yank myself free, taking the stairs two at a time.

She calls my name, but I barely hear her. I reach the top of the stairs and turn left down the hallway. She's behind me, begging me to stop.

"Caleb, she's sleeping. You're going to terrify her. Don't . . ."

I fling open the door and take in the soft pink light. Her bed is in the corner, a white four-poster. I walk in slowly, my steps muffled by the carpet. I can see her hair fanned out on the pillow, shockingly red and curly. I take another step in and I can see her face—pouty lips, chubby cheeks, and my nose. I kneel next to the bed so I can see her, and I cry for the second time in my life. I cry quietly, my body shaking from my sobs.

Leah's pleas have stopped. I don't know whether she's

behind me or not—I don't care. Stella's eyes flutter open. For being woken up in the middle of the night by a stranger, she is surprisingly alert and calm. She lies still, her blue eyes watching my face with the gaze of a much older child.

"Why are you cwying?"

The sound of her voice, raspy like her mother's, startles me. I cry harder.

"Daddy, why are you cwying?"

I feel like someone has just poured ice water over my head. I lean back, suddenly sober. I take in her disheveled curls, her full chubby cheeks, and I melt for my daughter.

"How do you know I'm your daddy?" I ask gently.

She frowns at me, her little lips pouting, and jabs her finger at her bedside table. I look over to see a picture of myself, holding her as a baby.

Leah told her about me? I don't understand. I don't know whether to be grateful or furious. If she wanted to make me think this little girl wasn't mine, why would she bother making Estella think anything different?

"Stella," I say cautiously, "can I give you a hug?" I want to pull her to me and sob into her beautiful red hair, but I don't want to scare *my* daughter.

She grins. When she answers, she lifts her shoulders up and tilts her head all the way to the side.

"Sure." She leans forward, arms outstretched.

I hug her to my chest, kissing the top of her head. I can barely breathe. I want to pick her up, put her in my car, and drive her away from the woman who has kept her from me. I can't be like Leah. I have to do what is best for Stella. I want to hold her to my chest all night. It takes everything I have to separate from our hug.

"Stella," I say, pulling away. "You have to go back to sleep now, but guess what?"

She makes a cute little kiddie face. "What?"

"Tomorrow, I'm going to come pick you up so we can hang out."

She claps, and again I'm tempted to pick her up and carry her out tonight. I curb my enthusiasm. "We're going to go eat ice cream, and buy toys, and feed ducks, and kick sand at the beach."

She slaps a hand over her mouth. "All in one day?"

I nod.

I help her snuggle back under her covers and kiss both of her cheeks and her forehead. I kiss her chin for good measure. She giggles, so I pull back the covers and kiss her toes. She squeals, and I have to press my fingertips to the corners of my eyes to stop the tears.

"Night, pretty baby."

I close her door softly. I don't make it five steps when I find Leah sitting against the wall. She doesn't look at me.

"I'll be here first thing in the morning to pick her up," I say as I walk toward the stairs. I want to get out of the house before I strangle her.

"She has school," Leah argues, standing up. I double back and come within an inch of her face. I am breathing hard, my chest heaving. She squares her jaw. I hate her so much in that moment. I don't know what I ever saw. My words are gruff and full of anguish.

"She has a father."

It's then that I hear the sirens.

27

The Past

"Hey, handsome, what are you doing here?"

I lifted my sunglasses and smiled.

"Cammie."

She smirked and stood on her tiptoes to give me a hug. My eyes darted past her and searched the crowd walking into the mall.

"Is she——?"

She shook her head. "Not here."

I felt myself relax. I didn't know if I could handle seeing her. Out of sight, partially out of mind was what was working for me at the moment.

"So what are you doing here? Shouldn't you be home with the pregnant wifey witch?"

We fell into step and I grinned at her. "I'm here for a pretzel actually. She had a craving."

"God, that's embarrassing—once the big man on campus, now the bitch's errand boy."

I laughed. Cammie was always good for a laugh. I held the door open for her, and the air-conditioning blasted me in the face. "What are you doing here?"

"Oh, you know me," she sang, stopping at a rack of skirts. "I like to spend money."

I nodded and stuck my hands in my pockets, feeling awkward.

"Actually," she said, turning to me, "I'm looking for a dress to wear to a wedding. Help me?"

I shrugged. "Since when do you need help shopping?"

"Oh, that's right." She tucked her lips in and shook her head. "You have to get back to your pregnant wife. Don't let me hold you up." She dismissed me with a wave of her hand and pulled a slinky white dress off the rack.

I scratched the back of my head. "White makes you look matronly."

She narrowed her eyes and put the dress back, while still looking at me. "Who asked you?"

She held up a blue silk dress for me to see and I nodded. She shoved it at me and I took it.

"So do you know what you're having . . . boy . . . girl . . . seed of Chucky?"

"We're not finding out."

She tossed another dress my way. I reshelved it when she turned away.

"I own a nanny agency, you know. So when the little bundle comes along, I'm sure I can find it a new mother."

She held up a Gucci dress and I nodded. "She'll be fine. You know I'm traditional about those things."

Cammie snorted. "You might be, but I highly doubt your lovely wife will be offering up the breast anytime soon."

I ground my teeth together, which she noticed right away.

"Sore subject much? Don't worry, C-Dizzle, I've seen

this before. Tell her you'll buy her a new set when it's all over. That should bring her around."

I cocked my head. That wasn't a bad idea.

I followed her to the changing room.

"So," I said, leaning against the wall outside. "How—"

"She's fine."

I nodded, looking at the floor. "Is she—"

She burst out wearing the blue dress and spun in a circle.

"Don't even bother trying the others on," I said.

She made a kissy face at the mirror and nodded. "You're right."

The door slammed closed. A minute later, she came out dressed and carrying the garment on her arm.

"Well, that was easy," she said.

I walked with her to the register and watched as she plucked out her credit card. "Now a gift and shoes and I'm all set."

"What's the dress for again?"

She leveled her eyes on me, a wicked smile playing on her lips.

"Didn't I tell you?" she said innocently. "This dress is for Olivia's wedding."

A tremor of shock passed through me. Suddenly, all of the colors around me were bleeding together, hurting my eyes. I felt sick, my chest constricting with each second that passed. Cammie's lips were moving; she was saying something. I shook my head to clear it. "What?"

She smirked at me tand tossed her blond hair over her shoulder. Then she patted my arm sympathetically. "Hurts, doesn't it, motherfucker?"

"When?" I breathed.

"Uh-uh. I'm not telling you that."

I licked my lips. "Cammie . . . tell me it's not Turner."

Her face broke into a smile. "Nope."

I felt the pressure in my chest release a little. A little. I hated Turner. I hadn't even met the guy. It was by sight alone.

"Noah Stein," Cammie said, grinning. "Funny story," she said, making her eyes really big. "She met him on that little impromptu trip she took to Rome. You remember? The one where she came baring her soul, and you turned her away."

"It didn't happen like that."

She cocked the corner of her mouth up and shook her head like she was disappointed in me. "You had your chance, big boy. Fate hates you guys."

"Leah had just lost the baby and her sister tried to commit suicide. I couldn't leave her. I was trying to do the right thing for once."

She jerked to look at me. "Leah was . . ." Her voice trailed off and her eyes glazed over. I cocked my head.

"Leah lost a baby?" she repeated. I saw something in her eyes that made me take a step closer.

"What are you not saying?"

She pursed her lips and shook her head at me. "When you went to Rome with Leah, were you trying to have a baby?"

Cammie was known for asking uncomfortable questions, but this was a little personal, even for her.

"No. We were just taking a break. Getting away from everything. Trying to work on—"

"Your marriage," she finished.

"Why are you asking me this?"

She suddenly looked up from the patch of floor she'd been staring at. "Just interested, I guess. Hey, I've got to get out of here."

She leaned up to kiss me on the cheek, but something wasn't sitting right with me. Cammie was an obnoxious spitfire. When she started acting awkward, something was wrong.

"Cammie . . ."

"Don't," she said. "She's happy. She's getting married. Leave her alone."

She started walking away, but I grabbed her wrist. "You said that to me once before, do you remember?"

Her face paled. She yanked her arm away.

"Just tell me when?" I pleaded. "Cammie, please . . ."

She swallowed. "Saturday."

I closed my eyes and dropped my head. "Bye, Cam."

"Bye, Caleb."

I DIDN'T GET Leah's pretzel. I got back in my car, drove to the beach, and sat on the sand looking out at the water. Leah called me five times, but I sent the calls to voicemail. Saturday was two days away. She was probably a mess. She always was when there was a big life change on the horizon. I rubbed my chest. It felt so heavy.

I watched the couples for a long time, walking hand in hand along the water. It was too late to swim, but some kids were playing in the surf, kicking water at each other. In a few weeks, I'd have one of my own. The thought was frightening and exciting—the way you felt before getting on a roller coaster. Except this roller-coaster ride would last eighteen years, and I wasn't sure if my riding partner really wanted to be a mother. Leah tended to like the idea of things more than the actual things.

Once, when we were first married, she'd come home from work cradling a sheltie puppy in her arms. "I saw him in a pet shop window and I couldn't resist," she'd said. "We can take him on walks together and get him one of those collars with his name on it."

Despite my skepticism about the duration of the dog's stay in my house, I'd smiled and helped her pick out a name—Teddy. The following day I'd come home from work to find the house filled with dog supplies—squeaking hamburgers, stuffed toys, and tiny fluorescent tennis balls. Aren't dogs color-blind? I remember thinking, picking one up and examining it. Teddy had a fluffy bed, a rhinestone-studded collar, and a retractable leash. He even had food and water bowls with his name on them. I studied this all with a sense of dread and watched Leah measure out half cups of food into his dog bowl. For two days she bought things for our new puppy, yet I never once remember seeing her so much as touch him. By day four, Teddy was gone. Given to a neighbor along with his fluorescent balls.

"Too much mess," Leah said. "I couldn't house-train him."

I didn't bother to tell her that it took longer than three days to housebreak a puppy. And so Teddy was gone before we could ever go on a walk with him. Please, God, don't let a baby be another puppy to Leah.

I stood up, dusting the sand off my jeans. I had to get home—to my wife. That was the life I chose, or what was chosen for me. I didn't even know anymore where my choices started and ended.

SATURDAY. I TOLD Leah that I had errands to run. I set out early, stopping at the liquor store for a bottle of scotch I knew I'd need later. Tossing it in the trunk, I drove the twenty minutes to my mother's house. My parents lived in Fort Lauderdale. They bought their house from a pro golfer in the nineties, something that my mother still bragged about to her friends. When Robert Norrocks owned this house . . .

She opened the door before I could knock.

"What's wrong? Is it the baby?"

I pulled a face, shook my head. She made a show of looking relieved. I wondered who taught her to make a performance of every emotion she felt. Both my grandparents had been pretty stoic people. As I walked past her into the foyer, her hand fluttered to her neck where her fingers absently found the locket she wore. It was a nervous habit I'd always found endearing. Not today.

I walked into the living room and sat down, waiting for her to follow.

"What is it, Caleb? You're scaring me."

"I need to talk to you about something," I tried again. "I need to talk to my mother about something. Can you do that without being . . ."

"Bitchy?" she offered.

I nodded.

"Should I be afraid?"

I stood up and walked to the window, looking out at her precious roses. She had every shade of pink and red. It was a mess of thorns and color. I didn't like roses. They reminded me of the women in my life: beautiful and bright, but if you touched them they made you bleed.

"Olivia is getting married today. I need you to talk me out of going to the church and stopping her."

The only indication that she'd heard me was the slight expansion of white around her irises.

She opened her mouth and then abruptly closed it.

"I'll take that as your blessing." I made to leave, but my mother jumped up and blocked me. She was pretty stealthy in heels.

"Caleb, honey . . . nothing good can come out of that. You and Olivia are—"

"Don't say it."

"Over," she finished. "That was my nonbitchy version."

I grimaced. "It's not over for me."

"It's obviously over for her. She's getting married." She reached up and cupped my face in her hands. "I'm so sorry you're hurting."

I didn't say anything. She sighed and pulled me down on the couch to sit next to her. "I'm going to put aside my extreme dislike for that girl and tell you something that you might find useful."

I listened. If she was putting aside her dislike, I potentially had mind-blowing advice coming my way.

"Three things," she said, patting my hand. "It's okay that you love her. Don't stop. If you turn your feelings off for her, you might turn everything off. That's not good. Second, don't wait for her. You have to live your life—you have a baby on the way." She smiled at me sadly as I waited for the grand finale. "And finally . . . wait for her."

She laughed at the confused expression on my face. "Life does not accommodate you, it shatters you. Love is mean, but it's good. It keeps us alive. If you need her, then wait. But right now she's getting married. It's her day and you can't ruin it."

Love is mean.

I loved my mom—especially when she wasn't being a bitch.

I jogged down the stairs to my car. She watched me from the doorway, tugging on her locket. Maybe she was right. I wanted Olivia to be happy. To have the things that were taken from her as a child. I couldn't give her those things because I was giving them to someone else.

I drove aimlessly for a while before eventually pulling into a random strip mall. Florida was a maze of peach-colored strip malls. Each one bragged a fast-food chain front and center like the mast on a ship. Flanking the token McDonald's or Burger King was always a nail place. I pulled into a spot in front of Nail Happy. The shop was empty except for the workers. When I got out instead of a woman, they looked disappointed. I pulled out my phone, leaning against the door. It was cool outside—not cool enough for a jacket, but Florida cool. My thumbs lingered over the keyboard.

I love you.

Delete.

If you leave him, I'll leave her.

Delete.

Can we talk?

Delete.

Peter Pan.

Delete.
I pocketed my phone. Punched a tree. Drove home with bloody knuckles. Love was fucking mean.

28

The Present

The day after I barged into Leah's, she got a restraining order. If I go anywhere near my daughter, I'll get arrested. I was almost arrested that night. The cops had me handcuffed when my brother showed up. Seth spoke quietly to Leah for a few minutes before coming over and taking off my cuffs.

"She's not going to press charges, little brother, but she's going to have us file a report, and tomorrow she's going to get a restraining order."

"Was that your idea?"

He smirked at me. We didn't exchange any more words. I just got in my car and drove away. Leah filed a report. She claims that I kicked down the door, threatened her life, and woke Estella up in the middle of the night—drunk. She is also back to claiming that I am not Estella's father. I wonder if she lied to Olivia to torment me. I don't know what goes on in that woman's head. Or what went on in my head for so many years. Either way, Leah's woken the beast. Olivia directs me to a family attorney. She says she's the best in the business. Her name is Marisol Cruz. She has deep brown eyes framed by rectangular glasses, and curly dark hair framing her face. Her smile is wide and genuine when she shakes my hand.

After listening to me speak for ten minutes, Marisol holds up her hand to stop me.

"You've got to be kidding me," she says. "The woman finds out that you want a divorce and tells you that the child you've been raising for six months isn't yours—and you believe her? Just like that?"

"I didn't have any reason not to. She didn't want a divorce. At that point, it would have only benefited her to let me believe Estella was mine."

"Oh, Caleb." She puts a hand to her forehead. "Didn't you see what was happening? You came out and dropped a couple bombs on her, and at some point in that conversation she decided that she didn't want you, she wanted revenge. And that's exactly what's happening."

I stare out her window at the traffic below and know it's true. But why hadn't I had the sight to see it? If someone other than myself was telling me this story, I'd laugh at their stupidity. Why do humans have such a hard time seeing their own shit clearly?

"She has you by the balls here, Caleb. There is no proof of what happened that night. But there is proof that for the last three years of that child's life you haven't seen her, paid child support, or fought for custody. Leah has you at abandonment. And now that she knows that, she's come back to let you know that Estella is yours, and she has the power."

God.

"What do I do?"

"You get a court-ordered paternity test. That's going to

take some time. Then we ask for visitation. It'll be super-
vised at first, but as long as you comply with the rules and
show up to see Estella, we can push for joint custody."

"I want full."

"Yeah, well, I want to be a swimsuit model."

"Okay," I say. "Do what you need to do. I'm in it. Whatever it is. Is there a way for me to see Estella?"

It's such a stupid question, but I had to ask. There is no
way Leah is going to let me anywhere near my daughter.
I have no proof, but I'm already thinking of her as my
daughter again. Have I ever stopped?

Marisol laughs.

"No way. Just sit tight and let me do my thing. We'll
have you back in her life soon enough, but it's going to be
a bit of a fight to get there."

I LEAVE HER office and go right to Olivia's. She's in shorts
and a tank top when I get there, mopping the floors and
looking annoyed. I lean against the wall and tell her what
Marisol said while she works. She's cleaning with gusto,
and when that happens I know she's trying to distract herself. There is also a bowl of Doritos on the table, and she
keeps walking over to it and pushing chips into her mouth.
Something's up, but I know even if I ask, she won't tell me.

"Do whatever she says," is all Olivia tells me. There are
a few minutes when we don't speak. Her crunching dom-
inates the room.

"She didn't seem sorry," Olivia says, finally. "It was the
strangest thing. She just showed up at my office to tell me
all of that. She knew I'd tell you. Seems sinister."

"She's up to something," I agree.

"Maybe she's out of money and she figures she needs to hit you up for child support."

I shake my head. "Her father built an empire. That company was a small portion of what he was dipping his interest into. Leah doesn't need money."

"Then she's out for revenge. Marisol is right. What are you going to do?"

I shrug. "Fight for Estella. Even if she wasn't mine I'd want to fight for her."

She stops mopping. A piece of her hair has slipped from the messy pile on her head. She tugs on it then slides it behind her ear.

"Don't make me love you more," she says. "My clock is ticking and you're talking baby."

I grind my teeth to keep from smiling.

"Let's make one," I say, taking a step toward her.

The whites of her eyes explode around her pupils. She hides behind her mop.

"Don't," she warns me. She reaches for the bowl of Doritos, without taking her eyes from me, and finds it empty.

"Do you think we'd have a boy or a girl?"

"Caleb . . ."

I take another two steps before she dips her mop in the bucket and whacks me in the stomach with it.

I stare down at my dripping clothes with my mouth open. She knows what's coming next because she drops the mop and runs for the living room. I watch her grab onto furniture as she slips and slides across the wet floor. I go after her, but she's such a cleaning addict she can practically ice-skate over wet marble. Amazing. I fall flat on my ass.

I stay there, and she comes out of the kitchen carrying two glass bottles of Coke.

"Peace offering." She extends one toward me.

I grab the bottle and her arm and pull her down on the floor next to me.

She slides around until we are sitting back-to-back, leaning on each other, our legs extended outward. Then we talk about nothing. And it feels so damn good.

29

The Past

My daughter was born on March 3 at 3:33 p.m. She had a shock of red hair that stuck straight up, like those toy trolls from the nineties. I ran my fingers over it, smiling like a goddamn fool. She was beautiful. Leah had convinced me we were having a boy. She'd stroked my face and looked at me like I was her god and practically purred, "Your father produced two sons, and your grandfather had three sons. The men in your family make boys."

I secretly wanted a daughter. I didn't express that to my wife as she bought and decorated the nursery in greens and yellows "just to play it safe." Though she wasn't playing it safe when I noticed a teether in the shape of a dump truck appear in the mounds of baby things or the tiny baseball-inspired onesie. Since I played basketball in college, the baseball selection could only have been a salute to her father, who never missed a Yankees game on TV.

She wasn't due for another few weeks. I'd read that most first-time pregnancies went past their due date—like it was an unwritten rule. Plenty of time, I told myself. Plenty of time to figure it all out.

Leah was climbing into her side of the car when she made a noise—small, broken—deep in the back of her throat. She froze halfway in, one hand slamming against the roof of the car, the other clutching at her stomach.

"I thought they were just Braxton-Hicks, but they're getting closer together. We might want to go to the hospital and save the beach for another day," she panted, closing her eyes.

I ran to the driver's side and started the car while Leah positioned all three air-conditioning vents at her face. I'd watched her for a minute, unable to comprehend that this was actually happening. She was holding on to the door handle like it was a lifeline. Another noise—this one louder—punched out of her like it hurt.

"My bag!" she panted. "Inside . . ."

Five minutes later, I pulled out of our driveway, tires squealing against the pavement.

"We're almost there," I kept saying. "You're going to be okay, we're almost there."

Every time she made a noise, I felt it. I was tied to her pain, helpless.

When the hospital finally came into view, I almost cried.

Inside, everything blurred. A wheelchair, a nurse, codes I didn't understand. They wheeled her away before I could follow. Somehow it all worked out. I was ushered into a room where Leah was already pushing. I was there to see my baby slide into the world.

The doctor's voice rang out clear and definitive. "Girl."

His announcement was loud, celebratory, as he placed a purple blob on Leah's chest. For a moment, the room seemed to hold its breath, the soft sound of monitors and distant footsteps fading into the background. I stood frozen, watching as tiny, wrinkled hands grasped at the air, her voice filling the room with fragile strength.

"Estella," I whispered, the name rolling off my tongue with a sense of finality. It had been waiting like a treasure buried deep inside my mind.

I am a father. To a little girl. Foreign, monumental words. I couldn't stop staring at her. Perfect Estella, the name felt like a prayer, soft and sacred. Her fingers, impossibly small, curled around my thumb. In that moment I started to worry. The world was too vast, too cruel, too undeserving of such a perfect creature.

I held Estella a little tighter. I'd already wondered how I would protect her from the ugly things in the world.

Dawnita, Leah's doula, popped her head into the room. She was wearing scrubs with shamrocks on them.

"How are you doing, Mama?"

Leah didn't answer her.

"Have you had a chance to pee yet?" she asked, her tone casual.

"No." Leah answered curtly. She closed her eyes and leaned her head back on the pillow.

"Okay, no problem. You will," Dawnita said, her voice steady "You're doing better than you think."

Leah's eyes opened.

"Okay," she said. "What do I do . . . ?"

Dawnita took Estella from my arms and placed her gently against Leah's chest. Leah moved slowly, carefully, every muscle stiff. She cradled the baby awkwardly at first, like she didn't trust herself not to drop her. When the baby latched on, she closed her eyes, pain registering across her face. But she didn't pull away.

"It feels weird," she said. "It hurts."

When Estella settled into a steady rhythm, Leah's whole body shifted. She looked relieved.

When Estella was finished nursing, Leah handed her back to me without a word. She sat on the edge of the hospital bed, her posture slumped, her gaze fixed on the wall.

"I need to go to the bathroom," she said.

She looked hollow and pale. I put the baby in the hospital crib, and helped her stand. "Are you okay?"

"No," she snapped. "Do I look okay?"

"You just gave birth, I don't think you're supposed to feel okay," I admitted. "How is your heart?"

Her expression softened. "I don't feel like myself."

She lowered herself onto the toilet.

"Baby, just give it a little bit of time. What you just did was one of the most incredible things I've ever seen. You're exhausted."

She glanced up at me, her eyes searching mine for something.

"What if it's not just that . . . ?"

What if it wasn't just exhaustion? What if it was something deeper?

"We'll figure it out," I say to her. "I'm not going anywhere."

Her shoulders slumped, and then I heard the soft steady sound of her peeing.

I stayed there with her, the silence stretching between us.

I knew it was true. No matter how messy things got I would figure it out. For Estella. For her. For me.

SHE WAS IN good spirits when we drove home from the hospital. She laughed at my jokes, and squeezed my hand at a red light. For a moment, it felt like we were finding our way back to normal, heading home with the newest chapter in our lives nestled in the back seat.

30

The Present

A week after we get back from the Keys I come back from a run, my mind clearer than it's been in a while. I'm walking through the lobby debating on whether or not to take the stairs, when I hear someone say my name.

"Caleb."

I stop mid-step, turning toward the voice. "Noah?"

I wipe my face with the hem of my shirt, giving myself a second to process.

Man, the guy looks like he's been run over by life.

Disheveled hair, tired eyes, and a rumpled jacket. I've looked like that a couple times in my life.

"Hey, Caleb."

He sounds resigned.

"What are you doing here?"

I lean against the wall still catching my breath.

Noah laughs humorlessly. "Why do you think I'm here?"

I stare at him. "There's a bar on the corner," I tell him. "Give me ten. I'll meet you there."

He nods and walks out without saying another word. I take the elevator to my condo.

Upstairs, I peel off my sweaty clothes and jump in a cold shower.

Whatever this is, it isn't going to be simple.

NOAH IS SITTING at a small table to the rear of the bar. It's an upscale place, like everything in this neighborhood. The ceilings are high, with clusters of pendant lights that look like glowing orbs, suspended midair. There are only two other patrons in the bar at this hour: one old, hunched over a whiskey glass, and the other young, scrolling through their phone like they're killing time. The faint hum of a downtempo track plays over the speakers. Noah doesn't look up as I approach, just keeps swirling the liquid in his glass. When I pull the chair back and take a seat, the sound of the legs scraping the floor pulls his gaze to me.

I wait for him to speak.

"You know what, Caleb? You play like you've got the best hand in the room, but everyone at the table knows you're bluffing."

I lean back in my chair, letting it roll off me.

"I told you to stay away from her." His voice is low.

"That was before you left her alone to deal with a stalker." My words hit their mark.

He cracks his neck before he looks up. "I'm here now."

I want to laugh. Like showing up late to the fire you started means you get credit for putting it out. "But she's not."

Noah's eyes flash. "Don't talk to me about my wife."

"I thought that's why we were here."

His fingers flex around the glass, but he doesn't break eye contact.

We take a moment to calm down—or to think—or whatever men do when they are compelled to beat the shit out of each other. We sit in heavy silence, neither about to back down.

"I was once in love with a girl the same way you're in love with Olivia," he says.

I stare at him, caught off guard. "Hold on right there," I cut him off. "If you were in love with a girl the same way I'm in love with Olivia, you wouldn't be with Olivia. You'd be with this girl."

Noah smiles, but it doesn't reach his eyes. "She's dead."

I feel like an asshole.

"Why are you telling me this?"

"Think about what you're doing, Caleb. She's not yours anymore. We made a commitment to each other, and it's like you said—I fucked up. We need to be able to work on what we have without you showing up every five minutes getting her high on nostalgia."

Nostalgia?

Like that's all Olivia and I are to each other—a collection of memories that she pulls out when she needs a distraction.

The day I met her under that tree, it felt as if I breathed her into me—like a spore settled in my lungs. I didn't notice it at first, didn't realize what happened. But as the days turned into weeks and the weeks into years, I began to feel it growing. The pull back to her.

No matter how much space we tried to put between us, we came back to each other. Noah knows it wasn't nostalgia; he wouldn't be here if it were. The comment pisses me off so much, I don't even think before I go for the low blow.

"So you're going to have a baby, then . . ." My words are calm but calculated.

The shock that passes through his eyes is enough to tell me I've struck a nerve. He knows she's discussed their private issues with me. "That's got nothing to do with you."

I don't know why he doesn't hit me. I would have hit me. Maybe that's the difference between us. He rubs a hand across the stubble on his jaw, which is more gray than I remember, and finishes his drink in one deliberate pull. He sets the glass down with the kind of precision that says he's in control.

"My sister had cystic fibrosis," he says. "I used to go with her to her support groups. That's where I met Melisa. She had it too. I fell in love with her and then had to watch her die before she had the chance to turn twenty-four. My sister died two years after her. I've seen two women that I love die. I don't want to bring a child into this world with the chance of passing them the gene. It's not fair."

The bartender hesitantly approaches our table, sensing the tension.

"Drinks?" She looks between us. I order a scotch on the rocks.

"Another of these," Noah says, holding up his glass.

I lean back in my chair. A headache is starting to pulse behind my eyes. The scotch arrives and I wrap my fingers around the glass. This is becoming more complicated by the minute, and the last thing I want to do is feel sorry for this guy.

I let the scotch linger on my tongue, sharp and biting,

before I swallow. The warmth spreads through my chest. "What does Olivia want?"

I don't know why I'm asking him that instead of her.

"She wants to save what we have," he says. "We met last night to talk things out."

The air feels like it's been sucked out of the room.

He doesn't flinch. Doesn't even blink. Something about the way he's sitting there—calm, steady, like he's got the answers, makes me uneasy.

Was that true? Why wouldn't she tell me she was going to see him. She didn't owe me an explanation, but . . .

I'd made the assumption that we were moving toward something, that we were going to be together.

I look up at him. If he's lying, he's damn good at it. But if he's telling the truth . . . I don't even know what to do with that.

I stand up. "I'll believe it when I hear it from her."

I've felt a lot of pain in my years with Olivia, but nothing compared to the moment I walked into that hotel room and realized she'd had a one-night stand with a stranger. It cut through me, jealous, ripping, unforgiving. Her self-destruction had gone too far.

The only thing that came close to that pain was showing up at her apartment to find out she left me.

I drop a twenty on the table and don't look back.

What I feel now? It might be worse. Because this time, she's leaving me and she has every right to. There's nothing I can do to morally justify her walking away from her marriage for me.

I'm stuck on a sick carousel ride, spinning in circles. Had they planned this? Him showing up to deliver her verdict?

The thought twists in my chest. No, that wasn't her style, she'd never send a man to do her dirty work.

The last few months, we've gotten to know each other as adults—raw, real, unvarnished by the chaos of our younger selves. This isn't nostalgia or a fleeting memory. It's us.

31

The Past

One week before my baby came into this world, I received a call from Olivia's office. Not Olivia herself— her secretary, Liz, with her clipped professional tone that somehow made everything sound more formal.

"Olivia asked me to call," she said.

"I figured."

"Three weeks ago," Liz continued, "Our office was contacted by a woman named Anfisa Lisov. Ring any bells?"

I told her it didn't.

"She saw a photo of Olivia online . . . with Johanna Smith."

Johanna Smith.

My grip on the phone tightened as I expelled the air from my lungs.

"Go on . . ."

"Olivia thought you should know, so here I am, delivering the weirdest phone call of my week."

"Liz," I said, trying to steady my voice, "Are you saying this woman knows Johanna—Leah—Smith?"

"That's what she claims," Liz replied cheerfully. "And if she's lying, she's a good actor."

"How? What is her claim?"

"That she's her birth mother."

No one knew Leah was adopted. We'd kept it out of the press.

"Why does she think Leah's her daughter?"

"She saw Leah's parents in the court photos and recognized them. Says they're the same people she handed her newborn over to."

"Wow. This is fucked."

"Well, hold your horses because I ain't done yet. Turns out this lady, Mrs. Lisov, is on her way to America to reunite with her biological daughter."

"Are you being serious right now?"

"As pie," Liz said.

"Why didn't Olivia just call me herself?"

"That question is above my pay grade, but if I had to guess it's because of the weird thing the two of you have going on."

I sigh. "Hey, thanks, Liz. I appreciate the heads-up."

This was bad—worse than bad.

Courtney, Leah's sister, was in an assisted living facility, in a coma. Her mother was a functioning alcoholic. Leah was balancing a fine line of sanity.

And she was having my baby. Whoever this Anfisa Lisov woman was, I couldn't let her near my wife. Not now.

"No problem." I hear her typing something on her keyboard.

"Can you give me all the contact information you have for her?"

"I'll email it over right now."

"Where is Olivia?" I ask. "Is she there?"

"She's in court," Liz said plainly. "This lady, Anfisa, she has a translator with her that might be acting as her attorney."

"Okay, I got the contact list, thanks Liz."

"Anything else, shoot me a call. I'm interested in how this is going to play out."

I tried sending an email to Anfisa using the address Liz gave me, but it bounced back.

The phone number was to an attorney's office in Kiev. I left a message in English on the chance someone in the office would understand it.

After hanging up I did what every sane person would do, I Googled *Anfisa Lisov/Russia* and the search came back with a picture of a striking woman. She had short red hair cut no longer than mine. She had written and published three books in Russian. I put the titles into Google Translate and they came back as *My Scarlet Life*, *The Blood-Soaked Baby*, and *Finding Mother*.

My pulse quickened as I scrolled further, but the trail went cold. She hadn't published anything in four years.

The faint vibration of my cell pulled me out of my thoughts. I grabbed it hoping it was Liz with some sort of update.

Olivia.

I stared at her name on the screen for a moment, my thumb hovering over the accept button. She rarely called me; she was more of a text and walk kind of person.

"Caleb," her voice was low. "Did Liz call you?"

"She did," I said. "Quite the surprise."

"She's some type of motivational speaker. She's authored three books . . ."

"I saw that."

"I spoke to her translator, older man—I have a suspicion it's her boyfriend but don't ask me why. Anyway, they're flying into New York, from what it sounds like she has a meeting with an American publisher. That's why they're stopping there first."

"Okay," I said. "I'll go to New York. Can you get me in touch with her translator slash boyfriend?"

"Sure," she said. "But how can you leave now—?"

"I don't have a choice. I don't want her showing up here."

"I have to go," Olivia said.

"Hey . . . it's good to hear your voice," I say.

"You too."

The line went dead.

I didn't know exactly what Anfisa wanted from this re-union, but I couldn't shake the thought that maybe she wanted a new story to tell. *My Crimson Life. The Blood-Soaked Baby. Finding Mother.* Reuniting with her birth child would be a fresh narrative after a four-year gap in her career. The only one I could talk to about this was Steve. When I called him, he picked up on the fourth ring, his voice breathless. "Sorry, was in the pool. Did Leah have—"

"No . . . no—she's still pregnant. I have something else I need to talk to you about."

"Go on—"

I told him the story—Anfisa, the books, the phone calls. It only took me ten minutes, but by the time I finished I felt drained.

"Maybe you're being too cynical about this Anfisa lady. You're jumping to conclusions on this book thing. How do you know she's not merely seeking a conversation with the child she gave birth to?"

He wasn't wrong. Maybe I was being cynical, but could I afford not to be?

"I guess there's only one way to find out."

We hung up, but the conversation replayed in my head. One thing I knew for certain: Leah would not want to meet this woman. She'd told me enough times that she had no intention of looking for her birth mother.

FOUR DAYS AFTER Leah gave birth, I was on a plane flying to New York. She was furious with me for leaving her alone so soon. I didn't see an option.

Anfisa Lisov.

Every detail I knew about her, every half-formed theory, looped through my mind. She claimed to be Leah's biological mother. Claimed she'd seen an article, and then footage of the trial—online. Claimed this was a serendipitous reunion waiting to happen. It felt wrong, too convenient, but I couldn't ignore the possibility that she might be telling the truth. That would make her Estella's grandmother.

I emailed with her translator, Mr. Orlov.

Dear Mr. Drake,

What a pleasure to make your acquaintance! Though I must say the timing is regrettably poor, Anfisa is very excited that you made contact. I myself was raised in Germany, though my father was born in Uryupinsk. I have proficiency in German, Russian, and English, which is how I met Anfisa. I translated her three works into German and now, many years later, I accompany her on her grand American adventure.

Anfisa, as expected, is very anxious to discuss both her daughter, and her grandchild with you. She comes from very humble beginnings, as is discussed in her books. Her daughter was a product of her sinister environment. Anfisa respects your wishes to keep this meeting between us for now and has requested you bring her photographs of Johanna so that she may look upon her child's face.

We will be in New York for four days, after which will fly to Canada to visit with relatives of Anfisa. Please let us know when to expect you so we can make arrangements.

Sincerely,

Yuri Olav

Yuri and I emailed back and forth until we settled on a day and time. We arranged to meet in Midtown, the lobby of her hotel. I spotted her seated near the large fireplace, her back straight against the plush armchair. I knew it was her by the picture I'd seen on the internet. She was older than in the photo, more worn around the eyes and mouth. Her hair, no longer red, was dyed a muted shade of brown. I eyed her face, looking for traces of Leah.

"Mr. Drake," she said, standing up. She was wearing bootleg jeans and a green and blue sweater that looked handmade. Her eyes were both warm and assessing as she took me in. "You are Johanna's husband? Yes?"

"I am. Nice to meet you, Ms. Lisov," I replied, taking her outstretched hand. "Call me Caleb. You speak English," I say, surprised.

She pinched the air with her fingers. "Little bit. Yuri has taught me."

"Caleb," she repeated. "I saw you on television. During the trial." Her accent was thick, but she spoke English well.

"Will Yuri be joining us?"

"He has . . ." She touched her stomach lightly and grimaced.

"Ah . . . enough said."

She looked nervous.

"How do I know you are who you say you are?" I asked.

She smiled. She held up a single finger, asking for a moment. Bending down, she rummaged through a leather handbag resting at her feet. When she straightened, she held something in her hand. She handed it to me.

It was a Polaroid of an infant lying on what appeared to be a scale. She looked brand-new, like Estella, her hands curled up into tiny fists, eyes sealed shut. Her hair was red.

I felt a strange pang in my chest; I missed my own baby. Why was I here? I looked at Anfisa in question. She pointed to the photo tapping the baby's leg.

A birthmark.

My stomach tightened as my mind raced. Leah had a mark on her shin bone. It was the same strawberry color. I hand the photo back to her. Could it be real? Or was it all just a carefully crafted lie?

"I was sixteen years old and I slept with men to survive. I went to the nuns and they told me they'd help. I didn't have a choice."

"I understand," I say—though I don't. The thought of someone taking Estella from me makes me lightheaded. You've written books about your experiences from what I understand."

She nodded, her gaze momentarily dropping to her hands folded tightly in her lap. "I'm writing another," she added, her voice edged with determination.

Here it comes.

"My daughter is very rich," she said finally, her tone flat.

I closed my eyes. Of course.

"I need money. Just enough to write my next book. And I want to write it in Canada. I have relatives. It will not take much," she said, without looking at me.

I shook my head. "Not so fast. You're going to have to take a blood test. If that comes back and shows you're my child's grandmother, I'll help you."

Her gaze locked on mine, sharp and unyielding. "Blood test? I've told the truth."

"Then it shouldn't be a problem."

She hesitated for a fraction of a second.

"Then I will."

I sighed. "But . . ."

"But I need some money now . . ."

I wrote her a check for five thousand dollars, if only to get her out of my hair for the time being.

The conversation ended there. But hours later, as the cab sped back toward the airport, the weight of the encounter began to settle in my chest. She hadn't asked to see the photo of Leah. Maybe it was an oversight, maybe we'd both forgotten to bring it up. She'd already seen Leah in photos and videos on the internet. The cab hit a pothole, jolting me back to the present. Steve's words haunted me: *How do you know she's not merely seeking a conversation with the child she gave birth to?*

For now, I would go along with whatever this was. I would not tell Leah.

32

The Present

I go straight to her condo. If she's not home already, I'll be waiting there when she arrives.

She is home. When she opens the door, it's as if she was expecting me. Her eyes and her lips are swollen.

She stands to the side to let me in, and I walk past her into the living room. She closes the door softly and follows me.

The condo is dim, all of the lights turned off. The plush rug muffles my footsteps. She has the patio door open and I hear the steady rhythm of the waves crashing against the shore. I glance around her dimly lit living room. Her coffee table is cluttered with the remnants of an evening spent in solitude—an empty wineglass, a discarded book face-down on the couch, her laptop propped on a pillow. I hear Olivia in the kitchen, the sound of the kettle being filled and put on the stove. I step outside onto the patio to wait for her. The wind is strong, carrying with it the salty tang of the ocean. The sky and water are indistinguishable.

She comes out carrying two mugs of tea. She made it the way I like it: milk and sugar.

"When you left and went to Texas, after we . . ." I break to let her catch up to what I'm saying. "I came after you. It took me a few months to get past my initial wounded pride, and to find you, of course. Cammie didn't want to tell me you were there, so I just showed up on her doorstep. I was on my way up the stairs to talk to you, when Cammie told me that you'd been pregnant."

Her expression changes then.

"It was a shock," I admit, my voice cracking. "To hear about it from her, not from you. And then to know you went through all of that alone—the abortion . . ."

Her sharp inhale cuts me off.

"Abortion?" The word tumbles out of her mouth.

Now . . . now her chest is rising and falling in uneven breaths. She puts her mug on the patio table.

"I didn't have an abortion." Her eyes meet mine wide and unflinching. "I had a miscarriage."

The words hit me like a punch in the gut. For a moment I can't speak.

"Why did you think I had an abortion?" Her gaze pierces through me, bottomless and searching.

I think back to that day—Cammie's tone, the things she said, the things she didn't say. She never outright said it, no. But she didn't need to. Her silences were surgical. Weaponized. She let it dangle in the air just long enough for me to grab hold.

And I did.

I grabbed it, ran with it, branded myself with it. Because that's what I do, isn't it? Jump straight to the worst-case scenario like it's the only one worth considering. Had I heard what I wanted to hear? Just to justify my own anger?

God.

Because deep down, some ugly, selfish part of me already believed the worst. I built a story out of silence. Out of a glance. Out of something Cammie almost said.

Olivia is struggling not to cry. Her lips move as she tries to form words. "I wanted the baby. It was never a thought. I was scared. I was trying to figure it out." Her arms are folded across her stomach, tight and protective. Her shoulders are hunched.

That's when it hits me—what she carried. Not just my baby. The silence. The guilt. The grief.

"I believe you. Look at me, Duchess."

She turns slowly.

"I'm so sorry," I say, the words hitting the floor between us. Useless. "Forgive me for that."

That's when she finally looks at me. Her eyes lock onto mine.

"What are you going to tell me?"

"You already know . . ." she says softly. Her mouth—pressed into that stubborn, trembling line—tells me everything.

I'm shaking my head before she's finished her sentence. "Don't do this," I say. "This is our last chance. We don't have the type of connection that can be put on a shelf. You're going to feel the loss every day."

Her resolves flickers, like she remembers, too. She's so beautiful it feels unfair. Electric eyes flickering with vulnerability. I step closer, just enough that I could touch her if she let me. My hands stay at my sides. For now.

She's blinking fast now, trying to get ahead of the tears. Arms still locked over herself, she's built a fortress. I know how to get inside. I've learned that there are holes in the wall, secret passages. I speak to the ancient side of her soul, the piece that has always known me. "Tell me you don't still feel it," I say. "Tell me you don't wake up at three a.m. with your chest aching and no idea why.

"You think you're choosing peace," I whisper. "But you're choosing numb."

Her gaze snaps to mine—sharp, defiant. "You think love's supposed to burn all the time?"

"I think we're supposed to burn all the time, Olivia."

I watch her, daring her to call it a lie. Her nostrils flare. I swear she stops breathing.

"I choose him."

I breathe through my nose, her announcement reverberating across my brain, burning my tear ducts, and landing somewhere in my chest, causing such incredible heartache, I can't see straight.

Through my crash, I lift my head to look at her. She's pale, her eyes wide and panicked.

I nod . . . slowly. I'm still nodding ten seconds later. I'm calculating the rest of my life without her. I am contemplating strangling her. I am wondering if I did everything I could . . . if I could have tried harder.

There is one last thing I have to say. Something I said before and was so terribly wrong about.

"Olivia, I once told you that I would love again, and that you would hurt forever. Do you remember?"

She nods. It's a painful memory for both of us.

"It was a lie. I knew it was a lie, even as I said it. I've never loved anyone after you. I never will."

I walk out.

Walk away.

No more fighting—not for her, or with her, or with myself.

HOW MANY TIMES can a heart be broken before it is beyond mend? How many times can I wish to not be alive? How can one human being cause such a crack in my existence? I alternate between periods of numbness and inconceivable pain all in the span of—an hour? An hour feels like a day, a day feels like a week. I want to live, and then I want to die. I want to cry, and then I want to scream.

I want, I want, I want . . .

Olivia.

But I don't. I want her to suffer. I want her to be happy. I want to stop thinking altogether and be locked in a room without thoughts. Possibly for a year.

I run. I run so much that if the zombie apocalypse were to happen, they'd never be able to catch me. When I run I don't feel anything but the burning in my lungs. I like the burn: it lets me know I can still feel when I'm having a numb day. When I am having a day of pain, I drink.

There is no cure.

One month gone

Two months gone

Three months . . .

Four

Estella isn't mine. The paternity test comes back. Marisol makes me come into her office to deliver the news. I stare at her blankly for five minutes while she explains the results: there is no way, no chance, no possibility that I am her biological father. I stand abruptly. "I need to go."

She nods, her face softening. "Take all the time you need."

I drive without destination, the city lights blurring past in streaks of color, and don't know where I am going. My hands are steady on the wheel, but my thoughts are anything but. Disbelief, anger, grief—they blur together.

Somehow I end up on Alligator Alley, the long, black ribbon slicing through the Everglades. There is something punishing about it. Flat, endless. Flanked by water and silence.

The house comes into view, and my chest tightens. It's still perfect. The dream. I pull into the driveway and cut the engine. It's just a house, I tell myself. Wood, and tile, and failure. I haven't been here since we left together.

Finally I step out and unlock the door. I don't bother turning the lights on in the house. I sit at the kitchen counter and make some calls. First to London, then to my mother, then to a Realtor. At some point exhaustion takes over. I fall asleep on the couch. I don't dream, I just shut down. When I wake up the next morning the light is flat and gray. I lock up the house, leaving a set of spare keys in the mailbox, and drive away without looking back. The realization settles over me, heavy but certain. I'm selling our house. After all these years.

I book a one-way ticket to London.

I pack. Just enough clothes to survive the first few weeks. A few books. A folder with documents.

I say plenty of lackluster goodbyes to friends and colleagues.

At the airport, I move on autopilot. Security. Boarding pass. Gate. All of it blurry at the edges. Like I'm already somewhere else. London. It feels real. I'm not just leaving a place, I'm leaving myself behind. I was a father in Florida. In London I am nothing and no one.

Somewhere over the Atlantic, I let it happen.

I let them both go.

33

———

Olivia

The Past

Birthday parties made me uncomfortable. Who the hell even invented them? Balloons, presents you didn't want . . . cake with all that fluffy, processed frosting. I was an ice cream kind of girl. Cherry Garcia. Cammie bought me a pint of that and handed it to me as soon as I blew out my candles.

"I know what you like," she said, winking at me.

Thank God for the type of best friends who make you feel known.

I ate my ice cream perched on a barstool in Cammie's kitchen while everyone else ate my cake. There were people everywhere, but I felt alone. And every time I felt alone, I blamed it on him. I set my ice cream on the counter and wandered outside. The DJ was playing Keane—sad music! Why the hell was there sad music at my birthday party? I slumped in a lawn chair and listened, watching the balloons bob. Balloons were the worst part of parties. They were unpredictable: one minute they were happy little balls of emotion, the next they were exploding in your face. I had a love/hate relationship with unpredictability. He-who-must-not-be-named was unpredictable. Unpredictable like a boss.

When I dutifully started opening presents, my husband standing to my left, my best friend jiggling her breasts at the cute DJ, I was not expecting the blue-packaged delivery.

I'd already opened twenty presents. Gift cards mostly—thank God! I loved gift cards. Don't give me shit about gift cards not being personal. There's nothing more personal than buying your own gift. I'd just put the last gift card I'd opened on the chair next to me, when Cammie took a break from flirting with the DJ to hand me the last of my presents. There was no card. Just a simply wrapped electric-blue box. To tell you the truth, my mind didn't even go there. If you work really hard at it, you can train your brain to ignore things. That shade of blue was one of them. I sliced the tape with my fingernail and pulled away the wrapping, balled it up, and dropped it in the paper pile at my feet. People had started to drift away and talk, getting bored with the present-unwrapping show, so when I opened the lid and stopped breathing, no one really noticed.

"Oh fuck. Ohfuckohfuckohfuck."

No one heard me. I saw a flash. Cammie took another picture and moved away from the DJ to see what was making my face contort like I'd sucked on a lemon.

"Oh fuck," she said, looking into the box. "Is that . . . ?"

I slammed the lid shut and shoved the box at her. "Don't let him see," I said, glancing at Noah. He was holding a beer in one hand, his face turned away from me and talking to someone. Cammie nodded. I stood up and bolted for the house. I had to walk around people who were still eating cake around the island in Cammie's kitchen. I made a right and darted up the stairs, choosing the bathroom in Cammie's bedroom rather than the one downstairs that everyone was using. I kicked off my shoes, closed the door, and stood bent over the sink, breathing hard. Cammie came in a few minutes later, shutting the door behind her.

"I told Noah you felt sick. He's waiting in the car. Can you do this, or do you need me to send him home and tell him you're staying the night?"

"I want to go home," I said. "Just give me a minute."

Cammie slid down the door until she was sitting on the floor. I sat on the edge of her tub and traced the lines of the floor tile with my toe.

"That was uncalled for," she said. "What's with you two sending each other anonymous packages?"

"That was different," I said. "I sent him a fucking baby blanket, not . . . that." I eyed the box that was sitting next to Cammie on the floor. "What's he trying to do?"

"Umm, he's sending you a pretty clear message."

I tugged at the collar of my dress. *Why is it so damn hot in here?*

Cammie pushed the box across the bathroom tile until it nudged my toe. "Look again."

"Why?"

"Because you didn't see what was underneath the divorce papers."

I flinched at the word *divorce*. Bending down, I retrieved the box from the floor and lifted out the stack of papers. Divorce was heavy. It wasn't official, but he'd obviously filed. Why did he need to tell me this? Like it made a difference anymore. I put the papers next to me on the lip of the tub and stared down at the contents underneath.

"Holy hell."

Cammie tucked her lips in and raised her eyebrows, nodding.

The Pink Floyd CD from the record store—the case cracked diagonally across, the kissing penny—green from age and flattened, and one deflated basketball. I reached out a finger and touched its bumpy skin, and then I dropped everything on the floor and stood up. Cammie quickly scooted out of the way, and I opened the door and stepped into her bedroom. I needed to go home and sleep forever.

"What about your fucked-up birthday present?" Cammie called after me.

"I don't want it," I said. I stopped when I reached her doorway, something eating at me. Turning back, I strode into the bathroom and crouched down in front of her.

"If he thinks this is okay, he's wrong," I snapped. She nodded, her eyes wide. "He can't do this to me," I reiterated. She shook her head in agreement.

"To hell with him," I said. She gave me a thumbs-up.

While our eyes were still locked, I reached out a hand and felt along the floor until my fingers found the penny.

"You didn't see me do this," I said, tucking it into my bra. "Because I don't give a fuck about him anymore."

"Do what?" she replied, dutifully.

"Good girl." I leaned over and kissed her on the forehead. "Thank you for my party."

Then I walked to my car, walked to my husband, walked back to my life.

I WAS IN bed an hour later, turned toward the ocean, even though it was too dark to see it. I could hear the waves rushing against the surf. The ocean was choppy tonight. Fitting. Noah was watching television in the living room; I could hear CNN through the walls. CNN was a lullaby to me at this point. He never came to bed when I did, and every night I fell asleep listening to the drone of the news. Tonight, I was grateful to be alone. If Noah looked too carefully—which he often did—he would see through my hollow smiles and pretend illness. He'd ask me what was wrong and I wouldn't lie to him. I didn't do that anymore. I was betraying him with my rogue emotions. I had the penny clutched in my fist. I couldn't put it down. Why couldn't my past leave me alone? Ten years was a long time to grieve a relationship. I'd paid for my stupid decisions with a decade. When I met Noah, I finally felt ready to put my broken love to rest. But you couldn't put something to rest when it kept coming back to haunt you.

I stood up and walked to the sliding glass doors that led to my balcony. Stepping out, I walked lightly to the edge of the railing.

I could do this. I kind of had to. Right? Exercise the ghosts. Take a stand. This was my life, dammit! The penny wasn't my life. It had to go. I lifted my fisted hand and felt the wind wrap around it. All I had to do was open my fist. That was it. So easy and so hard. I wasn't the type of girl to back away from a challenge. I closed my eyes and opened my fist.

For a second my heart seized. I heard my voice, but the wind quickly took it away. There. It was gone.

I stepped back and away from the railing, suddenly cold. Backward I walked to my bedroom, one step, two steps . . . then I lurched forward, throwing myself against the railing to peer over into the space between me and the ground.

Oh my God. Had I really done that?

I had, and my heart was aching for a goddamn penny. You're a fool! I told myself. Until tonight you didn't even know he still had the penny. But that wasn't really true. I'd seen inside his Trojan horse when I'd broken into his house. He'd kept it all those years. But he had a baby, and babies had a way of making people throw out the past and start new. I walked back into my bedroom and shut the door, and climbed into bed, and climbed into my life, and cried, cried, cried. Like a baby.

THE NEXT MORNING I took my coffee out there. I was dragging, and I told myself the fresh air would be good. What I really wanted was to stand at the site of where I murdered my penny. God, would I ever stop being so melodramatic? I was halfway to the balcony with my coffee clutched in my hands when my foot passed over something cold. I backed up a step, looked down, and saw my penny.

Gah!

The wind. It must have blown it back toward me when I threw it. I didn't pick it up until I was through drinking my coffee. I just sort of stood there and stared at it. When

I finally crouched down to retrieve it, I knew. You couldn't get rid of the past. You couldn't ignore it, or bury it, or throw it over the balcony. You just had to learn to live beside it. It had to peacefully coexist with your present. If I could figure out how to do that, I could be okay. I took the penny inside and pulled my copy of *Great Expectations* off the bookshelf. I taped the penny to the title page and slid the book back in. There. Right where it belonged.

34

The Present

The apartment is on the third floor of a building off Charlotte Street. The building is an old Victorian terrace, the kind that's been standing here for over a century. A faint patina of soot clings to the brickwork and ivy snakes up the corner. From the living room window, I can see the tops of trees swaying in Fitzroy Square Garden, and beyond that, the blurred rush of cabs and cyclists below. The kitchen is tiny, tucked on one side of the living room. Open shelving holds an uneven collection of plates, mugs, and bowls I picked up at Camden Market. Against one wall there is a pile of unopened boxes, and a folding chair I borrowed from the landlord. The navy blue couch came later, a lucky find from Camden. Same as the coffee table I dragged home from a secondhand shop on Portobello Road. There are scratches on the surface—someone has carved their initials, and a date, into the wood. I like that. Stories untold. I haul the table up three floors by myself, my back isn't happy, but it's worth it. The bedroom comes next, I order a wooden bed frame and then stop by Heal's on Tottenham Court Road for bedding. The rest comes piece by piece. A lamp from an open-air market, a set of ceramic mugs from a vendor. A vintage record player I find on Golborne Road, sitting in the corner of a dusty old shop.

I shop at Tesco, Sainsbury's and Marks & Spencer. Stock my tiny fridge with ready meals: tikka masala, shepherd's pie. I'm oddly impressed with coronation chicken, and for a while, I eat it for every meal.

One evening I finally tackle the box labeled "Books." When I cut open the tape and pull back the flaps, the smell of paper hits me. The first book I see is *Great Expectations*. I close the flap and put it aside for another day. The only thing I have shipped to London from the house is the painting that hung at the top of the stairs, near the bedrooms.

I take a position as a consultant at a boutique management firm near Holborn—two stops away on the Tube. The job is practical, and my workday is structured without being rigid. It allows me to slowly piece myself back together without any expectations.

I run through Regent's Park, a 2.8-mile loop that passes a lake. I try not to compare it to the beaches of Miami. Ducks are nice too. On weekends, I see my father, who hasn't changed much. He looks like an older version of me. He acts like we've been together every day for the last five years— which is nice. No awkwardness, no fumbling for the right words, just an easy rhythm of him being himself.

He starts his day with a double espresso and a cigarette on the balcony of his penthouse. He reminds me of a jaded, overcaffeinated king surveying his kingdom.

He takes me to his private members' club and introduces me to his friends, either tech billionaires or artists. I'm grateful for the gesture. I'm often a tagalong to The

Wolseley, Le Gavroche, and Scott's where I spend the night trying not to check my phone.

The most unlikely of the group is Fred, a tattoo artist in Shoreditch. My father met him at an art exhibit, where Fred curated the show. From there somehow Fred became part of the circle.

He invites me to his studio one weekend, a sprawling place tucked into a corner. It smells of ink, leather, and weed. The walls are covered with sketches, photos, and posters, all of it somehow cohesive.

It's at Fred's studio that I meet Leila. Sweet . . . quiet except for when she's watching Chelsea play. She's getting a tattoo of a raven when I pop in to say hi to Fred.

"That's either a breakup tattoo or you're really into Poe."

"Bit of both. But mostly because I like that birds outlive men. Especially American ones."

"Wow. Barely introduced and already a hate crime."

"It's not hate. It's pity. Poor you, thinking football means shoulder pads and tailgating."

"You could try to change my mind . . ." I'm flirting. It feels . . . good.

"Chelsea plays Arsenal on Sunday. Come watch us win," she says.

Fred gives me a pointed look.

"She's doing you a favor, mate."

Leila is willing to live on the edge of my life. She doesn't ask for more than what I can give. We date for a few weeks—easy dinners, pub nights. But convenience only works until someone wants more. It doesn't take long for things to fizzle out. But for once there are no explosive arguments, no dramatic showdown, no teary confessions in Rome. Just a mutual understanding. It's a nice change of pace. I keep waiting for her to send me an angry Instagram message telling me how she really feels, but it never comes. Not every connection needs to feel like a meteor crash.

LONDON IS GOOD to me in the ways that matter. Good job. Good suits. Good manners. Most days it's enough. I can pretend that this life fits me. I take long walks, mostly at night. Headphones in, hoodie up. On weekends I go to museums, and sometimes the movies. There are no ghosts in my flat. No arguments lingering in the walls.

My life feels clean and quiet. And maybe that's what healing looks like.

And then my phone rings. It's an American number. One I don't recognize, but something about it punches straight through the quiet I've built here. I look at my father across the table as he stirs his tea. He motions for me to take the call. "I'll be back . . ."

The cold hits me as I step outside the café, the London sky low and colorless. I swipe to answer. I immediately recognize the voice.

"Marisol," I say.

"Hello, my dear. I have news."

"Okay . . ." My mind is spinning. I glance at my watch. It's around two o'clock stateside.

"Are you sitting down?"

"I'm anxiously standing up."

"When your ex-wife took Estella into the clinic to get the blood work done, she used Leah Smith on her paperwork instead of Johanna. That's what caused the whole mix-up."

I cut her off. "What are you saying?"

"You got someone else's results, Caleb. Estella is yours. Ninety-nine-point-nine percent yours."

I don't speak. I can't. I'm standing on a narrow London street and it feels like the ground just cracked open. "Oh my God."

"During the intake process, someone at the clinic mis-filed Leah's paperwork."

"How can something like that happen?"

"Oh, you'd be surprised how common administration errors are, especially when these people are dealing with large volumes of tests. It was probably some overworked technician."

"How did you find out?"

"Leah. She didn't feel like the paternity test added up so she had another done."

"When?"

"Two months ago."

"Why am I only finding out about this now?"

"She wants child support. I think she's going to paint herself as the devoted mother; they'll make it seem like you left when it mattered most."

"I did," I say.

Since I'm living in another country, Marisol tells me I won't have to be there in person for all the court dates. Technically. Legally. But I fly back anyway. The first time I'm there, Leah doesn't look at me. Not once.

I sit behind my lawyer and say nothing. My heart thunders. When the judge calls my name, I stand and speak.

The judge notices that I show up.

All three hearings, suit pressed, never late. Maybe that's what tips it. Or maybe it's just luck.

He grants me three weeks a year. Twenty-one days.

Since I'm still living in England, he agrees Estella can spend the time there—as long as she's accompanied by a family member. It's a small victory. But it's mine. She's mine.

35

The Present

I spend forty minutes in a toy store trying to decide what to get Estella. In the movies when parents are reunited with their children, they have a pastel-colored stuffed animal in their hands—usually a bunny. Since a cliché is the worst thing a person can be, I browse the aisles until I find a stuffed llama. I hold it in my hands for a few minutes, smiling like a fool. Then I carry it to the register.

My stomach is in knots when I climb onto the Tube. I take the Piccadilly line to Heathrow and mistakenly get off at the wrong terminal. I have to double back, practically sprinting through corridors, scanning arrival boards like my life depends on it. By the time I find the correct gate, my mother has texted: We've landed.

Panic hits.

What if she doesn't remember me? Or if she decides not to like me and cries the entire trip? *God.* I am an absolute mess. I see my mother first, her blond hair in a perfect chignon even after the nine-hour flight. When I look down, I see a chubby hand attached to my mother's slender one. I follow the length of the arm and see messy red curls bouncing excitedly around a face that looks exactly like Leah's. I smile so hard my face hurts. I don't think I've smiled since I moved to London. Estella is wearing a pink tutu and a cupcake shirt. When I see that she's smeared lipstick all over her face, my heart does the most peculiar thing: it beats faster and aches at the same time. I watch my mother stop and point toward me. Estella's eyes search me out. When she sees me, she pulls free of her grandmother's hand and . . . runs. I drop to my knees to catch her. She hits me with force—too much force for such a little person. She's strong. I squeeze her squishy little body and feel the ducts in my eyes burn as they try to summon tears. I just want to stay here, crouched on the tile floor of Heathrow, holding my daughter like it's the most natural thing in the world. But she pulls back, grabs my face with both hands like she's conducting an interview, and starts talking. No shyness. No hesitation. She tells me about the flight in vivid detail—something about orange juice, and the bathroom soap. She clutches the llama plushie in the crook of her arm like it's her sidekick.

I glance at my mom, who's smiling now. I wink at her, but I can't look away from Estella for long.

"And then I ate my butter and Doll said it was gonna make me sick . . ."

Doll. That's what she calls my mother. My mother thinks it's the greatest thing in the world. I think she's just relieved to have escaped the normal *Granny* or *Grandma* monikers that would make her feel old.

"You're a genius," I say while she's taking a breath. "What three-year-old speaks like this?"

My mother smiles ruefully. "One who never stops speaking. She gets unfathomable amounts of practice."

Estella repeats the word *unfathomable* all the way to baggage claim. She gets the giggles when I start chanting it with her, and by the time I pull their luggage from the belt, my mother's head looks ready to explode.

"You used to do that when you were little," she says. "Say the same thing over and over until I wanted to scream."

I kiss my daughter's forehead. "Who needs a paternity test?" I joke. Which is the absolute wrong thing to say, because my small person starts chanting *paternity test* all the way through the airport . . . until we climb into the cab outside and I distract her with a pink bus that's driving by.

During the cab ride home, Estella wants to know what her bedroom looks like, what color blankets I got for her bed, if I have any toys, if she can have sushi for dinner. She's so bright and friendly, a little social butterfly in the making.

"Sushi?" I repeat, tickling her. "What about spaghetti or chicken fingers?" She squeals in delight.

"Sushi," she says again.

My mother raises her eyebrows. "You'd never need a maternity test," she says out of the corner of her mouth.

"Hey, thanks for doing this, Mom, I love you."

"Love you too," she says reaching across the seat to squeeze my hand.

AFTER WE DROP their things at my flat—a whirlwind of pink luggage, and my mother making polite critiques about my apartment—we head out for sushi. Estella insists on sitting between us like a tiny diplomat. And then, my three-year-old picks up a pair of chopsticks and starts eating like she's been doing it since birth. Tiny fingers, full confidence, no hesitation. She doesn't even glance around to see if we're impressed.

I'm dazzled.

"She's consumed an entire crab roll while defying jetlag. What a trouper."

My mother smiles and pats my hand. "The proud father. It's nice to see you happy."

"It's nice to feel happy. I didn't know that it was possible."

On their way out of the restaurant an older couple stops at our table to fawn over Estella. "Her hair is just beautiful," the woman says. "You can't replicate a color like that."

I glance at Estella who looks back at me like she's used to this sort of thing from strangers.

"Thank you," she says, politely. And then less seriously she adds, "Thank you, very much," in what sounds like an Elvis impersonation. That gets another round of laughter.

"Lovely, just lovely," the woman says. "Enjoy every moment with her."

I feel my throat tighten. Enjoy every moment. That's exactly what I need to do.

Estella falls asleep on my shoulder on the walk home. "She's so little," I say, plucking a piece of rice from her hair. "Is it just me or is she cuter than the average kid?"

"She looks just like you when you were that age. Without the red hair of course." She reaches over to touch Estella's curls fondly. "The only good thing Leah has ever brought to the table is this child."

"You like telling people your grandchild has red hair."

"I do," she sighs. "I'm the only one of my friends who has one. I feel like God's favorite."

"You would," I tease.

Estella is easier to carry up the stairs than the coffee table. She's light as a feather in my arms, her hair fanning across my shoulder. I lay her down carefully, trying not to jostle her. She doesn't even stir. I take off her shoes and jacket and tuck her into bed. Enjoy every moment. I find my mother asleep on the couch, her head tilted at an awkward angle. She's already in her pajamas. I gently shake her awake.

"The bed is all yours," I tell her. I offer her my hands and when she places them in mine and I pull her to her feet. Her skin feels thin and papery, her grip not as firm.

"This old lady is tired."

I watch her walk to the bedroom, her hips and knees stiff with the telltale signs of time. The vitality that once defined her stride has softened. I wasn't just missing Estella's life by being in London, I'm missing hers. And Steve's.

After a traditional English breakfast, I take them to Hyde Park. Estella climbs the massive wooden ship in the Diana Memorial Playground, and then we feed the ducks.

"I want to ride the train, Daddy." Her face is pressed into my neck and her voice is sleepy.

"Tomorrow we'll ride the Tube," I tell her. "We'll do lots of gross things tomorrow that Granny doesn't like."

"Okay," she sighs. "Will Mommy be mad?"

"No. Mommy wants you to have fun."

A few minutes later I feel her snoring against my neck. My heart beats and aches and beats and aches.

I SPEND THE weekend alone with my daughter. My mother, aware of the delicate balance we're trying to strike, decides to visit friends and relatives.

We start with the zoo in Camden. The next day I take her to ride the London Eye and she falls asleep on my lap. Upon her request, we eat sushi every day for lunch. I talk her into spaghetti one night for dinner, and she has a meltdown about it. She wails, her face turning as red as her hair, until I start singing "The Wheels on the Bus." She agrees to eat her spaghetti in the bath. It feels like a two for one special, so I agree to it. When I get her out of the bath, she rubs her eyes, yawns, and falls asleep right as I get her pajamas on.

I take her to meet my father. He has us meet him at his country house so he can show Estella his horses. My mother politely declines to join us, choosing to stay home and catch up on her shows. He carries Estella from stall to stall where he introduces her to the horses. She repeats their names: Sugarcup, Nerphelia, Adonis, Stokey.

He's good with Estella. She mimics his accent and tugs on his ears which makes him laugh. That's the good thing about my dad, he makes you feel like you're the only person in the whole room worth having a conversation with. The negative side being that he will go a year without having a conversation with you.

But I'll let my daughter have today, and I'll protect her the best I can tomorrow. Broken people give broken love. And we are all a little broken. You just have to forgive and sew up the wounds love delivers and move on.

We go from the stables to the kitchen where he makes a

show of making us huge ice cream sundaes and then squirts whipped cream into Estella's mouth right from the can.

The last two days of her visit, I work from home, dreading goodbye. I have four months left on my contract. Four months of torture before I can head home and see her every week.

Estella cries when we part at the airport. She's clutching the llama to her chest, tears soaking its matted fur.

"I don't wanna go," she whispers. "I wanna stay with you."

My chest caves in. I drop to my knees in front of her. "I know. I want that too."

My mother stands a few feet away, composed but tense.

"Mommy will be so sad if you don't go home," I tell her. "Grandma is going to give you a special present when the plane takes off, okay." That gets her attention. She grabs my chin with her hand and kneads it like dough. "Who is the present from?" she asks, squinting at me like this part is important.

My heart breaks in entirely new ways.

"Sugarcup, Nerphelia, Adonis, and Stokey," I say, referencing my dad's horses. "And me."

She stares at me a moment longer, then nods solemnly, like she's accepting the terms of a fragile truce. She hesitantly goes to my mother. I pass her the little gift bag with the horses I bought for Estella from Hamleys.

"Mum . . ." I start, my voice trailing off.

"You stopped calling me mum when we moved to America."

I look into my mother's eyes, and feel bad about every negative thought I've ever had about her. She always shows up for her kids.

"Don't worry," she says, her tone soft as she pats my arm. "I have her on the weekends for the next few weeks. I'll keep my eye on things. We'll take good care of your girl until you're back."

I nod, the lump in my throat making it impossible to respond. I kiss them both on the cheek.

I stand there, rooted to the spot, and watch as they make their way through security. The Tube ride home feels endless. I sit with my head in my hands for most of the ride.

My flat feels eerily quiet with them gone. I put the TV on for noise and start cleaning up the toys we couldn't fit into her suitcase.

36

The Present

I open the email at work. Just another notification. Just another subject line.

Until it's not.

I read it once, then again. A third time, slower. My hands start shaking. There it is in black and white, judge's signature at the bottom.

This Christmas, I get Estella.

Relief doesn't come in a wave—it hits like a flood. Fast. Total.

I'm still staring at the screen, barely able to grasp what this means—when my phone buzzes on the desk beside me.

Leah's name lights up the screen.

I glance at my watch. It's seven o'clock in the morning; she's probably just seen the email herself.

I hesitate for a second before picking up, bracing myself. There's a pause.

"Leah."

No greeting, No soft lead-in.

"A child should never be away from her mother on Christmas."

"You got the ruling?"

"She doesn't even know you. You can't just do this to me."

"A child should never be away from her father on Christmas either," I shoot back. "But you made sure that happened for two years."

She didn't like that. I can almost hear her grinding her teeth. "She has plans, Caleb! You can't just show up here and uproot our lives."

I lean against the outside of the building as I wait for the light to change. A pigeon struts confidently past my feet stopping to peck at a discarded hot dog bun.

"She's three years old, Leah, she doesn't have plans, you do."

"Yes! We do. We have plans. Her clap club has a Christmas party, and there's a birthday party. These are things she's looking forward to."

"Fine. I'll take her. I'd be happy to take her to clap club and the party."

"This is going to confuse her, you're being selfish."

I take a deep breath.

"She's not going to feel confused. She's used to being around my parents. I'll stick to whatever schedule you give me. But I am her father, Leah, I plan on being in her life."

She hangs up on me.

THE DAY BEFORE I fly home I call my mother. She answers the phone out of breath.

"We are thrilled you're coming. It's been so exciting around here getting ready. We're having a traditional roast on Christmas. Estella is helping me make chocolate pie and cookies. She's so excited, you should see her, Caleb, she's dancing around in her little tutu. She's asked if we could put the star on the tree together when you get here. She's got it all planned out—what to wear, which cookies are yours."

"I can't wait," I tell her. And it's true.

"Listen, I've got to go, Steve just came back from the store and I need to unpack the groceries. See you tomorrow?"

"Love you, Mum."

ON THE MORNING of my flight, my suitcase is zipped, my boarding pass loaded. And then my phone rings.

Unknown number. Miami area code.

My stomach tightens instinctively.

"Hello?"

"Caleb Drake?"

"Yes, who's calling?"

"My name is Claribel Vasquez. I am a counselor at Boca South Medical Center." Her voice drops off and I wait for her to continue, my heart beating wildly.

"There's been an accident," she says.

I go still.

"Your parents . . . your daughter. They—" She doesn't finish. Or maybe she does, but I can't hear it. My breath won't come right—tight and shallow.

"Are they alive?"

She pauses. It feels like an hour, ten hours. Why is she taking so long to answer me!

"There was a car accident."

"Estella?" I demand. "My daughter . . . ?" I squeeze my

eyes shut. My body folds forward. My phone is pressed to my ear, useless.

"She's stable."

Relief crashes over me. I nod.

I'm afraid your parents didn't make it." The words don't echo. They just land. Final. Painful. It feels like a door has been slammed in my face.

I try to sit, but there's nothing to sit on. So I slide. Back against the wall, legs giving out. I hit the floor hard.

"Is Leah there . . . her mother, is she there?"

There's a pause. The kind that's never a good sign.

"No, we haven't been able to contact her mother."

The words slide into my gut like ice.

Not there. Not with Estella.

"Estella came out of surgery about an hour ago. There was some internal bleeding, but her doctor says she's stable. The doctors are monitoring her now."

"So she's alone?"

"She's not alone," Claribel says, quickly, like she hears what I'm really asking. "I'm with her right now."

I nod even though she can't see.

"How soon can you get here?"

I tell her my situation.

She asks me to hold while she runs to her desk to jot down my flight number and arrival time. "I'm Estella's case worker so I'll be here to meet you when you get to the hospital." I thank her, and head to the airport.

BY THE TIME the 747 touches down on American soil, carrying me in its belly across oceans and time zones, my three-year-old daughter had already survived surgery on hers. As the plane taxied to the gate, all I could think about was her tiny body lying in a hospital room by itself. I catch a cab right to the hospital. I text Claribel to check on Estella. She tells me Estella's condition hasn't changed and says she will be waiting for me in the hospital lobby. Then I try calling Leah again, it goes straight to voicemail. I texted my brother from the plane, but he still hasn't answered me.

Claribel texts that she's wearing a red skirt. I see her as soon as I walk through the doors.

She has a heart-shaped face and warm brown eyes. She shakes my hand.

"Nice to finally meet you face-to-face. I'm sorry it's under such terrible conditions, my condolences about your parents." She doesn't wait for me to respond. "Estella is doing great, she's responding well to the medication."

"Is she awake?"

"Not yet. They're keeping her medicated for the time being. They want her body to heal."

She walks me to the elevator.

When we reach the fifth floor, Claribel steps out. I follow her to a set of double doors where she swipes a card through a keypad next to the door and it opens. The smell of antiseptic hits me in the face. She touches my arm lightly as we step through.

"It's going to be hard to see her. Just keep in mind there is still a lot of swelling on her face."

I breathe deeply as she opens the door, and I step inside. There is a symphony of medical equipment beeping in the room. I approach her bed slowly. She is a tiny lump under the covers. When I see her face I start crying. There are tubes everywhere—up her nose, down her throat, snaking into her tiny, bruised arms.

Claribel stands at the window and politely looks away while I cry over my daughter. I am too afraid to touch her, so I run my pinkie over her pinkie, the only part of her that isn't bruised.

There are so many doctors. I listen to them talk about her organs, her chances of recovery, the months of rehabilitation she's facing. I'm on my third cup of coffee, but I'm having trouble focusing on what they're saying.

A few minutes later, Claribel slips back into the room, her phone in hand. She looks tired. "I spoke with Sam," she says softly. "He said he's Leah's assistant . . ." Her voice drops off. "Leah is in Thailand. That's why no one has been able to reach her."

"Thailand," I repeat. She hadn't mentioned anything about a trip abroad. I'm depleted of anger for the day so all I can do is take a steadying breath.

"We got in touch with her. She's on her way back."

"Great," I say rubbing a hand across my face.

Claribel clears her throat.

"She went with her boyfriend. Since you were supposed to have Estella for Christmas."

I haven't eaten or slept in thirty hours.

"Hey, they're going to take her down to get a scan. While she's gone you should go down to the cafeteria and grab a sandwich. You look like you're going to pass out. I don't feel like cleaning a man of your size off the floor."

I nod. "Yes, ma'am."

"I'm not going to be here tomorrow, but you have my number, text me if you need anything."

I nod.

"Merry Christmas, Caleb," she says, about to head out the door.

I blink. Christmas. Right. That was tomorrow. I hear my mother's voice in the back of my head, talking about a roast dinner, and the chocolate pie . . .

It feels like a weight is pressing on my chest. I blink at Claribel as a wave of realization crashes over me. They were dead. I wasn't ever going to talk to my mom or Steve again.

"You okay?" she asks.

"Yeah, just tired. Thank you . . . I mean it. I don't know what I would have done without your help. Merry Christmas."

She gives me an encouraging smile. "See you in a day. Hang in there."

I wait until they wheel Estella out of the room before forcing myself to move. My legs feel heavy. I don't feel like eating but I know Claribel is right. I can't take care of Estella from a hospital room. It doesn't make it easier to leave.

The cafeteria is packed. I join the shortest line and grab the first thing I see: a turkey sandwich wrapped in cellophane, and two bottles of water. I carry my sad meal back to Estella's room and eat the whole thing in four bites, barely tasting it. I'm dozing in the chair when they bring Estella back. I sit up as the nurse maneuvers the bed back into place.

"Is she okay?"

"She's fine. One of her doctors will look over her scans in the morning and discuss them with you."

When she's gone I stand by Estella's bed and stroke her hair, speaking softly to her in case she can hear me. I tell her everything I bought her for Christmas: more ponies for her stable, a music box, and my favorite book as a child—*Where the Wild Things Are.*

"I'll get it out of my suitcase and read it for you tomorrow," I tell her softly.

I DON'T MEAN to fall asleep again, but I do. When I wake, there is a nurse in the room, adjusting the wires and checking Estella's vitals. I rub a hand across my face, my vision blurry. It all comes crashing back.

"How is she?" I ask. My voice barely above a rasp.

The nurse looks up from Estella's chart. "Vitals are stable."

So clinical and yet so comforting. Stable. I'll take it.

She smiles sympathetically when she sees me rubbing my neck. "Those chairs are uncomfortable. Your wife requested a cot, they're sending one up now. You'll be able to stretch out a bit. Feel free to use the shower in the bathroom too if you need it."

I freeze. "I'm sorry. Who?"

"Your wife, honey." She pats me on the shoulder. "She said she'd be right back."

My wife. I'm not sure whether to laugh, correct her, or panic.

"Where is she?"

I wasn't going to argue with her in the same room as Estella. Not now. The frustration was clawing at me. I want to grab her by the shoulders, look her in the eyes, and make her explain why she thought it was okay to fly ten thousand miles away without telling anyone.

"She said she was getting coffee," the nurse said. "Could have gone down to the cafeteria or the Starbucks in the lobby."

"Thanks."

My feet kick-start and I'm walking again. My mouth feels like sandpaper. The hallway stretches out in front of me, sterile and harsh under the fluorescent lights. I follow the corridor past the nurses' station.

I can hear the muffled shuffle of footsteps echoing off the linoleum, the low murmur of hushed voices. Somewhere in the distance, a pager beeps sharply, cutting through the quiet.

I scan the hallway, searching for a flash of red hair—that same unmistakable shade Estella has.

Nothing. No one. I rub my eyes. What am I even doing? I can't leave Estella.

I stumble back toward the elevators, jabbing the button harder than necessary. The doors shudder open with a hollow ding. I step inside, jaw clenched so tight my teeth ache. The whole world feels slanted.

The elevator doors sigh open. I don't even look up at first. I just walk. Heavy. Dragging. One step at a time, toward my daughter's room.

And then I see her.

At the end of the corridor, leaning against the wall like she's been there for hours, a cup of coffee in each hand.

Olivia. The sight of her knocks the air out of me. For a second I think I'm imagining her. She looks up and sees me. She straightens, one of the coffees trembles in her hand. We just stare at each other. No words.

"They told me my wife was here," I say, my voice rough. "I was looking for Leah."

She lifts her eyes to mine, gaze cool and steady. "Sorry to disappoint."

I chuckle.

I want to toss the coffee cups aside and pull her into my arms. "How did you know we were here?"

"I can't tell you that."

"Marisol?"

"She would never," Olivia says half-heartedly.

I kiss her forehead, breathe her in. She hands me a cup. "Let's go back in and sit with Estella."

There's a cot set up in the corner of the room. I sit on the edge and Olivia sits on the chair.

"How is she?" She hands me an open container of cheese and fruit. "Wait. Eat the peanut butter and the apples and then you can tell me."

I do what she says before filling her in on what the doctors have told me.

"Drink the rest of that water."

I try to smile around the bottle. My face feels stiff. She's wearing sweats, her hair down and wet. I wonder if she came in a hurry. I open my mouth to ask her, but she cuts me off.

"We'll play twenty questions tomorrow, London boy. I'll sit with her while you sleep."

I want to argue, but the largest sentence I can formulate is, "You're treating me like a child."

She makes me lie on my back. "Everyone needs to be treated like a child sometimes."

When she leans over me I smell her perfume.

"I have this—" She pulls a light blue sleep mask out of her pocket and puts it on my chest. "I'll wake you up if anything changes. Do you have your earbuds?"

I shake my head. "They're dead. I forgot to charge them."

"No problem." She walks back to the chair and digs around in her bag until she finds her pair. "Okay put them in."

I can't hear much of anything when they're in my ears. She messes with her phone until I hear the sound of rain. I give her a thumbs-up and she smiles.

"I love you," I say out loud, but I don't know if she hears me, I can't even hear myself.

37

The Present

Olivia stays at the hospital with me the next day. When I wake up from her enforced nap she's still sitting in the chair. I sit up, flinching at the brightness of the lights.

"How long have I been sleeping?"

"Four hours. She's fine."

"Okay," I say.

She sits with Estella while I shower in the little bathroom. When I come out, she has food set out on the little table. "I ordered takeout this time."

I check on Estella before I sit down.

"Where's your brother?"

"I don't know, my phone died too. He was supposed to be there on Christmas."

"You don't think that's weird? Both of them being MIA at the same time?"

I spoon eggs into my mouth. I'd thought it. I hadn't processed it yet. "I really don't want to think about it."

"Okay," she says gently. "Eat your avocado . . ."

ON THE DAY after Christmas, Olivia helps me make the funeral arrangements for my parents. We set up the Zoom call from Estella's hospital room.

The funeral director introduces herself as Kristy.

"I know it can feel overwhelming, but we'll handle the logistics for you," she says, her words measured like she's said them hundreds of times before. And maybe she has.

That's all I catch before my mind goes blank. *Bobbing like a balloon.* I'm here but I'm not. Olivia gently touches my arm when she needs me to choose something. A casket. Flowers. Has anyone notified their friends and family? Yes. I'd texted everyone from the plane.

When the Zoom call finally ends, I sit there, staring at the blank screen. Olivia sits on my lap and wraps her arms around my neck. I don't even think before I hug her back. She's the only thing that's keeping me from falling apart. She makes me lie down and close my eyes. And somehow, I fall asleep. When I wake up, she's still there. Sitting by Estella's crib like a sentry. Her hair is a little messy, her expression unreadable but composed. The most beautiful woman I've ever seen. She waits until I've eaten, slept, and showered before she lets herself leave. The room feels colder the second she's gone. I stare at her empty chair. How did I ever let her go? What version of me was so prideful that I thought there was anything safer than her?

Leah calls me from the airport, her voice frantic. "Caleb, I'm so sorry, I just landed. I couldn't get a flight home because it was Christmas. I sat at the airport for two days crying. It was terrible. Humiliating—"

She keeps going, like if she says enough sad words they'll

stack into an excuse. I cut her off. "They're reducing Estella's sedatives right now. You need to get here."

"They're waking her up? Oh my God don't let them do anything until I get there. Please, Caleb." Her voice shreds through the speaker. "I'll never forgive you if she wakes up and doesn't see my face."

I grind my teeth. "Just get here." She wants to be part of the moment now that it's almost safe.

An hour later, Leah rushes through the door, breathless. She's wearing a sweatshirt and denim shorts. Her ponytail is hanging on by sheer desperation. She cuts through the room toward the bed, single-minded urgency. When she sees Estella, her whole body folds in on itself.

Her sobs are loud and unrelenting. "Oh my God, this is all my fault. I should have been here! I can't believe this is happening."

She's saying everything I said in my head two days ago. I want to feel relief that she's here, maybe even sympathy. But I just feel tired.

I give her space, leaning against the wall with my arms crossed. The nurse working at Estella's bedside glances at Leah, her movements slowing as she watches her. I glance at the whiteboard near the sink.

Sandra, she wrote in neat letters earlier. She's been kind. Steady.

"Leah . . ." I say finally. Her head snaps up at the sound of my voice. She glares at me.

Her tear-streaked face is flushed with anger and embarrassment. "Don't act like the hero. I don't want to hear it."

I know from experience that nothing I say can defuse

the situation. We'd had dozens of fights during our marriage, and they all ended the same way—Leah angry, accusing, and hysterical.

Sandra intervenes.

"Ma'am, I understand this is hard for you, but if you
can't remain calm, we're going to have to ask you to step
out of the room. We need a quiet environment to focus on
Estella. If you need a moment, feel free to step outside and
take a breath."

Leah's head whips toward Sandra.

"Step out? You're asking me to leave? I'm her mother. I
haven't slept, I haven't eaten, and now you want me to leave?"

Sandra doesn't flinch. "Let's focus on your child?"

"So I'm not focused on my child? Are you calling me a
bad mother?"

I'm two seconds away from saying something I regret
when Sandra puts her hands on her hips.

"Ma'am, I'm not calling you anything, but I'm about to
call security if you don't get yourself under control."

Leah's faces flushes red. I think she's going to lash out
again, but then her expression changes. The fight drains out
of her.

"Fine." She sits in the small chair next to Estella's bed,
her eyes fixed on her daughter.

The tension ebbs and for a moment the room is quiet
again, save for the beeping of the machines.

"Oh . . . oh . . . there she is—hi, honey, hi, Estella, can
you hear me?"

Leah gasps, jumping out of her chair. I reach the bed in
two strides. The nurse leans over Estella, as she checks her
vitals.

Her voice is soothing. "Mommy and Daddy are right here. You want to open your eyes so you can see them?"

Her eyes are fluttering. It looks like she's struggling to open them.

"What does this mean? Is she going to be okay?"

Estella's hand twitches and we all make sounds of joy.

"She's responding well," Sandra says in our direction; she hasn't taken her eyes off the monitor. "Take your time, you're doing great. Dad, get over to where I am and come stand by her."

She moves so I can be on one side of Estella and Leah on the other.

"Hey, sweetheart, hi—" My voice catches when her eyes open.

She looks right at me. "Hey," I say again, softer this time. "There you are, baby girl. We've been waiting for you."

Leah leans forward, her hand reaches for Estella's. "Hi, honey," she whispers.

I glance at Sandra, who's standing a few steps back, her face serene.

"She's going to be okay," she says, winking at me.

A WEEK LATER Olivia is standing at the window in Estella's hospital room, watching the rain. She's wearing jeans and a white tunic, her hair wet and smelling of flowers. I am overtaken with gratitude.

"How long will she be gone?"

"They said the full-body MRI will take sixty to ninety minutes, but they have to monitor her while she's in recovery."

She leaves the window and joins me at the small table, sitting across from me.

"You don't have to leave before she gets here. I'm not trying to hide you."

"It doesn't feel right. Leah wouldn't want me around her and I don't want to cause problems."

"I don't care what Leah wants," I say. "I want you here."

"Okay, so let's talk," she says, resting her clasped hands on the table. "You're blaming yourself . . ."

"It's my fault. I shouldn't have left. I should have been here myself to drive her where she needed to be. If I'd been here all along none of this would have happened."

She purses her lips, nodding slowly. "The day I saw you in the music store it was raining like this. Do you remember?"

I nod. I remember everything about that day: the rain, the drops of water clinging to her hair, the way she smelled like gardenias.

"Dobson Scott Orchard was standing outside of the music store."

"Come on . . ." She stares at me unblinking, and I balk. "Are you being serious?"

"I'm not kidding. He offered to walk me to my car with his umbrella."

I search her face for the joke, but I already know she wouldn't joke about something like that.

"My God, Olivia. Why didn't you tell me?"

She shrugs. "I've never told anyone, also who would I tell?"

"Cammie . . ."

She rolls her eyes. "Cammie doesn't count, of course I told Cammie—"

I lean back in my chair, shaking my head. "Then what happened?"

"I debated taking him up on his offer, but I chose to go inside and talk to you instead."

"Wow. I honestly don't know what to say. The next time I saw you, you could have been on the news."

"Well . . . maybe. We could speculate for an hour about all the ways it could have gone. Trust me, I have spent many hours of my life imagining it in horrific detail . . ."

I make a sound in the back of my throat. I don't want to think about that.

When she continues, her voice is lower than before. "The sum of all the things we shouldn't have done in our lives is enough to kill us with the weight, Caleb Drake. Neither you nor I nor anyone else in this life could possibly know the chain reaction our decisions cause. If you're to blame, then so am I."

"How?"

"If I'd done what my heart said and said yes to you, you wouldn't have left for London. Luca and Steve would be alive and your daughter wouldn't be in the hospital in a medical-induced coma."

We are quiet for a few minutes as I think over her words. It's frightening to think about.

"So why did you take Dobson's case?"

She breathes deeply. I hear the air leave her in a great sigh. "I felt a connection to him. That may sound sick, but I don't know how else to describe it. I needed to be there to see how the story played out."

"What the fuck?"

We both look up at the same time. Leah stands in the

doorway, eyes wide and glassy, cheeks flushed like she'd been powerwalking. She looks at Olivia like she's radio-active.

Then at me.

Then back at her.

"Why is she here, Caleb?"

Olivia and I exchange a glance—just a flicker, but it says everything.

"I asked her to be," I say, my voice low. I am done playing polite. "Why are you here, it's not your shift? We agreed to certain times."

Leah blinks like I've slapped her. She didn't expect me to push back.

"I am her mother. I don't need permission to see my daughter."

Olivia looks between us, her eyebrows raised. She's not rattled. "I'm going to get out of here and give you guy some space."

She rises from the chair slowly, unbothered, like she has all the time in the world.

I give her a quick thank-you glance before she slips out the door.

THE FUNERAL IS three days later. I ask Olivia to go with me.

"Your mother hated me," she said, on the phone. "It feels weirdly disrespectful to go."

"She didn't hate you. I promise. Besides, your father would have hated me, and I still would have gone to his funeral."

"Fine," she says.

I've pushed every thought of my parents from my mind in order to give Estella what she needs, but when I walk through the doors of the funeral home and see their coffins side by side, I lose it.

I excuse myself from an old neighbor who is approaching me with condolences and walk briskly to the parking lot. There is a low-hanging willow to the rear of the property. I stand underneath it and breathe. That's where she finds me.

She doesn't say anything, just comes to stand next to me, taking my hand and squeezing it.

"This isn't happening," I say. "Tell me it's not."

"It's happening," she says. "Your parents are dead. But they loved you. They loved your daughter. You have so many good memories."

I glance down at her. She saw two parents die and no doubt only one of them provided decent memories. I wonder if she had anyone to hold her hand after her mom died.

"Let's go in," she says. "I got you."

I squeeze her hand.

Leah is sitting next to my brother. When she sees me with Olivia she looks rageful.

I take my seat near Seth.

My mother's favorite roses are—were—English Garden. There are several tasteful arrangements around her casket, interspersed with lilies, next to a blown-up photo of her and Steve embracing each other, happiness in both their eyes and smile. Both caskets are closed, but I can't stop myself from picturing them inside. I try not to do it, to remember them alive instead, but just seeing those rectangular boxes makes me sick.

When the service is over, I flank one side of the door, and my brother takes the other. We don't speak to each other—haven't really since the whole nightmare began— but we nod at each other when it's time to do our duty. People filter by slowly, murmuring their condolences as they pass. I want it to be over.

When the room clears out, we move to the graveside. Olivia stands with me. It's so sunny everyone is hidden behind sunglasses, but I can feel Leah staring at us, silently fuming.

When the priest finishes, the quiet stretches out like a thread about to snap.

So this is it. This is how it ends. Not with some grand moment of closure, not with time to prepare, but just . . . silence. Two caskets side by side, like a cruel joke. I thought I had time. Time to visit more. Time to say I love you. Now all I had was this moment and a shovel full of dirt.

38

The Present

Caleb!" I turn to see Leah marching across the parking lot. I stop to let her catch up. Olivia visibly stiffens beside me.

My mind jumps to Estella; I slide my phone out of my pocket. No missed calls from the hospital. I exhale.

She's out of breath when she reaches us. Seth isn't far behind. The look on his face says he'd rather be walking in the opposite direction.

"What is it, Leah? Everything okay?"

"I don't want you coming to the hospital. You're a shitty, irresponsible father. And don't think Estella will be making any more trips to see you. I'm taking you to court for full custody."

I shake my head. I know exactly what she's doing and I don't want to play this game. Out of the corner of my eye I see a flash of movement.

Olivia steps forward and shoves Leah. "The hell you will."

Leah freezes, her eyes wide in shock for half a second. Then angry.

"You did not just do that," she rages, fists at her side.

Seth reaches her just as she lunges forward. He drops her bag and grabs her around the waist swinging her in the opposite direction.

Olivia is calm and still.

"Don't do that again, Duchess. You're a lawyer, you know what could happen."

"You're not my father so you don't need to be concerned about my behavior," she snaps.

The parking lot is empty except for a Toyota Corolla I'm assuming belongs to the funeral director.

Seth lets go of Leah and she lunges for Olivia. I roll my eyes. I didn't have the energy to deal with this. I push Olivia behind my back and hold my hand out to Leah.

"No," I say. "You don't touch her. Enough."

Leah holds her phone up, waves it around.

Was I really married to this woman?

Leah holds up her phone like she's going to hit me with it. I glance at Seth. "Can you get her."

When I look back down Olivia is snatching the phone out of Leah's hand. Before I can intervene she throws it on the ground and stomps on it with her heel, cracking the screen. Once . . . twice . . . three times. I grab her. "You really have a death wish today, Olivia," I say between my teeth.

Leah's mouth is open. "I'm going to destroy you," she says.

"Good luck." Olivia looks bored.

I can't believe she's being so calm about this.

"There is nothing more you could do to me. But I swear

to God, if you fuck with Caleb, I'm going to put you in prison for one of your *many* illegal activities. Then you'll be the one who won't see Estella."

Leah closes her mouth.

"Mind your business," Leah spits. "Homewrecker."

Olivia laughs.

"I don't even hate you," she says. "You're so pathetic, I can't. But don't think for a minute that I don't know what you've been doing."

I look at Olivia in question, but she's walking toward her car.

Goddammit.

No one was getting a proper goodbye from me today.

"Get her home," I say to Seth. "Make sure she gets some sleep."

Seth nods to me, then says something close to Leah's ear. She glares at me one more time before letting him steer her to his truck. It's my afternoon with Estella. I roll my head, crack my neck, and get on with it.

Olivia calls me from her car. "Sorry about that," she says.

"Hey, it was fun to watch what can I say?"

There is a long, awkward silence. Then she says, "Noah and I are divorced."

The world freezes for one second . . . two seconds . . . three seconds . . .

"Remember that coffee shop? The one we went to after we ran into each other at the grocery store?"

"Yeah," she says.

"Meet me there tonight at seven?"

"Deal," she says.

WHEN I WALK into the coffee shop, she's already there. She's sitting at the same table we sat at years earlier. In front of her are two cups.

"I got you a tea," she says. "Tell me how Estella is."

I bring her up to speed.

When I stop speaking Olivia has a look on her face.

"What?" I nudge her leg with mine.

"You light up when you talk about her."

"Yeah?"

"Like a very proud dad."

"Stop flirting with me and tell me what happened with Noah."

She tucks her hair behind her ears and gives me the saddest shrug. "I got pregnant."

I try to pretend that I'm unfazed by this little piece of news, but I can feel the awkwardness all over my face. I'm jealous, I'm hurt. I keep my mouth shut and wait for her to go on. Her face twists, her eyes squeezing shut. A crease forms between her brows.

"I lost the baby."

She swallows hard. I don't know what to say.

"Don't say anything or I'll start crying." I nod. She clears her throat.

"He agreed to have a baby with me. Great. I was excited. New chapter, the whole shebang. But . . ." She draws the word out. "When I lost it, he looked so relieved. Ugh! I hate crying." She pauses to dab at her eyes. "Then he said maybe it was for the best."

I flinch.

"Yeah exactly," she sniffs. "Just so . . . Noah."

"Wasn't there a show called *That's So Noah*?"

She gives me a look. "It was called *That's So Raven*. What planet are you from?"

"England."

She laughs.

"Keep telling the story, Olivia Kaspen."

"We made it a few more months, Caleb Drake." She blows the air out of her cheeks. "Did the therapy thing . . . Did the vacation together . . ." Her voice trails off.

"Do you want to take a break?"

"No, I want to finish—I just couldn't do it anymore. It was like something snapped. I asked him to leave."

"Why?"

"I felt like he wanted to go back to the way things were. Our old life. I didn't know how to do that. I was pissed that he expected me to."

"Understandable."

She sighs. She's a prolific sigher of sighs.

"It sounds awful when I say it out loud. I hate myself for not being able to see past this one thing that happened to me. Women have miscarriages every day, I'm not special."

"You always do that—diminish your feelings because someone somewhere has it worse than you."

"Someone does have it worse than me . . ."

It's my turn to sigh. "Just because someone else is drowning in deeper waters doesn't mean you're not allowed to struggle to swim. It's not a competition."

She looks at her phone, her eyes turning into saucers. "Hey, I gotta go. Shit—my meeting." She jumps, grabbing her bag off the back of her chair.

I ball up the trash.

"Olivia?"

"Yeah?"

"If I make this shot, will you go out with me?" I hold the ball of trash like it's a basketball and look from her to the trash can.

"Yeah," she says, smiling. "Yeah, I will."

This time I make the shot.

39

The Present

I move back to Florida, sell my condo, and spend the next six months living in my parents' house while I get it ready to put on the market. Five thousand square feet of . . . stuff.

One day when I'm going through my mom's closet, I find a manilla envelope buried beneath her scarves. I open it to find a stack of love letters. I assume Steve wrote them to her, but when I get to the signature, I see my father's name. Interest piqued. I sit cross-legged on the closet floor and read them—seventeen in total. I take a screenshot of one and send it to Olivia.

O: Whoa!

I know. It's disturbing. But also . . .
enlightening? Might need therapy.

O: How many were there?

Seventeen. Some of them are emotional.

I didn't know he was capable of being
that open with his feelings.

O: Do you think they were in love?

My mom was in love with him, she wouldn't have
kept these otherwise. It's hard to say he was in love
with her when I saw how he treated her. Idk. Broken
people give broken love. We're all a little broken.

I fold the letters back into the envelope.

O: Don't forget tonight. Six o'
clock. Gotta go. Love you.

I bag up the last of the donations and fold the envelope, sliding it into my back pocket. It doesn't feel right to throw the letters away. I check the time. I have two hours until I have to meet Olivia and the Realtor. I close my mom's closet doors for the last time and head downstairs to shower.

It takes a minute to collect the toys scattered across the shower floor. Barbies, a plastic spatula, sunglasses, and three of her beloved horses. Estella starts kindergarten in the fall. She's growing so fast, too fast. Everything is always covered in glitter including me. She already knows how to write a handful of words, and lately her favorite has been *RUN*. She's been writing the word on Post-it notes and leaving them all over the house. Last night I found a toy spider on my pillow, a parting gift before she went to Leah's house. I plan on suggesting she play the same prank on her mother. Fair is fair.

We don't make an offer on the house we see. Nothing has quite felt like us—not that we really know what us is yet.

We'll figure it out. Might take some time. But we are both okay with the surrender of not knowing.

We have little fights all the time. The kind of arguments that feel monumental in the moment but fade into laughter or grudging silence. She hates that I don't throw away my trash—water bottles, cookie bags, candy wrappers. She finds them all over the apartment and makes a big show of crinkling them up and throwing them in the trash.

I hate the way she soaks the bathroom floor when she gets out of the shower. Every. Single. Time.

She always makes the bed. I always do the dishes. She drinks milk straight from the carton and that kind of pisses me off, but then she reminds me that she has to live with my snoring and I call it even. But holy hell is she fun. How did I not know that we could laugh this much? Or sit in absolute silence and listen to music together? How did I live without this for so long?

I lean over her neck as she works and kiss her on her sweet spot. She shivers. "Stop it, I'm trying to work."

"I don't really care, Duchess . . ."

I kiss her again, my hand sliding down the front of her dress. Her breath catches. I can't see her face, but I know her eyes are closed. I step around the front of her chair and she lets me pull her to her feet.

I struck my match, she poured out her gasoline. We burn now. All the time.

I lead her to my bed, stopping at the foot to pull her against me. I kiss her for a long time.

I unzip the back of her dress and slip the sleeves from her shoulders.

"I won't leave you," I say. "I won't ever love another woman."

She smiles up at me, her eyes soft and hazy. The only time Olivia's eyes are not alert and pointedly cold are when she's pinned beneath me—or when she's recovering from being pinned beneath me.

EPILOGUE

One night while we're in Paris, we make vows to each other lying in the bed of our hotel room.

I touch the pressed penny she wears on a chain around her neck.

"I'm worried," she says, brushing my cheek with her fingertips.

"Right now? About what?"

We spent the day walking. No schedule, no itinerary— just the two of us hand in hand with the city wrapping around us. There was an artist on Rue de Rivoli who paints only in shades of blue and somehow manages to capture the entire spectrum of emotion in a single canvas. We ate a late dinner, stumbled across a band playing in the street, and danced under a streetlight.

As far as I was concerned it was perfectly relaxing.

"That if we die we won't go to the same place."

"That is not what I thought you were going to say."

"But what if we don't."

"Wherever we go in the next life, we'll be together."

She doesn't look convinced.

"Do you think if we get married we'll have more chance of staying together?"

She bites her lips. "Maybe. I don't know. I just want us to have all of our bases covered."

"You know I'd marry you in a heartbeat."

"No—not like that. Maybe just our own ceremony."

"When we get home?"

"Right now."

"Wearing sheets?"

When she smiles it makes my chest ache.

"I'll do whatever I have to do to protect you. I'll lie, cheat, and steal to make you okay. I'll share your suffering, and I'll carry you when you're weighed down. I'll never leave you, not even when you ask me to. Do you believe me?"

She leans in, pressing her forehead to mine. "Yeah, I do. That was really pretty."

She nods, then clears her throat.

"I trust you. You're strong enough to protect your heart and mine, and your heart from mine. I love you so much. I'll give you everything I have in this life and the next."

"In this life and the next," I repeat.

We smile like fools. And that's it. Our hearts are married.

We buy a house on a lake, and remodel it. We fight. We make love. We take Estella to Disney World, Texas, San Diego, and London, We adopt a puppy and Estella names him Ginger Cookie. We call him Gookie for short.

Olivia has a black thumb and kills all of our plants. I buy new ones at the hardware store and replace them when she's not looking. She's very proud of her (my) tomatoes.

We try to have a baby, hope stitched into every plan and

possibility. But Olivia miscarries twice, each loss a devastation. When Olivia is thirty-five, the universe throws us its cruelest twist yet. She is diagnosed with ovarian cancer. The word lands like a bomb. *Cancer.* Not now. The aftershocks ripple through every corner of our lives. The treatments are brutal, but nothing hurts more than the day the doctor tells her she needs a hysterectomy.

She cries for a year. Most days I just begged God to keep her alive and make it go away. That's what I asked him—*Make it go away*—like I was five years old and there was a boogeyman in my closet. Maybe God heard my prayers because the cancer never comes back. We emerged from that chapter scarred but still standing. But the fear never fully leaves you.

I wish I could have kept my promise and given her a baby. Sometimes, when she's at the office late, I sit in what would have been the nursery and think about the past. It's a pointless game of torture, but I suppose it's a consequence of being a flawed, stupid man. Olivia doesn't like it when I think. She says my thoughts are too deep and they depress her. She's probably right. And I would hate for her to see what I see: the fact that if we'd just done things right, if I'd fought harder, if she'd fought less, we would have been together sooner. We could have had our baby before it was too late—before her body made it impossible. But we didn't, and we're both a little wilted around the edges because of it.

I've come to the conclusion that there are no set rules in life. You do what you have to do to survive. If that means running away from the love of your life to preserve your sanity, you do it. If it means breaking someone's heart so yours doesn't break, do it. Life is complicated—too much so for there to be absolutes. We are all so broken. Pick up a person, shake them around, and you'll hear the rattling of their broken pieces. Pieces our fathers broke, or our mothers, or our friends, strangers, or our loves. Olivia has stopped rattling quite as much as she used to. *Love is a God-given tool,* she tells me. *It screws things back in place that were loose, and it cleans out all the broken pieces that you don't need anymore.* I believe her. Our love has been fixing each other. I hope to only hear a tiny jingle when I shake her in a few years.

LEAH REMARRIES A few years later, surprising exactly no one with how quickly she finds her footing, and has another baby. He's born with a head of dark hair. She names him Damien.

"That's the name of the kid from *The Omen* . . ." Olivia says when I tell her. "The movie about the son of Lucifer . . ."

When Estella is nine, she comes to live with us.

There is no fight about it, no custody dispute—just a quiet mutual understanding. She thrives when she's with us. Her laughter fills the house; she plays more pranks on me than I can count.

Olivia and Estella have their secrets—little inside jokes and whispered conversations I'm not privy to. They share a sense of humor. I find myself the target of salt in my sugar, a sabotaged playlist on Spotify that only plays "Barbie Girl." One day they switch the settings on my phone to French and it takes an entire day to switch back. Seeing their uninhibited laughter that makes them double over is worth every mouthful of salt. Some nights I come home and they're sitting side by side on the sofa, legs propped on the coffee table, watching Bravo.

"Mom would do that—"

It's hard not to laugh in those moments.

It's a joke in the family that no one has the same hair color. Raven, red, and blond.

We are raising a really beautiful little soul. She wants to be a writer and tell our story someday. We are gonna be okay. That's what happens when two people are meant to be together. You just work it out even when the edges don't line up perfectly.

We make love every single day—no matter what. She is the only woman I've seen that gets more beautiful with age. She is the only woman I see.

★ ★ ★ ★ ★

ONE PLACE. MANY STORIES

Bold, innovative and
empowering publishing.

FOLLOW US ON:

@HQStories

Praise for Tarryn Fisher

'The ending shattered me in a way only Tarryn Fisher can!'
Colleen Hoover

'A compulsive, brilliant, enthralling thriller . . . a novel that totally captures absolute love and utter deception, total obsession and cruel betrayal. I was hooked to the very last page'
Adele Parks

'Dark, disturbing and deliciously addictive'
B. A. Paris

'No one writes as authentically as Tarryn Fisher'
Anna Todd

'This page-turning psychological thriller by Tarryn Fisher will leave you guessing right until the end'
HELLO!

'A perfect page-turner . . . a must-read'
Woman & Home

'Gripping'
Bella

'Compelling page-turner'
My Weekly

'A glorious thriller – you'll be asking for more!'
Chat

'A tortuous romance mystery that will keep you guessing'
Sunday Post

'A fantastic thriller that asks the question: how well do we know the people we love? Filled with twists and turns you won't see coming'
PopSugar

'Fans of B. A. Paris will love this addictive page-turner'
Woman's Weekly

Tarryn Fisher is the No. 1 *New York Times*, *USA Today* and *Sunday Times* bestselling author of fifteen novels. She is best known for her bestselling novels *Never Never*, *The Wives* and *The Wrong Family*. Born in South Africa, Tarryn now calls Seattle, Washington home, where she resides with her husband and children. She writes primarily in the romance, thriller, and new adult genres and specialises in writing villains.

Also by Tarryn Fisher

Good Half Gone
An Honest Lie
The Wrong Family
The Wives

Love Me with Lies Series
The Opportunist
Dirty Red
Thief

With Colleen Hoover
Never Never

For a complete list of books by Tarryn Fisher,
visit her website, www.tarrynfisher.com